# HALFWAY
# THERE

MIDLIFE MULLIGAN, BOOK ONE

## BY EVE LANGLAIS

"I DON'T WANT TO BE WITH YOU ANYMORE."

The declaration hit me, a hammered fist to the heart. I stopped breathing as I stared at my husband of more than twenty years. Married straight out of college, we were supposed to grow old together.

"I don't understand."

I really didn't. Where had this come from? I'd been the best of wives. Having seen my parents going at it from a young age, I'd decided early on in my relationship that I would be the peacemaker, meaning I tended to agree with anything Martin said—even if I didn't agree. It wasn't worth the fight, especially since he didn't like to lose.

"What's not to understand, Naomi? It's quite simple. I want a divorce. You know, that thing you file for when a person doesn't want to be in a marriage anymore." He spoke tersely. Not for the first time.

Usually, I let it slide right over me. A long time ago I'd made sure his insults couldn't touch anywhere important. It wasn't working this time. He'd said the one word I couldn't ignore.

"Did you say a divorce?"

When had he decided this? Because I'd had no inkling when I woke up that morning—at the same time as him because he didn't like it if I slept longer than he did. As per our routine, he said not a word as he rolled out of bed and went to the bathroom. While he did his business, I slipped on some slippers and headed downstairs to make his coffee with freshly ground beans. Once it started percolating, I tackled the toast. Not too dark, slightly buttered with the real stuff, not margarine —which he held in low regard. By the time he came downstairs, his routine precise down to almost the minute, I'd plated it along with his sausage and sunny side up eggs. Martin was particular about his meals, and I'd had more than two decades to perfect them.

I stared at this man who let me make him a freaking breakfast, knowing he was going to tell me he wanted out of our marriage. A spark of anger lit inside, but I ignored it.

For now.

"Yes, I said a divorce." His voice held a hint of

impatience. "You can't tell me you didn't see this coming."

Actually, I hadn't. Martin was always unhappy. About everything. It might have gotten worse in the last few years, but I'd attributed it to him turning fifty. He had a few years on me, which might seem odd since we met in college, but he didn't go to school right after he graduated.

"I never thought about us ever separating." A lie, actually. I had, more than once, imagined a life without his miserable comments and attitude. On many occasions, I'd cursed his existence in my head. I'd wondered what it would be like if he didn't come home from work one day. He wasn't in the best shape. Men his age died of heart attacks all the time.

The moment the thought even crossed my mind, I'd feel guilty. How dare I wish for his death! So what if he didn't make me happy like the heroes in my romance books? This was my marriage, my reality, and unlike so many other couples, I would make our relationship work. 'Til death do us part.

I kept my gaze from straying to the wooden block of knives.

"Well, I have thought of leaving for a while now," Martin declared, and I was offended.

What did he have to complain about? The spark of annoyance flared brighter. "I've always done everything you asked of me." Ironed his clothes.

Made his meals. Cleaned his house. Had sex once a week. Blew him if I was on my period. I took care of everything but wiping his ass and doing his job as a real estate agent.

For a moment the words of my best friend, whom I'd not talked to in over ten years, played inside my head, *"You're a doormat. A slap in the face to feminists everywhere."*

My cruel reply at the time? *"You're just jealous I'm married and got out of small-town hell and you didn't."* A horrible thing to say, and I'd burned with shame after. I couldn't have said why I didn't apologize.

Most likely because she'd told the truth and I didn't want to admit I was wrong. How long since I'd last spoken to Tricia? Too long. Because of the man currently expounding on the reasons why he didn't want me.

"Even you can't be so stupid as to realize we have nothing in common."

I simmered, and words I rarely dared speak aloud spilled forth. "And whose fault is that?" I'd tried everything they told me to do in the books, setting up date nights with dinner followed by an activity. Except it didn't quite work as planned.

Bowling was a failure. Martin refused to wear the shoes that other people had worn. Just like he'd outright said no to painting because it was dumb, pottery was messy, escape rooms were juvenile. He had a reason to hate everything, meaning date night

4

most often failed, if he even bothered to come home. Since his promotion a few years ago, he'd been working longer hours. When I dared to say something, he pointed out he was the breadwinner in the family.

Not entirely true. I had a part-time job that brought in some extra money, but mine didn't pay the larger bills, and I hadn't always worked.

Martin put in the long hours so I could stay home with our children. I appreciated it when the kids were growing up. Felt the guilt that because he worked so hard, he missed the pivotal moments in their lives. But because of his sacrifice, I'd been there for them with every milestone and every hurt. The one thing I could never fix was their obvious pain at their father's indifference.

When they were young, Daddy came home, ate dinner, and sat in his chair. It didn't change much as they got older, except the yelling got louder and more frequent.

I consoled myself with the reminder that at least they had two parents living together and a home. According to many books, I did the right thing.

Yet the moment Geoffrey and Wendy graduated high school, they moved out. Not just out of the house but out of the state. Some days I lied to myself and blamed it on the fact they wanted to go to college somewhere cooler than a small town in

Vermont. The truth was they left because they couldn't stand being part of our family.

Being near Martin more specifically. With me, as they entered their teen years, they became indifferent. As adults, we were almost strangers.

I heard from them occasionally, but those conversations where short and stilted, painful beyond belief, so I was almost relieved it didn't happen more often. The guilt would hit me that I didn't reach out. Then the pity party would start because my own children hated me.

Could I blame them? I also hated myself.

I hated Martin, too. However, panic at the thought of him leaving made me say, "If you're unhappy, we can get some counseling. Fix things." Because as much as I disliked him, now that he'd offered me an out, I suddenly didn't want it.

The thought of being alone...

I tried vainly to think of something, anything, to cancel out the roaring in my ears. The heavy sensation pressing on me from all sides. The debilitating dismay as I saw my life, my future, being flushed away to make room for what Martin wanted.

It was always about what *he* wanted.

For a half-second, a rebellious thought overcame my anxiety. *Why is everything always about him? What about* me?

The ember of rage flared brighter than ever, yet I remained cold.

"I don't want to fix things." His short, clipped words brimmed with anger. "Get this through your thick skull. I don't want to be with you anymore. You're boring. Fat. Stupid. I mean look at you." He waved a hand, and his face twisted in disgust. "You don't even try to look nice anymore."

Another verbal slap and a part of me wanted to argue, and then I glanced down at my outfit. An oversized shirt to hide the bulging middle and stretchy leggings in a soft faded cotton. I'd stopped wearing denim a long time ago due to chafing. I'd gained a lot of weight during my pregnancies. Even more in the past few years as boredom put me on the couch.

While I'd gotten a job once the kids hit high school, Martin had refused my request to go back to work full-time. He said it would make him look bad. I was secretly glad, given the idea of working more than twenty hours a week for minimum wage meant I'd have a hard time keeping up with the housework. Perhaps had I gotten a better paying job I might have splurged and hired some help. Except, as Martin liked to remind me, I wasn't qualified to do anything. I was a wife. A mom. A homemaker.

"—a slob. Why do you think we don't have sex anymore?"

I bit my tongue before I said what first came to mind. I wasn't allowed to speak about his problems below the belt. "I've offered."

I had, out of some sense of obligation and because sometimes my books had some steamy parts that reminded me of how I used to like sex when I was younger.

"And I said no to those offers because you disgust me. The sight of your body turns me off."

The cruelty of his statement stole my breath. Martin had always possessed an acerbic manner, and it only got stronger as we got older. But this level of meanness… When did the hating begin?

The cold in me intensified as my rage overflowed. How dare he speak to me like this? Something in me rebelled. "I thought we stopped having sex because you couldn't get it up anymore."

It was mean. Horrible of me. Making fun of a condition that came with age and a relief that I no longer had to pretend.

The smirk on his lips should have warned me. "A limp dick only with you. Turns out I just needed the right woman. A real woman."

Okay, that sucker-punched me even more than the body insults. I barely had any breath to speak. "You're cheating on me?"

"I've moved on, and so should you."

"To do what?" I practically yelled. I'd revolved my whole world around him. As miserable as it was, I had nothing else.

"Do whatever you want, but do it somewhere

else. I want you out of my house. Take your stuff and go."

"Where?" This was my home. This couldn't be happening.

"I don't really care so long as you're gone by the time I come back."

Hold on a second. "Where are you going?

"None of your business."

My lips trembled. "You can't just leave me."

"I can. And don't you dare start your crying. This is your fault." With those final words, he slammed out of the house.

And I broke.

I sat down on my immaculate kitchen floor and sobbed. It wasn't pretty. Or quiet. Or even dry.

Snot ran down and dripped from my chin, mixing with my salty tears. I took great, hiccupping gulps as my body shook and I cried. Cried hard.

If asked, I'm not even sure I could have said why I was so sad. In many respects, Martin was right. Our marriage hadn't had any kind of true intimacy or love in a long time. Yet, it existed. It gave me purpose and meaning. A reason to get up early every morning.

Did it matter if I was happy? I wasn't even sure what happiness looked like. How did one define happiness? I had a roof over my head, clothes, food, my own car. But those things came at a cost. My dignity. My self-worth.

When was the last time I'd truly smiled? Laughed? I didn't even have my children anymore. Martin had chased them away, and I, too meek to confront him over it, allowed it.

Allowed that man to guide my every move and thought. He was right about one thing. I was dumb. In one fell swoop, he took my life and my future away from me.

*I am nothing.*

I was a nobody. No one needed me. Not a single person I could turn to or count on because I'd driven them all away.

Would anyone really care if I were gone?

My children would mourn me, but not for long. They'd escaped, and I knew they blamed me for allowing Martin to be Martin. As a father, he was the hockey dad on the sidelines, screaming obscenities at referees and other parents. Every year he was escorted from an arena and I got pitying looks. I wasn't surprised when Geoffrey stopped playing.

As for Wendy, his little girl, she wasn't so little. A chubby girl growing up, she'd retained some of the weight as a teen, and her father mocked her. *"You'd need a dozen of those fairies with magic dust to make you fly."*

It was one of the few times I stood against him. Where I tried to protect my daughter.

*"Don't call her fat."*

*"Don't tell me what to do in my house with my kid,"*

he'd sneered. *"Do you want her to end up looking like you?"*

Rather than fight, I'd buried myself in a room with a book and a pint of ice cream. I did that a lot. Hiding from the ugliness in the hopes it would go away.

It never actually worked, and yet I couldn't break the cycle. I still recalled how I'd hated it when my parents split up. I couldn't do that to my kids. Then, once they were gone, I stayed. Why?

I actually knew the answer to that. Fear.

I was a fat, middle-aged woman with no job skills, nothing. Where would I go? What would I do? I couldn't start over.

Except now Martin had left me no choice.

He'd told me I had to pack up and go. The very idea had me hyperventilating. Where would I go?

My first thought was to call the kids, and I immediately dismissed it. I couldn't ask Wendy or Geoff. They didn't deserve to have their lives disrupted, not to mention I didn't think I could handle the "I told you so" from my daughter.

But if not them, then who? My family had died a long time ago.

*I'm all alone.* There was no worse feeling in the world.

I fixed my gaze on the gas stove. I'd heard it didn't hurt. What would it be like to go to sleep and never wake? At least then I'd stop being a disappointment to everyone, most of all myself.

Without even realizing I'd moved, I found myself standing in front of the stove, my hand on the knob. The scent of gas filled my nostrils.

*Dring. Dring.*

My phone, with its old-fashioned ring tone, broke me free from the depressed mood that gripped me. I smelled the rotten egg of the gas and snapped the valve shut.

Never would I kill myself. In that I was certain.

I stepped away from the stove—and my moment of insanity—and rubbed at the hair straggling across my face, stuck to damp, snotty cheeks. Gross.

*Dring. Dring.*

I chose to rinse my face with cool water rather than run for the phone. It would hit voicemail before I reached it. Besides, I didn't want to talk to anyone.

They might hear the shame.

And if they asked if I was all right—

Well, that was a question I'd rather not deal with right now. Only once I'd patted my face dry did I peek at my phone. Unknown. Damned telemarketers.

I shuffled from the kitchen into the living room, catching sight of myself in the mirror. Halting, I stared long and hard. Stared at myself in a critical manner that I'd not dared for a long time. I hated the woman looking back at me.

A woman who had let herself go. When was the last time I had my hair cut? The wispy ends of it were dry and split. Gray lined the brown. And it was thin. So thin compared to my youth when I could barely put my fingers around it.

Look at the state of my brows! Shaggy caterpillars that only narrowly missed joining. Just call me Bert.

My shirt probably wouldn't even make the repurpose bin if donated. It was little better than a rag. In my defense, I'd not expected to get up this morning and get dumped on. But at the same time, I couldn't recall the last time I'd bought myself something because it looked pretty. It had been a while since I'd bothered trying to doll myself up to look attractive.

For that I blamed Martin. He didn't care, so neither did I.

And now look at me. The old lady in the mirror had a trembling lower lip and her skin was blotchy.

It would have been easy to start crying again. Just as easy to forget my previous vow of not giving up and go straight for the pills Martin kept in the upstairs bathroom. Wash them down with some booze and then a nice soak in the tub and I wouldn't have to deal with this…nightmare.

My gaze strayed to the stove again. I knew all

the ways I could go. Easy, painless methods, unlike what I'd have to deal with today, tomorrow...

*Scratch. Scratch.*

It came from the living room. The strange noise drew my gaze to the back of the house. A curtain covered the sliding glass door because Martin hated sunlight in the morning. For once, I didn't actually mind it, as the gloom suited my mood.

I heard it again, a strange noise coming from outside. I crossed the room in an instant. Yanking the curtain aside, I saw a little furry face. The ears on the smoky gray fluffball were bent. Its fur was matted and wet as if it had spent time in the rain. It had one blue eye, one green, the mismatched set gazing mournfully at me. It raised a paw, and its sharp little claws dragged on the screen.

How had a kitten gotten into the yard? The fence was too high for it to climb.

"Meow." The cry emerged soft and muffled.

I still slid open the door and then pulled mesh along the metal track before kneeling. "Hello there, little one. Where did you come from?" I saw no collar. Nothing to identify whom it belonged to.

I reached out and stroked a finger over its head. It trembled. Poor little thing.

"What am I going to do with you?" It probably belonged to someone. Maybe they'd come looking for it.

"Meeee-uuu." The long, plaintive sound tugged

at me, and I scooped the wet thing, cradling it to my own damp chest.

"Don't cry," I soothed, the gesture and comforting of the trembling body reminding me of my kids when they were little. A time when I used to be if not happy, then content. Back when they still loved and looked up to me.

The little head bumped into my chest. I stroked a finger over its damp head, and the kitten broke into a ragged, rumbling purr.

"Let's get you warm and dry." I brought the kitten into the house, ignoring the inner voice that said Martin wouldn't like it. He hated animals. Forbade us from having any.

Martin could stuff it.

"I wonder if someone is looking for you," I murmured, bringing it into the kitchen.

I only briefly thought of going and asking door to door if someone had lost it. The thought of facing that many people…I couldn't do it.

Instead, I created a small poster and stapled it to the fence out front with its peeling paint. It had been years since Martin gave a hoot about anything pertaining to the house. Probably too busy giving his attention to another woman.

Jerk.

With my civic duty done, I made a quick trip to the store, bought everything I needed for the cat and myself, paid for it on a credit card. Then I went and gassed up, where the same card was declined.

I frowned at the machine. Perhaps it had malfunctioned. I went inside and the cashier gave me a bored look as it was declined again.

A good thing I had a few dollars to pay for my gas. I got back into my car, hot with embarrassment, which turned to fury once I got off the phone with the credit card company. Martin had cancelled my credit card.

Glancing at my phone, I wondered if it would be the next casualty. I had no doubt vindictive Martin would try to take everything from me. He'd leave me with nothing.

Then what would I do?

Starting my car, I found my spine and yanked it out of hiding.

If Martin wanted a divorce, I'd give him a divorce, but I was done bending over backwards for him.

He wanted a fight. I'd give him a fight.

## 2

"I can't believe the judge is letting you stay in the house," Martin hissed.

It was a few days later, after my lawyer—who assured me Martin would be paying for her services—got a court order that said it was mine to live in until the divorce was final. My lawyer also got me back a portion of the money Martin had cleared out of the joint account, which was good, because my puny paychecks didn't go very far. I'd not yet asked for more hours. I'd been too busy digging out every single piece of paper I could find to give my lawyer, Mrs. Salvatore—who specialized in ensuring spouses didn't get screwed during separations.

I could thank my new kitten for finding Mrs. Salvatore—*"Call me Rosy"*—given I'd almost thrown out the flyer with her name and number on it. My little furball had attacked the piece of paper when it fluttered to the floor on the way to the recycle bin. The headline had grabbed me with its bold statement. *You deserve more.*

I did.

One phone call to the lawyer and some of my anxiety had lessened. Today, winning in court, a bit more eased. I still had a home.

Martin didn't like losing, though. "You'll regret not leaving."

I'd regret even more letting this man tell me what to do. I angled my chin. "Don't worry. I don't plan to stay in it forever." I hated it with a passion and couldn't wait to abandon it. "Once we sell it and I receive my half—"

"Half? I paid for it. It's mine!"

Maybe in his mind, but according to the law, I was still entitled to at least half of it. And given Martin had been spending his nights with his girlfriend—another kick in the face—the judge had no sympathy for him.

"I'll have your things boxed and placed on the front porch." No point in mentioning the fact there might be a little spit mixed in.

Now that I'd had a chance to really mull things over, I'd gone from crying to fighting. Not to save our marriage but to salvage my part in it.

I'd come into it with a small inheritance from

my grandmother, who'd died while I was away at college. After I graduated and we married, I was the one who paid the down payment on the house, and while I didn't contribute to much of the mortgage afterwards, my role at home was recognized by the courts. I was entitled to half, which angered Martin to no end.

"I should have killed you." The spittle almost hit me in the face.

"Is that a threat?" My heart raced, and I almost trembled with fear, but I wouldn't let him intimidate me. It turned out standing up to him was easier than expected, if ugly.

So very ugly.

A good thing I had Grisou to keep me company. I'd chosen that name for my kitten because the French Canadian endearment reminded me of my grandmother.

Thinking about her reminded me of the discovery that I still owned her cottage. Kind of. It was held in a trust that passed down to me after her death. I'd completely forgotten about it. I'd only gone once after she died. Martin said it was too far, and he hated the rustic nature of it.

It was a strange offer that arrived in the mail with an offer to buy it that inadvertently reminded me of its existence. My lawyer had immediately researched it and was confident I'd get to keep it.

Something about a legal trust and some clause saying it had to stay in the family. Meaning Martin couldn't touch it. Even if I died, it would go to Wendy and Geoff.

I wondered how it fared. Probably not too well given how long it had been since my last visit. Guilt filled me at the thought. I'd spent happy times in that cottage with my grandmother. It was even my home in high school after my dad disappeared—presumed dead—yet, I'd abandoned it.

So many things I'd given up for Martin, and for what? Other than the children, who barely spoke to me, what had I gotten out of it?

Low self-esteem. An extra hundred or so pounds. And the loss of my youth.

At forty-six, it was too late for a do-over. If only life came with a mulligan like it did in golf.

Arriving at the house I'd shared for much too long with Martin, I parked in the driveway and grimaced. I didn't want to go inside. I hated everything about it. The taupe color of the walls. The set of leather furniture in the living room. Martin's idea, not mine. Cold in the winter and sweaty in the summer. I preferred something with fabric that I could sink into, like the big chair my grandmother positioned by her fireplace. From it, she used to tell me stories while I drank hot cocoa, fantasy tales about how the woods were home to fairies and other impossible creatures. About the monster in the lake and the elves that roamed the woods.

I'd loved her fiercely and still remembered how hard I cried when, after my mother died, my father moved us far enough that it became hard to visit. I went from seeing her all the time to once or twice a year. Then Dad didn't come home, and she was the only person I had left. Not that I cared. By the time I went to live with her as a teenager, I was a moody thing, prone to depression.

She left everything to me. Her only grand-daughter.

Funny how I couldn't stop thinking of her lately. Her and the cottage. I recalled the tranquility of the woods surrounding her place and the gentle sound of waves lapping the shore of the lake.

It had been too long since my last visit. Way too long. I doubted it was still the same.

As I entered the house, Grisou came bolting out of nowhere and flung himself at my calf. Four legs and too many teeny-tiny claws clamped onto my pants, penetrating fabric and digging into skin.

Ouch. I winced, but I didn't shake my leg to fling him off. I'd learned my lesson. He would only cling tighter.

Instead, I gave him my sternest gaze. "What did I say about climbing my leg?"

"Miii-ooo." His happy sound as he inched up

me until his head butted into my chin. He instantly started to purr.

How could I be mad? I couldn't. On my darkest day, he'd appeared like some kind of guardian angel and saved me. Or at least gave me something to smile about.

I rubbed at his ears, and he purred so lustily his whole body vibrated. I laughed, a sound that was less and less rusty by the day. "You are such a cutie." I forgave him the pinpricks on my leg.

With him clinging to my shoulder and neck, I headed for the kitchen. After the afternoon I'd just had, I needed a drink.

Whereas only days ago I would have gone for the soda in the fridge—the sweeter, the better—I now aimed for water. Ever since Martin dumped me, I'd been resisting the temptation to eat my anxiety away. It hadn't worked for more than two decades.

Time for a change, even if it was painful—like the hour I'd spent plucking my brows. Not something I'd recommend. My skin still hadn't forgiven me.

My phone rang, which was startling given I'd only gotten it a few days ago. As expected, Martin had cancelled the other line. So far, only the kids and my lawyer had it.

It wasn't them calling.

I frowned at the number. Unknown. Just like the

call I got the day Martin left me. Probably a tele-marketing scam. Like that guy who told you he worked for the IRS and you'd better send money or the cops would be knocking down your door. Maybe I should answer and given them Martin's number to call instead.

Tempting.

I ignored it.

It went to voicemail, and the notification went off. I'd check it later. First, I changed clothes and got on the treadmill, which had been gathering dust in the basement for years.

I huffed and puffed as I quick-marched on it, hating every minute. Those people who talked about the euphoric high they got from exercising? Liars. But I was determined to stick to it. Not because Martin had called me fat but because I *was* fat and it was time I did something about it.

When we'd married, I'd weighed one hundred and fifty pounds. By the second kid, I was over two hundred and never came back down. Over the years I crept up. Two twenty. Two forty. I got depressed. Two sixty…and my husband left me.

I didn't want to be a sad, overweight divorcee who stayed in the house and never did anything except collect cats. Although I now understood why you would. There was something very satisfying about having Grisou around.

"Next week, I'm going to learn how to throw

axes." I'd seen a flyer in the grocery store a few months ago. It seemed the most frivolous skill I could learn, and yet, I tingled with excitement at the idea of trying. If the apocalypse came, I'd be ready.

"I am also going to try belly dancing at the rec center and eat at that new sushi place," I informed Grisou, who'd followed me to the basement and curled up in the blanket on the chair I'd set up for him.

The cat stretched and blinked in reply. It was nice having someone who agreed.

Off went my phone again just as I finished my wretched bout with the machine of leg torture. Seeing a number I recognized, I almost dropped the cellphone as I tried to answer.

"Hi, Wendy." I tried to act casual. My daughter rarely called me, but this would be the second time this week. The first being the day after I told her Martin and I were separated.

"Hey, Mom. Just calling to see how you were doing."

The first time she'd done this, I'd gaped in surprise. Now, I had a reply. "Doing fine. You?"

Look at me acting calm and collected. Meanwhile I wanted to jump for joy. My daughter cared what happened to me.

I'm sure Geoff did, too. Hard to tell, given my son took the news of the divorce with his usual aplomb. "That's cool." Not exactly encouraging, but at least he didn't freak out.

When I'd told Wendy, she turned quiet as I babbled, "…it happens all the time to couples who've been married a long time. You know. They grow apart. And, um, want to move on."

"Are you having an affair?" Wendy has asked.

"What? Of course not!" I'd exclaimed.

"Is he?"

At the time, I'd said no, not wanting to be that woman who turned her kids against her ex. But I had a feeling Wendy knew.

"Mom?"

My daughter snapped me back to the present, and I stuttered, "Sorry, I got distracted by the cat. What did you say?"

"Wait, cat? Since when do we have a cat?"

"I found him, and no one has claimed him." Nor did he show up on any lost pet networks for the neighborhood or have a microchip. I'd checked, worried I'd get attached and that someone would take him from me.

"Hunh. I always wanted a cat."

"I know." What else could I say? We both knew why we never could have one before.

Rather than address it, Wendy said, "Weren't you supposed to attend court today?"

"I did."

"And?"

How to explain her father had turned into a giant douchecanoe that painted me to be the stupidest of cows? And that the judge saw through his less-than-rosy words to grant me some modicum of support.

"I'll be staying in the house while things get settled."

"Ha, I'll bet the prick didn't like that."

The exclamation had me almost gasping in surprise. "Your father was understandably upset."

"My father is an ass."

"Wendy!"

"Please, Mom, we both know it's true. I've said it for years."

She had, and I'd stubbornly rejected the statements and told Wendy to respect her father. No wonder she'd moved away from me.

I found myself blurting out, "I'm sorry for how he treated you."

There was silence. Had I gone too far?

Then a whispered, "He treated you way worse."

Tears filled my eyes because, in that moment, I grasped just how much my daughter had seen. How had I ever fooled myself into thinking otherwise? Of course, she saw. It was right there every time Martin opened his mouth and berated me. Every time I catered to one of his whims.

My stupidity hit me like a piano to the head. I'd been so determined to keep the family together at all costs that I'd ignored everything else. In my mind, the kids being shuffled between households was the most horrible thing because I'd remembered it being terrible for me. It didn't get better when I was stuck with my single dad. Surely having parents who were together was the right choice.

Wrong. In staying, I'd made my children's lives worse.

"You must hate me," I stated, the truthful claim raw. I should have protected her better. Her and Geoff.

"How could I hate you when you hate yourself so much already?"

My lower lip trembled, and I might have truly started bawling had Grisou not nudged my hand. My words emerged choked. "I don't hate myself."

"Really?" There was a sarcastic lilt to it.

I closed my eyes and sighed. "Okay, maybe a little. I should have been stronger."

"Kind of hard when someone keeps beating you down."

"Your father never hit me." I couldn't have said why I defended him.

"Abuse doesn't always come from fists."

When had my daughter gotten so wise? Please tell me she'd escaped soon enough to not be the weak mess I turned out to be.

"I'm working on getting better." I didn't say how much it scared me.

But she somehow knew. "It won't be easy. Especially since you're still living in that house."

"I don't have a choice. Where would I go?" The moment I said it, I saw the corner I'd backed her into. "I'm fine. I don't need to move anywhere. Not yet at least."

"Please don't tell me you're planning to live in that house forever."

"No!" I almost shouted the word. The idea seemed too much like a prison. "I'm just going to stick around long enough to handle the legal aspects of the divorce."

Martin was pushing hard for it to happen fast, and that worked for me. The sooner I could distance myself and start over, the better.

"You don't have to be in that house to do that. Your lawyer can deal with most of it."

"I'll be fine."

Which wasn't a complete lie. Was everything one hundred percent perfect? No. But I could celebrate the small victories. Every day I got up counted as a good thing. Every decision I made on my own was a step in the right direction. I would get past this bump in my life.

We spoke a little longer about Wendy and her job, which she hated—"I feel like I'm going nowhere." I refrained from saying she was right. She was venting, and I'd read enough books on being a better me by this point to know she just needed me to listen.

She spoke of her roommates and the fact they were stealing her milk again. "Like I won't notice it went from full to barely enough for my cereal."

I listened and sometimes had some words of wisdom to give, such as putting dish soap and a fabric softener sheet in a pot that had burnt crud on the bottom.

We chatted more than we'd talked in…ever, I guess. I'd never realized how much we'd tiptoed around the house, fearing Martin's wrath. I'd allowed myself to miss out on having a relationship, a true one, with my kids because of fear.

I wanted to duck my head and hide in shame. But I wouldn't. Hiding was how I'd gotten to this point. No more. I was done being a doormat. I could and would survive this and emerge stronger.

If only being alone wasn't so damned scary. I reminded myself that thousands, probably even millions, of women managed to live independently. Many, like me, had to start over. If they could do it, surely, I could too?

*I can do this.*

As pep talks went, it bolstered me when the panic wanted to set in. Each time I went to submit a job application to somewhere that might pay me more, I would stand outside the building, take a deep breath, and remind myself people did this every day.

Then I walked in.

On day two of pounding the pavement—so to speak—I got a full-time job as a cashier at a local big box store, the kind small businesses railed about when really they should be getting mad at the consumers. The buyers chose to go where their dollars stretched furthest. It was human nature. I now worked for the enemy of all small towns, but I was getting forty hours a week instead of twenty. I went to work, and I came home. I couldn't say I did much more. All the pep talks in the world wouldn't let me try the things I kept saying I'd do.

I didn't go axe throwing because anxiety convinced me I'd drop the blade on my foot.

I almost went painting, arriving at the restaurant early enough to have a meal, a salad with grilled chicken. My healthy food choices were at least sticking, but my resolve didn't.

As I saw people arriving in twos and threes, smiling and in chatting groups, I realized how pathetic I'd look. Me, all alone, surrounded by strangers.

I fled. I couldn't stand to sit there and feel judged. Or worse, pitied.

I was a mid-forties woman with no friends.

None.

And I didn't have the slightest clue how to make

any. At work, things were busy. The employees rarely got time for more than hellos and how are you doing. I lied a lot. "Doing fine. How are you?"

Technically, I *was* fine. I got up, I exercised, fed the cat, fed myself something diet approved. I'd found a few low carb books at the local Salvation Army and, after studying them, found that was the diet that kept me the most sated.

As the weeks passed, the weight came off. I found my energy rising, enough that I started getting a little stir crazy. It had been since before my kids were born that I didn't want to flop onto a couch at night. Now, eight o'clock hit and I got restless.

Pacing the living room, not able to find a show that kept my attention, I decided to go for a walk. At night. By myself in the dark.

Bravest thing ever.

Maybe the stupidest. My mind had a list of bad things that could happen if I walked out that door.

Grisou eyed me as I put on my shoes.

"Don't worry. I won't be gone long." I feared the dark. However, my need to move outweighed that anxiety.

I locked the front door behind me and began a quick walk down the front walkway onto the side-walk. I shoved my hands into the pockets of my sweater, my pace rapid, meaning I soon huffed. Yet I noticed I didn't breathe as hard as before. In just a few weeks, I'd already become fitter. Climbing the stairs didn't make me pant or set my knee to aching. Getting up in the morning didn't involve as much groaning.

I'd even noticed the improvements in the mirror and in the way my clothes fit looser. Enough that if it kept up, I might soon have to buy some pants—which I couldn't afford but I'd find a way. Dropping a pant size was exciting to me. After all, it indicated I'd accomplished something.

Count the small victories, or something along those lines. I'd read that in some self-help book.

My sneakered feet hit the pavement with solid, rhythmic slaps, but in between them, I heard an echoing scuff. Someone else was out. No biggie. People were allowed to walk. That didn't make them predators out to harm me.

Still, I couldn't help but quicken my pace, arms swinging, my face turning hot and the sweat running. The only glow I got from exercise was the kind that stank and made me moist. So gross. I'd shower when I got home.

As I turned the corner, cutting my planned square of a walk into a rectangle, I listened intently to see if the other person kept going straight or away from me. I heard nothing. They must have moved on.

The next half a block was lined with front yards, some lit with lights planted in stakes or as

posts, illuminating short grass and tended shrubbery. Cars were parked at random, some people
either not home judging by darkened windows or
their vehicles in the garage. I didn't see anyone else
ahead of me, merely glowing windows that often
flashed as if someone watched television. While I
didn't look behind, I heard no signs of pursuit. I
relaxed.

Too soon, apparently.

Scuff. The soft noise alerted me to my mistake.
My slackened pace picked up again, and I practically ran to the corner. If I turned left, it would
bring me back to the house.

In between my pants of breath, the sound
almost a whistle as panic set in, I glanced over my
shoulder. Something loomed on the sidewalk, dark
and hulking. I saw no face, nothing distinct. I wasn't
even sure I saw a person, yet I felt an incredible
chill.

Terror filled me. Danger. It stalked me. I was
convinced of it.

Sobs tore from me as I kept running, trying to
pull my phone from my pocket. I should have had it
in my hand. It jiggled as I ran. How was I supposed
to call for help if I couldn't see to dial?

I dropped it then almost ran away and left it.

But I couldn't afford another phone. I had to
stop running and crouch to grab my cell. Tears
pricked my lids as I noticed the cracked screen. The

pounding of steps approached, and I pressed at the power button then tried to log in.

Nearer and nearer.

*Invalid passcode. Try again.*

I couldn't get the passcode right; my shaking hands kept getting it wrong.

Nearer and…

The person went past, their feet moving in a smooth cadence, their head angling to look at me, questioning, yet not stopping.

For which I thanked him silently in my head. I think if the jogger had spoken, I might have screamed.

Instead the man went on his way, soon disappearing from sight, and I walked with my cracked phone, feeling so stupid.

The peeling fence of the house appeared. The yard was less overgrown than the week before, as I'd gotten outside with some shears and taken care of stray branches.

As I turned onto the walkway, the hairs on my neck rose. The temperature dropped suddenly. A chill puckered the skin of my arms, and when I exhaled, I could have sworn I saw mist.

Halfway up the walk to my house, I stopped and pivoted. I looked behind me to the street, dark because the light across from my place had stopped working. The night was quiet. Not even the sharp bark of a dog broke it.

My breath emerged cold again, as if a sudden frost draped the land. Possible given it was mid-September.

I'd have to dig out the warm stuff and see what I had. In previous years I'd stayed in the house a lot. Not this winter. Maybe I'd go skating on an outdoor rink.

Turning, I walked to my door, and the cold deepened, as did the sense of menace. My walk turned to a sprint, and I ran for my door, key emerging from my pocket with fluid grace and sliding into the lock. I turned it. *Click.*

Relief flooded me. I thought for sure it would fail. The door opened and I fell inside, quickly flipping to slam it shut. I turned the dead bolt then stood there waiting.

I swear if I'd heard a knock, I would have peed myself.

Nothing happened other than Grisou meowing at my feet. As I bent over to grab him, he darted sideways with a growl. He faced the door and his body arched, his fur rising in bristles.

Another deep sound emerged from him, and I stopped breathing. I stared wide-eyed at the door and saw my breath misting again.

Inside the house.

I might have wet myself a bit. Grisou stalked a few cat-sized paces to the door, still uttering that low rumbling noise.

I prepared to die. I imagined the door slamming open and something killing me. Bullets coming through it. Perhaps an explosion ramming splinters into my body.

Instead, the air lost its chill and my cat calmed down. He turned his back to the door and began twining around my ankles, purring.

I scooped him up and noticed everything felt fine. No more misty air. The hair on my neck behaved, and all apprehension had fled. It was the only reason I dared approach the door and look outside. Not much to see with the street still dark. I nuzzled my cat and murmured, "We're both paranoid, I think."

He made a tiny noise that made me laugh.

I cast one last glance outside and frowned. "Would you look at that. The light is working again."

It should have been reassuring to see the illuminated sidewalk, and yet I couldn't help but wonder why the light had failed to shine before.

Bulbs didn't just start suddenly working again. Not unless you re-screwed them in.

I walked away from the door, heading into the kitchen and the table with its daunting pile of papers. Income records, a listing of our assets, everything I could find in the house. I was sorting them into piles for my lawyer in case she needed them.

The letter, with its offer to buy my grandma's cottage, sat by itself. The third one I'd received at this point from a company called Airgeadsféar. Never heard of them and I wasn't interested in selling. My lawyer said I didn't have to reply. I just wished they'd stop sending me offers since I couldn't stand seeing them. Not because they wanted to buy the place. It was weirder than that. The logo on the top corner, some strange symbol, made me uncomfortable. Stupid, I know. Yet every time I saw it, my skin crawled.

Snatching it from the table, I marched to the stove. It didn't take much to ignite a corner, but I didn't expect the noxious black smoke.

"Idiot!" Was I trying to set off the fire alarms? I tossed the sheet into the sink and turned on the water, which made things only worse. I opened a window before the alarm started chirping at me then leaned against the sink and closed my eyes.

What was wrong with me? Freaked out by a piece of paper. Why hadn't I just tossed it or shredded it? Ignored it like an adult?

A cold breeze came through the open window.

I slammed it shut and glanced into the sink at the burnt mess. Wouldn't you know that stupid symbol was the one thing to survive and taunt me?

I rammed it down the garbage disposal and then set it churning.

My phone rang as it gargled. Unknown number.

Probably the same one that kept leaving me blank, staticky messages.

The garburator choked and whined. Then stopped.

Great. Just another broken thing in my life.

Thanks to my anxiety, I took a sleeping pill that night.

3

---

THE FOREST SNAGGED AT ME. THE SHARP TIPS OF branches reached out to scratch bare arms. My breath came in hot, fast pants, the air so cold the mist fell like tiny icicles.

I had to escape. Move faster.

My legs ached. I saw no refuge. Nowhere to hide.

*It* came after me. I couldn't have said what. I could hear it, though, taunting me even though there was no actual sound.

*Run, run as fast as you can. If I catch you, I'll—*

It never finished the horrible rhyme. A chill rushed through me, tickling my skin, whispering icily on flesh.

"Leave me alone!" I yelled, stopping my mad dash to whirl and yell at nothing.

*Little bitch. Little bitch. Let me in.*

The awful words ended in laughter.

"Go away!"

*Never.* A hand fell onto my shoulder, digging in sharply, and I screamed—

It was the nudging of a cold wet nose that woke me.

"Grisou," I grumbled, not entirely angry. The terror of the nightmare clung to me, and I was glad to be shed of it.

My kitten nudged me and let out a bossy growl. The kind that said I really should be up and paying attention. I'd really rather not. The sleeping pill I'd taken wanted me to shut my eyes.

"Mee! Uuu!" The cat uttered a strident cry, unlike any I'd heard.

As I opened my mouth to speak to him—never mind the folly of a cat understanding, let alone replying—I knew why he'd woken me. I smelled smoke.

My eyes popped fully open. Despite the slight odor of smoke, the fire alarms in the house were silent, making me wonder, was there truly a fire? Then again, could I say with certainty we'd even changed the batteries? It used to be we did it religiously when the clocks moved forward and sprang back. But then we invested in those that came with built-in ten-year batteries. How long ago?

Didn't freaking matter. Alarm or not, smoke seeped into my room. A glance at my shadowy closed door made me wonder what I'd find on the other side. The smoke filling my room made wonder if I'd caused this. Me and that stupid letter I'd burned. But surely I'd doused it thoroughly?

I glanced to my nightstand. Three a.m. My phone sat in the charging dock, and yet I didn't see the little green light indicating it was charging. Nor did I hear the hum of the ceiling fan.

A power outage *and* a fire? Or had the fire caused it? Let the experts figure it out. I snatched my phone, and there was only one number to call.

It took two rings before anyone answered. "Nine one one, what's your emergency?"

"I think my house is on fire."

"Think, ma'am?"

"There's a lot of smoke in my room."

"Ma'am, are you inside the house?"

"Yes."

"Have you seen any flames?"

"Not exactly, but my bedroom is getting pretty smoky." A part of me realized I should be more panicked, and yet I couldn't help a surreal feeling. This wasn't happening.

"Ma'am, you need to exit the premises if possible." The voice remained calm.

"Okay, but what about the fire? I don't even have a working hose." It leaked something horrible, so I'd tossed it to the curb and not yet replaced it.

"I've already notified the fire department. You need to leave the premises."

"Right. Should I bring anything?" I tried to remember the fire drill lessons I'd done with the kids.

There was a hint of impatience in the dispatcher's next statement. "Ma'am, you can't delay. Please get out if you can *now*."

"What if I can't?" I knew I was being dumb. Stalling. When I didn't get a reply, only silence. I glanced at my cellphone. The screen showed no signal. How did that happen? I lived in suburbia, not the boonies.

"Seriously?" I grumbled. At least the fire trucks were on their way. "Come on, kitty. Let's get out of here."

Having no idea what I'd find, I took only a moment to put on a robe and slide my feet into slippers. A hand on the doorknob had me hissing in pain. Hot. So very hot. I wouldn't get out that way.

I glanced to the window. Located on the second story, it wouldn't be easy getting down to the ground. Still, I moved to the glass and struggled to open the sash. It had been a while since it had to creak its way up the track, and it protested every inch of the way. I welcomed the fresh air that immediately poured in.

There was no screen. Glancing out, I bit my lower lip. How would I get out? If I jumped, I'd break something for sure. My mattress would never fit through the opening. But maybe I could soften my landing?

Moving quickly, I yanked the comforter off the bed and tossed it outside. In the distance I could hear sirens. Would they get here in time?

The smoke in the room thickened, and I could have sworn I heard the crackling of flames. I quickly tossed pillows outside, only to stare in dismay as they flopped to the side.

It was then I had the brilliant idea to use a sheet and climb down. It worked in the movies. I yanked it from the bed and, given it wasn't very long, knotted the flat sheet to the fitted one. Then I scrambled to tie it to the doorknob of my closet. There was nothing else nearby that would work.

I coughed even as my eyes watered, stinging with the smoke and heat. Time to go.

I tucked the kitten into my robe pocket, tossed the makeshift rope out the window, and then sat myself on the ledge. It still looked like a long way down. I gripped the sheet and gave it a tug.

It didn't move. I yanked it harder, and it pulled free.

Horrified I stared at the loose end. I'd have to tie it again. Looking back, I saw the door to my room glowing, the outline of it a terrifying orange.

Just then the first emergency vehicle arrived. I sighed in relief.

Rescue was here.

They even brought the trampoline which, as a big girl, I'd been avoiding my entire life. With good reason as it turned out because when I hit it, I bounced. Arms and legs splayed, I flew from the protection of it, right into a fireman, knocking him to the ground.

My hefty frame squashed him, with my robe riding up over my copious ass, showing off my granny panties. It was the picture that made the local paper.

## 4

I HAD TO FIND A NEW PLACE TO LIVE AND NOT JUST because of the embarrassment of having an image of my ass distributed to everyone in the town. The house had burned to the ground. A complete loss, along with everything in it.

Overnight, I became homeless. Quite literally. It came as no surprise my soon-to-be ex-husband had cancelled the insurance on the place to save a few dollars. The property was practically worthless now. Sure, we'd get something for the land, but the real value had been in the home.

The realization hit me as I sat on the sagging motel bed that while the judge had ruled Martin had to pay me alimony, between it and my low-paying job, I still couldn't afford to stay here long. I had to find somewhere else.

The question being, where?

I didn't have more than a few hundred dollars and the car to my name, which thankfully had been parked in the driveway, a spare key hidden in one of those magnetic boxes stuck inside a wheel well.

All my clothes, personal effects—especially pictures of my kids growing up and my grandma— were gone. I'd gone from thinking I'd lost everything to *truly* losing everything. Was this a sign I should just give up?

Despair had me hunched in on myself.

Why did life have to kick me in the face when I was already down?

I'd been trying so hard. And now this. I couldn't handle it. I couldn't—

"Meee-uuu." Grisou sat at my feet and cocked his head.

I glanced at the furball that saved my life because had he not woken me I would have succumbed to smoke inhalation. For a moment, that evil monster inside me said maybe it would have been better.

"Shut up," I mumbled. I wasn't giving in to that nasty voice. Yes, this was a setback, but I'd survive. I just needed a plan.

"What are we going to do?" Again, a question my cat couldn't exactly answer.

I had a list, starting with calling my daughter and begging a place to stay. Our conversations had been getting better of late. We were off to a

46

promising start, closer than we'd been in years. So why did I dread calling to tell her about the fire? Why didn't I want to ask for help?

Easy. I didn't want to ruin what had blossomed. It was too fragile to handle my midlife crisis. I couldn't turn to her. Leaving who?

Martin was aware of what had happened. He'd shown up while the house burned, fully dressed and none too pleased when he saw me. He'd not been concerned about my welfare one bit but more how this would affect the divorce.

"I can't believe you burned it down," he'd snapped. "Half of that house was mine, and now it's worthless."

Did he seriously think I'd done this?

I didn't dare admit I thought it might be my fault. Surely the letter I'd set on fire hadn't caused the fire.

"If you ask me, I think *you* did it. Couldn't stand the fact the judge was on my side, so you tried to burn it down with me inside of it," I snapped, overcome by guilt. It seemed ridiculous until I said out loud. *Had* Martin tried to kill me?

Once I would have said no, and yet the ugly side of him had only grown since our separation. Who knew what he was capable of? After all, he'd told me it would have been easier if I'd died.

For a second after my statement, his eyes widened and his mouth worked, but no sound came out. Eventually he spat, "Is this how you think you'll win in the divorce? Accuse me of trying to murder you so you can walk away with everything? Think again, bitch."

"Don't call me names."

Rather than listen, he streamed a litany of nasty things at me, including the C word.

As he ranted, weariness tugged me. My eyes still stung from the smoke, my lungs ached, and my spirit was bruised. "Go away, Martin."

"Oh, I plan to but not before reminding you that this changes nothing. You're not getting more money out of me because you're homeless. As a matter of fact, I'm going to ensure my lawyer takes the value of the home you ruined into consideration when we settle."

"Go suck on a cactus." I leaned my face on my knees and ignored him.

Thankfully he left before I really lost my mind. I wasn't feeling kind. As a matter of fact, I finally understood why some people resorted to violence when frustrated. I wanted to break something. Martin's face would have been satisfying. Instead, I remained sitting on the edge of the ambulance until the drivers kicked me out. Since I wasn't going to the hospital, they were needed elsewhere.

Standing on the curb, I felt like an island with my wool blanket around my shoulders. Neighbors hung out in clusters on their lawns. A few had tried approaching, but I'd hidden my face each time to make sure they went away. Only one got close enough to say, "Can I help?"

Rather than scream, *No one can help me,* I silently shook my head.

The fire crew tamed the fire, and hoses got wound up and put away. The lone police car remained, lights strobing, the pair of officers already done with me. They'd file a report, and that was that. No crime here as far as they were concerned unless the investigation into the cause of the fire said otherwise.

Squirming in my pocket, a rather impatient kitten poked its head out. He uttered a plaintive meow.

"I know, little one. I'm kind of lost, too." What should I do? Dawn peaked on the horizon. I'd soon be able to call my daughter and say what?

*Hey, Wendy, the house burned down and I have nothing to my name but dirty slippers and pajamas. But don't worry. I'm fine.*

Except I wasn't. Why did life keep crapping on me?

My phone, tucked in the cat-free pocket, vibrated as a call came in. It apparently had decided to start working again. Stupid, glitching piece of crap. Pulling it out, I noted, once more, an unknown number on the screen. Seriously?

I'd been getting one or more a day. Annoyed,

I'd answered a few times, only there was never anyone there. Just static on the line. Super annoying. I blamed the phone company that recycled numbers much too quickly these days. Obviously, I was on some kind of telemarketing call list.

The phone stopped ringing, and I sighed as I eyed the ruin of my home. "Now what?"

Help came from a local charity group, who arrived in a rusted minivan bearing a bag of clothes. Mismatched and ill-fitting but better than my smoky ruined robe and pajamas. They also set me up and paid for a week at the hotel, plus offered me a box of groceries and the address to the local food bank.

They'd given me a small respite. My boss proved less than impressed I showed up late. Some sympathy was shown when they heard of circumstances, and yet it showed what value I had to them. None. Still a nobody.

I spent the next few days looking for a low-rent apartment when I wasn't working. I didn't have many requirements. Didn't matter. It proved harder than expected to find a place I could afford in a tight economy.

By day four I was getting worried. Which when my daughter called.

"Have you found a place?" she said before I had a chance to finish saying hello.

"No."

"Have you looked into basement apartments or one room rentals?" she asked.

"I haven't found any I can afford."

"If I had the room, I'd have you come stay with me."

Wendy had already offered—bringing me to tears. But I refused. To save money, she shared a house with two other people, which meant having me stay more than a night or two would be imposing. She'd suggested we share a new place, but without a decent job, I didn't dare. Not to mention, what if I said yes and us living together destroyed the fragile bond forming between us?

Best I say no.

"What about the cabin?"

I blinked. "What cabin?"

"Great-grandma's."

*That* cabin. It hadn't even occurred to me. It had been over two decades since I'd gone to see it. Twenty years. I doubted anything was left.

"Leave here and go back to Canada?" Over the border into my home country. I could technically do it. I had dual citizenship.

"Why not? I thought your lawyer said you owned the place no matter what."

"No way is it still standing."

"So you'd rather live in your car?" was her sarcastic retort.

I winced. I might have jokingly told her I could

sleep in it until I found a place. Not such a joke as my time at the motel neared its end.

"But my job and—"

"Mom, I don't mean to be a bitch, but you're a cashier. They have cashier jobs in Canada. Or maybe you'll find a better one."

"Or it could be I won't find one at all."

Wendy didn't say anything. She didn't have to.

My anxiety and pessimism were getting in the way of common sense. "You're talking about me leaving the only place I've known for over twenty years."

"I didn't realize you loved the shit hole so much." Her sarcasm shone.

"You're bossy."

"I prefer to think of it as giving a damn about you."

Tears pricked my eyes. "I don't know why you do." The guilt at the things I should have done for her made me wonder why she bothered at all.

"Because you're my mom, and even if you're a dumbass, I love you."

"I love you, Winnie." My nickname for my round-cheeked girl with the brightest smile.

"Yeah, well." She cleared her throat. "About the cottage. It can't hurt to go take a look. Maybe see if you can find a secondhand tent to bring with you in case the cottage is a write-off."

A tent pitched by the lake. Maybe I could fish.

This time of year, I might even find a few apples left on the tree my grandmother used to keep in the yard. If the cottage was in disrepair, I'd have to either fix it myself—and quickly before winter—or find something cheap in town. Maybe a job that I could walk to so I saved on gas.

Was I nuts?

Maybe and yet, I suddenly wanted to do this. The longing for something familiar, for the way my grandmother used to make me feel warm and protected, was suddenly all I wanted.

"Meee-ow!" Grisou flipped off the dresser and raced around the room, excited, as if he approved of this insane decision. I really was turning into a cat lady.

But I didn't care.

After more twenty years away, I was going home.

## 5

Quitting my job was easy, although I worked until the last instant, trying to ensure I had as much money as possible in my account. I hoped I wouldn't run into trouble on the way. If my car broke down, I'd have to ditch it and see if I could hop a bus. I couldn't afford to fix even a tire at this point.

It didn't take long to strip the motel room of my presence. I packed my car with my meager new belongings and still had room in the trunk, which was big enough for a body. A good thing Martin hadn't come by.

If I'd worried about how Grisou would travel, I shouldn't have. For the most part, he lay stretched in the back window, sunbathing.

As the miles between me and my old life stretched, I relaxed. The tension in my shoulders eased and the knot in my stomach unwound. I wouldn't have to worry about running into Martin here. The distance meant I wouldn't be tempted to drive by the ruins of the house and wonder how I'd survived. The phantom smell of smoke finally cleared my nostrils.

It chilled me to realize how close I'd come to dying. Despite how I'd felt initially—Was it two months ago now?—I wanted to live more than anything. It was terrifying being on my own, and yet I was happier than I'd been in a long time.

Could I get any more content? I was about to find out.

Despite all my anxiety, the border guards gave me no trouble. I'd expected them to pull me over and strip my car. Perhaps impound my cat. Accuse me of smuggling. Make me submit to a cavity search.

Instead, they perused my passport with a polite smile and waved me on. It seemed too easy.

The entire two-day trip went well. Though I was tempted, I didn't dare do it in one shot, given my lack of sleep over the past few days. I spent the night parked in one of the service areas. My cash wouldn't stretch to a motel or even a campground, so I slept in my car, doors locked, a tire iron gripped in my fist, dreaming of fireflies of all things, except they looked less like bugs and more like tiny glowing people with wings.

I blamed the gas station salad I'd picked up for dinner. I should have known something was off about it. That didn't stop me from getting some fake scrambled eggs and desiccated bacon the next day. The mini mart required a purchase to use their bathroom. The tepid water from the rusted sink splashed my face and left it, if not clean, at least slobber free. The store sold coffee strong enough to put hair on my chest and a gag-worthy breakfast burrito, of which I ate the egg and bacon but tossed the wrap. With caffeine in my veins, and a belly no longer grumbling, I was on my way.

I still couldn't believe I'd actually done it. Look at me, the brave adventurer. The heroines in my books never had to stop to pee every two hours, nor did they walk funny after getting out to stretch their legs. Getting old sucked.

I didn't remember the highway or recognize the area. I only knew I was getting close by the butter-flies in my stomach. What would I find? Had I come all this way for nothing?

I saw the lake first. How could I not, given Maddiogo Lake stretched more than twenty miles end to end. While long, it was narrow in a few spots. My grandma's cottage sat at the north end inside one of the small bays, screened from the water by a line of trees, the dark green metal roof serving as camouflage. Standing in her yard next to the shore, you could see the opposite side of the lake and where the trees were cleared, spot the sparse scattering of houses.

Driving through the sad remains of downtown Cambden, I realized it was no longer the place I remembered. The town had been erected around the single lane highway more than a hundred years ago. While never busy, it at least had a slight bustle to it. I imagined it all ended when the highway was rerouted a few years ago.

Like many a small town, once the traffic moved away, so did most of the businesses, following the dollars that transient travelers brought. It meant the shuttering of local shops, lots of vacant buildings, and a diminishing population. Another town about to ghost the world.

As I drove down Main Street, I noted the many boarded-over windows and faded signs. Lots of for-sale properties, too, yet oddly enough almost all stated they were sold, the stickers slapped across faded signs bright and obviously recent. It made me wonder who was investing in a town that the world had seemingly forgotten. It reminded me of that damned letter I'd burned.

The fire marshal had deemed the fire an accident. It apparently started in the basement by the water heater, which happened to sit below the garburator and kitchen sink. Coincidence? Better faulty wiring than the alternative.

A good thing I'd not accepted the offer to buy

the cottage. If I had, I wouldn't have anywhere to go. It made me wonder if the same person who'd offered to buy my grandma's place was the same one snatching up properties in town. And why.

Then again, if I had the money, I'd want to own it, too. To breathe life into an old-fashioned place where neighbors looked after one another. Or so I liked to believe. I'd never know. While I was moving in, the rest of the town had moved out. It made me wonder if Tricia still remained in the area. It also brought a twinge of guilt.

How long since I'd called the best friend of my youth? Back in the day, we'd been inseparable. Hanging out together as toddlers and going to kindergarten together.

Even though I'd moved, my dad had brought me back for visits and I'd gotten to see her. When I came to live with my grandma, we had sleepovers every weekend, usually at my place on account her family situation wasn't the greatest.

We shared everything until I went to college. We'd started out writing each other letters. It seemed so archaic now. Long distance phone calls were too expensive back then. I'd just about flipped when I got my first phone bill at my dorm. The phone company charged by the minute, and I'd spent an hour telling Tricia about Martin. Back when he wasn't such a jerk.

Tricia had seen his potential for being a prick,

though. She tried to warn me, but I was so desperate to have someone to love. Needed it so badly I ignored the signs.

And then, when I began to realize just how bad it was and how right she'd been, I'd stubbornly gone into denial. I'm sure a therapist would say I did it out of shame. Partially. I also did it out of contemptuous malice. Although I never understood why I'd want to spite Tricia. Was it because she'd seen what I wouldn't recognize? Because, whenever we spoke, I felt guilty that I'd abandoned her and my grandmother?

Needless to say, we grew apart after that. I didn't even have her number anymore and could only wonder if she still lived in her mom's old place.

Taking the road that rounded the lake, I moderated my speed, mostly to watch for wildlife. I remembered that there were deer and bear that lived in the area. Yet it wasn't the furry four-legged critters I ended up screeching to a stop for but a turtle moving laboriously across the road. Drumming my fingers on the steering wheel, I glanced between the trees and eyed the water. The beautiful deep blue. The freshness of the air coming through the rolled-down window.

It was quiet out here. No traffic noise, no people. Just me and my cat.

Why had it taken me so long to come back? I'd always loved this place as a young girl. Been devastated when my grandmother died just before I graduated college. I'd only returned once afterwards. I wanted to blame Martin for it, but the truth was I couldn't handle being inside that cottage without grandma there.

I'd not wanted to deal with the grief, so my children had missed out on the adventures I'd had growing up. Frog hunting and fishing. Learning how to make jam from the wild raspberries we picked. S'mores by the fire. The twinkle of fireflies as they danced in the forest. Although my grandmother used to claim those were fairies.

*"Daddy says fairies aren't real."*

*"Not real?" she'd exclaimed. "Why the very idea! Your mother used to like catching them with me. Hold on a second and I'll show you."*

*She'd gone into the house and returned with a mason jar, the lid in one hand, the jar in the other. Off she marched to the forest, her worn jeans tucked into hiking boots. Her long gray hair dangled in a fat braid down her back.*

*She returned with a tiny golden speck floating in the jar. Too bright for me to stare at for long, and even when I did peek, the wings fluttered too quickly for me to truly see anything.*

*Grandma said, "I told you it was a fairy."*

Young me believed her. Why wouldn't I when she claimed to show me proof?

Fairies weren't the only thing she tried to convince

me to believe in. She had the best stories, like the one about the lake monster, Maddie. Depending on who you asked, she was a three- or five-eyed, horse-headed monster with a green, weedy mane that flowed down a serpentine body. A reporter doing a study of lake monsters in Canada claimed she was a mix of the legendary Mussie in Muskrat Lake and the famous Ogopogo. Although a different professor of folklore history claimed it was more likely a relative of Caddy, another monster out in British Columbia.

Whatever the case, Grandma claimed Maddie woke only every hundred years to feed, and we weren't due for another forty years yet. But she did also warn to beware of those that disturbed Maddie's rest.

I'd never seen the monster, given it was supposedly asleep. As an adult, I didn't believe in fairy tales anymore. I'd also given up on miracles until I pulled into the gravel driveway to my grandma's place and saw the cottage.

It looked just as I remembered, which should have been impossible. I'd not been by in over two decades. It should have had peeling paint and a sagging roof. At the very least been overgrown by the shrubbery.

Yet the pale cream siding appeared almost freshly painted. The porch and its railings remained a matte black. The hunter green metal roof was unbowed. A gray stone chimney jutted from the peak.

It took me a moment to move as relief shook me. I'd been so convinced I'd find a ruin. It seemed impossible that it looked untouched. I pinched myself and blinked in case it was a mirage. Yet the cute cottage remained.

Given the state of it, I wondered if someone lived here. Pretty brazen, given I owned the place. Then again, if they'd been maintaining it, could I really complain?

Exiting the car, I leaned on the door for a second and just looked around. Nostalgia hit me like a ton of bricks, crushing me in memories.

The tree with the rope and the tire swing. How many times had I gone too far, felt the rope do that slack thing then drop, jolting me each time so my stomach sat in my throat? The tree was taller now, but the swing remained. As did the wrought iron bench in the garden. The birdhouses I'd painted in my youth and given Grandma as gifts had been replaced with simple feeders. I guess it was too much to hope cheap plywood and glue had lasted that long.

Before shutting the door to my car, I scooped up Grisou. He scampered to my shoulder and perched. I should have probably worried about him bolting. If he did, I'd never find him. Yet he seemed content, and having him close kept me calm as I crossed the gravel driveway to the flagstone path leading to the cottage.

The front door was closed. Would it be locked? I had no key with the fire having destroyed everything, and I wasn't even sure I should enter. While I'd not seen signs of anyone around, the upkeep suggested otherwise.

Raising my fist, I knocked. Waited.

Knocked again.

If someone did live there, they could have gone out. It was Wednesday. A workday for most people.

I chewed my lower lip as I stood caught in indecision. I couldn't exactly leave. I had nowhere to go. This was my property. Surely that trumped any squatter rights?

The knob turned under my grip, and the door opened. Unexpected and therefore I hesitated. "Hello?"

I shuffled forward, pausing by the threshold. It wasn't just wondering if I'd be invading someone's home that held me back. What would I see inside?

Taking a deep breath. I walked in.

And sobbed.

## 6

I'd been prepared for the worse. Mouse poop all over. Walls and ceilings ripped open, exposing moldy insulation. Perhaps even rotted floorboards that might snap under my weight. Instead, I beheld a miracle.

Everything inside the cottage seemed frozen in time with the ghostly lumps of furniture covered in dustsheets dotting the room. Some shapes were familiar, some not. It also laid to rest the speculation that someone lived here. The house was stuck in limbo, waiting for its owner to come home.

Waiting for me.

Could I be so lucky? Was grandma's stuff still intact under those covers?

I tore the tarp of a long shape that looked like a sofa. The dust cloth pulled free and revealed a familiar floral pattern. The cushions still appeared firm and the material intact. They knew how to make quality stuff back then.

My fingers trailed over the fabric of the armrest. I remembered sitting on this couch when I was a tween back when I liked to be close to my grandma, who always smelled of the perfume she kept on her dresser. That scent somehow lingered even as I recognized it was utterly impossible. It had been too long; however, as I sank onto the couch, I could have sworn her scent surrounded me, wrapping me in a hug. If I closed my eyes, I could pretend I heard her whisper.

*Everything will be all right now that you're home.*

Now if only I could believe it. Would I finally outrun my bad luck and be able to have a proper do-over of my life?

Grisou wiggled from my arms, and I set him free to explore. He bounded over the cushions and then off the arm to the floor. I took a moment longer, looking around, wondering which tarp I'd tackle next.

The silence was nice. The open front door let sunlight pour in. The windows had their curtains drawn. I rose from the couch and shut the cottage door before my kitty went exploring outside.

Next, I tackled curtains, pulling them back, seeing less fluttering dust than expected. I'd almost say someone had been regularly cleaning the house.

My phone rang. A glance showed it was Winnie. I answered with a cheerful, "I made it."

"How's the place look?"

"I won't need to sleep in my car." As I spoke to her, I tugged another dustsheet. The wooden secretary still had the roll top lid that I'd opened every day after school to give myself room to do my homework.

"What kind of shape is the cottage in?"

"It's in excellent shape. It looks just like I remember, Winnie." I pulled off more tarps, revealing blasts from my past.

"Well, damn, that's awesome, Mom."

"It is." My luck finally appeared to be changing.

"Listen, I should go. I start work in an hour. Talk to you later."

"Yeah, later."

Winnie hung up, and I stared at my phone. Smiled. This was turning out to be the best day ever.

I tucked my phone into my pocket as I began surveying the space. As an adult, I noticed the things I'd never paid much mind as a child, starting with the furniture.

Each piece appeared handmade, the wood sturdy, and yet the legs and even the edges were inlaid with intricate carvings, loops and swirls, almost as if embedded with some kind of fancy writing. The same pattern existed around all the door and windowsills, as if the artists wanted to etch their mark into everything they could.

I didn't think the same person had done all the carvings. Running my fingers over the patterns, it was as if I could feel the different signatures. The writing desk by the front door had a fine filigree compared to the deep marks in the floor by the front door, etching out a circle only barely big enough to stand in. There was a shallow set of sigils in the bathroom, embedded in the tiles that formed the shower.

There was water in the toilet bowl—the same baby blue as the sink—and it flushed when I pulled the handle. I almost dropped to my knees to give thanks. I wouldn't have to squat in the woods. Everything was just as I remembered.

*Everything.*

It kind of freaked me out to see just how much had survived the years, because it didn't seem normal. The towels of pure white wrapped in paper in the linen closet should have holes in them. The fridge, an oldie with a rounded frame, green exterior, and vintage appearance, with its door propped open and immaculate shelves, shouldn't have started working the moment I plugged it in. Dear God, I'd never paid an electric bill here. Would my reappearance result in some massive overdue account?

I almost yanked the plug back out but stopped

myself. *Que sera, sera.* What will be will be, as my grandmother always said. If I had a debt, then I'd be a Lannister and find a way to pay it.

How I loved immersing myself into impossible stories. I used to get all my adventures from books, but as the internet took over, I found myself expanding my horizons and watching racy shows on HBO like *True Blood* and *Game of Thrones*.

If only I had something special about me that would allow me some grand experience. It would be nice for once to be the heroine I saw on television or read in a book.

Then again, everything scared me. I'd probably be the person who peed themselves as they huddled, rocking on the floor.

The kitchen cupboards, when opened, showed what you'd expect for the most part. Plates, bowls, cutlery, but no food. That might have been a little too much to expect.

I found the tiny bedroom on the main floor that used to be my mom's and then became mine, first during visits then when I lived there full time.

Before his death, my dad—who never liked my grandmother—always chose to stay in a motel, unless I was here for a few weeks in the summer. Then he left and only returned to pick me up. I didn't mind; I loved this cottage and my grandma.

Yet, at the same time, I couldn't wait to leave.

I'd chosen to go somewhere far away for college, so why the tears rolling hotly down my cheeks?

I wiped at my face even if no one could see me. I hated crying. I'd cried too much of late. And it didn't help I was an ugly crier. Blotchy face, red nose, snot running, and eyes bloodshot, as if I'd been on a bender.

Crying meant I was letting despair win. I needed to stop doing that. Things in my life could be so much worse. I could have been sleeping in my car tonight and getting my ass bitten by bugs when I crouched in the bushes to pee.

Instead I had a bed. Not a very big one but a bed just the same. The twin-sized bed remained pressed against the pine-planked wall painted a pale pink. The boy band posters were gone. I'd owned more than a few, especially of Bon Jovi, before they broke up. In my youth, I loved a man with a mane of long hair and tight jeans, yet I'd settled for the complete opposite in Martin.

The mattress was stripped of sheets, which wasn't a big deal. I had a sleeping bag. Yet when I opened the closet, I found the faded fabric bedding I recalled with its pink roses and thorny vines. There was a pillow in there, too, along with my collection of Nancy Drew books.

"Holy cow." I dropped to sit on the floor and tugged the box of books closer.

Nancy Drew was my hero. As a young girl, I'd admired the intrepid girl detective. What a pity her courage in the stories hadn't rubbed off on me.

The first book made me smile. The title, *Nancy Drew: The Ghost of Blackwood Hall*. I always did like that, just like most Scooby Doo episodes, sometimes the mysteries that seemed supernatural had an explanation.

As I made the bed, I couldn't help but feel as if I'd won the lottery. I couldn't wait to get under those covers and read a book. The simple pleasure of it made me impatient for night to come.

It was too early, though, and I had more to explore. I returned to the kitchen and checked the pantry, finding more dishes, pots, pans, and an old toaster that matched the fridge. I also found a giant cannister of rice.

Was it still good? Surely it had an expiry date. I dug my hands into the grains, letting them run through my fingers. I couldn't eat it on my diet. I sealed the lid on the cannister. I had some grocery stuff in my car.

I brought my few belongings inside and stowed them, including my letter from the lawyer that told anyone who might have a problem with my presence that I owned the place. She'd dug up the deed with my name on it.

The cottage was mine. Every bit of it, including

a possibly massive hydro electric bill. I wasn't prepared to even think of any property taxes owing. Tomorrow I'd worry. Today, I'd let myself feel relief. I had a roof over my head, a woodstove to stave off the cold of the coming winter, a toilet. Even a shower. What else did I need?

For some reason, I saw my daughter's, my son's, even Tricia's face. A taunt that a house wasn't the most important thing. How about friends and family? Perhaps with one worry out of the way, I could concentrate on fixing those bonds.

I'd gone all around the main floor a few times but hadn't seen my cat. I pursed my lips. Glanced upstairs. The one place I'd not gone because, in my mind, that was my grandma's space.

But she was gone, and I'd have to confront her room eventually. I'd been inside it only once after she died. When I'd come with Martin I couldn't exactly tell him to sleep on the main floor on the tiny bed when there was a full-sized one upstairs. I'd walked up those stairs ahead of him, slowing as we neared the top. I'd taken one look at her room, smelled her, and burst into tears.

Martin didn't argue when I ran off and slept downstairs. That was the last time I'd been here.

Which reminded me, the time I'd come before, the dustsheets hadn't been there. Everything had been clean but left as if my grandmother had just stepped out. Someone had obviously done something to preserve the place.

My mind automatically went to Tricia. She lived closest, and while we'd drifted apart, she'd loved my grandmother and might not have wanted to see the refuge of her teenage years go to ruin.

Whoever had taken care of it deserved my thanks for preserving a place that meant so much to me. Meant so much I'd ignored it for more than half my life.

For shame. I almost heard a bell at the word.

Glancing at the stairs, I found my courage and marched up them. At first I kept my eyes closed, afraid of what I'd see. What if they were still there? The gallery of framed pictures on the wall containing images of my mom and grandma at various ages. Some of me as a little girl, my smile wide and carefree.

Not yet. I couldn't look at those yet. The very fact I looked for an excuse not to had me opening my eyes. I faltered as the past rushed to haunt me. Everywhere I looked there was my face, my grandma, my mom and dad, young and happy, pregnant, getting married, and then there were the pics of me.

What froze me, though, were the images of my kids. Baby pictures. First birthdays. School pictures.

All images I'd thought lost forever in the fire. How did they come to be here?

I almost bolted back down those stairs to jump into my car and drive away. There was something uncanny at work here. Only a stalker would have had access to my pictures. Or someone had broken into my house before it burned down and stolen them. Except the images weren't familiar. The events, yes, but I recalled most of my albums. I'd flipped through them often enough, sitting on the floor of my closet, hiding from my angry husband, losing myself in the memories.

Had someone been cataloguing my life? And if so, how did I not notice them? Not to mention, why? Why take pictures of me and the kids and put them on these walls?

"Meow."

Hearing the familiar voice of my kitty, I trotted up the rest of the steps and through the open hatch in the floor before entering the attic proper. I gaped.

Whereas the main floor was unchanged, here was a different scenario. The layout itself remained the same. The attic had long ago been converted into a giant bedroom with bathroom on one end and a closet on the other.

I loved grandma's bathroom. It featured a giant claw foot tub. A hot soak would be so nice.

Walking farther into the room, I didn't notice any real smells. Definitely no perfume.

The bed was stripped, the mattress covered in a plastic sheet. The brass four poster I recalled was gone, replaced with a wooden frame. I'd never seen the sleigh bed before but immediately admired it.

The rocking chair by the woodstove and the stool I used to perch on? Replaced by bean bags, of all things, the fabric a patterned chenille.

The tall dresser might have been the same, but it had been stripped of its varnish and painted white then distressed for an antique look. The braided rag carpet was gone, and only the bare plank floor remained. The long dresser with the big mirror atop it had also changed into another distressed piece. The mirror inside its thick silver frame had been tilted lengthwise and hung on the bathroom door. A space that appealed to me and didn't actually remind me much of my grandma at all.

Still, given what I'd found downstairs, it was a relief to open the closet door and see no clothes. No shoes. The drawers when checked were empty. The bathroom was clean of toiletries. It made me wonder where grandma's things went. She didn't have much jewelry, a few necklaces and rings mostly, but as a young girl, I'd loved the antique silver brush she used to comb my hair.

Turning away from the bathroom, I laughed to see Grisou splayed on the bed. Sly critter. He'd not been there a moment before.

"There you are, naughty boy."

He poked his four furry legs in the air and waited for a belly rub.

I flopped onto the bed beside him and gave him one. I then proceeded to talk to him. Again. How many times a day did I have to talk to him as if he'd answer before I was officially the cat lady? Or was it the number of felines I owned that determined it?

"Who do you think took care of the place?" I asked.

I really hoped I wouldn't have to fight someone over it. Although I might owe them a bit of money, given they'd saved the place from ruin.

Could it be that the trust grandma set up not only paid for the taxes on it but the upkeep too? I'd have to get my lawyer to check it out.

"Come on, furball. Let's see if we can light the stove and make ourselves some dinner."

The can of Spam fried in a pan and served with my cheesy orange pasta was delicious. That night, I sat on the porch, listening to the crickets, while Grisou—on a harness he instantly disdained—hunted the moths fluttering to reach the outdoor light. Out in the woods, lights blinked on and off. Fireflies at play. A gentle breeze rustled, the only sound I could hear. No neighbors. No traffic. Finally, just calm and quiet, with none of the ugly.

Peace settled within me. When I heard a big splash coming from the lake, I told my anxiety to calm down. Fish couldn't walk on land, and I'd left my monsters behind.

That night in the tiny bed with its rose-bud sheets, I slept soundly for the first time in what seemed like forever.

Until the rude awakening.

## 7

I'D FORGOTTEN TO PULL THE CURTAINS SHUT, AND the dawn light streaked across my face, doing its best to pierce my eyelids. I felt so nice and cozy. I didn't want to get up yet.

"Mee-uu?" A tiny questioning sound.

I grumbled, "Not yet. Give me a minute to enjoy this."

As if my kitten would let me sleep now that he knew I was awake. He ended up purring in bed with me, his head insistently butting at my hand. I absently scratched him. Greedy little bugger. He just loved his morning snuggles. But I wanted to sleep. When he moved away, I rolled over.

Something furry tickled my nose.

"Grisou," I complained.

His head rubbed softly against my fingers and yet somehow also still tickled my nose. My eyes popped open as I brushed at my face. Panic set in as I felt bristles against my fingers.

Rolling out of bed, I stumbled and stubbed my toe hard enough to make me cry out and blink back tears. The pain didn't stop me from whirling around.

There it was. Sitting on my bed. Brown furred and whiskered.

A mouse!

I screamed. It squeaked. Grisou let out a sound of satisfaction and gave chase, which led to more squeaking and more screaming.

A broom was involved at one point, as was some sobbing and shrieks as my cat chased the mouse. I chased the cat and eventually got said mouse to exit the door I'd opened.

Out of breath and heart pounding, I then slammed it and stared at my cat, who sat demure as you could please, licking a paw and washing his face.

"That was terrifying," I murmured. As was the sudden knocking at my back.

I almost peed my pants.

What the hell? I glanced at the portal. It was much too loud to be the mouse. And mice didn't knock.

People did.

The solid door had no peephole, so I couldn't see who stood outside, but apparently, I was about to have my first visitor. Lovely. Here I stood wearing an oversized gray sweatshirt, loose pink track pants, and I'd yet to brush my hair or teeth. I really needed a bra, too. Gravity had not been kind.

Maybe they'd go away.

There was more knocking. "Hello? I know you're in there," said a distinctly male voice.

How did he know? Was he spying on me? I glanced at the staircase and its collection of pictures. Had I found the person who had catalogued my life? Wait, wouldn't that be he'd found me? Was I in danger?

Or just being paranoid?

"What do you want?" I managed to croak.

Through the door I heard him say, "I heard screaming. Is everything okay?"

Oh, dear.

I opened the door and had to look up. Even though the man stood a few feet away, he was tall. Good looking, too, with his square, clean-shaven jaw. He wore a plaid shirt tucked into snug, worn jeans. He also carried an axe, its head resting on my porch.

A lumberjack perhaps? Murderers also liked to use axes.

Gulp.

I tore my gaze from the weapon to his face. Despite the early morning hour, with dawn barely cresting, shades hid his eyes. A ballcap sat low on his head with silver-blond hair curling out from under it. What my son as a teen would have called hockey hair. Maybe I was still asleep because, in many respects, he was a fantasy come true.

"Good morning," I said more brightly than the situation warranted, trying to forget the fact I looked like a hot mess.

"Were you the one screaming bloody murder?"

My cheeks flushed. "Um. Yeah. That was me. Not being murdered though. I had a mouse situation."

"A mouse," he repeated. "You shrieked as if being eviscerated."

"It touched me," I explained. "And then my cat chased it around the house."

He stared at me with those dark lenses and said nothing.

"I got rid of it, though," was my next defensive attempt.

"Killed it, you mean." His lip curled.

I recoiled. "Of course not. I shooed it back outside where it belongs. Last I saw, it dove off the porch and headed for the woods."

"You know it will be back." A bald statement.

"Says who?"

"Says me. Mice don't give up their homes that easily."

"He'd better. Grisou is a fine hunter." I might

have lied on that score. A fine hunter would have never let a mouse into my bed in the first place.

"I take it, despite the shrill noises coming from you, that you are uninjured?" He eyed me up and down, making me realize I looked absolutely horrible.

It wasn't just the outfit. Despite my new regime, I remained overweight. It would take more than a few months to reverse decades of damage. The running around had also left me flushed, smelling of sweat, and with my hair a wild mess of gray and muddy brown. I had no style and usually kept it tied back in a ponytail.

The more he stared, the more self-conscious I felt. I couldn't have said why. I had no need to impress him. Nor did I care what he thought. At least I shouldn't have cared. But then again, if I was going to meet someone at my most wretched, why did they have to be so damned good looking?

The fact I noticed no longer came as a shock. Since I'd split with Martin, I'd begun looking at men differently. Sizing them up. Wondering what kind of people they were. What hid under their clothes.

To my surprise, my libido woke. Not that I did anything about it. Masturbation embarrassed me. Stupid, I know. People did it all the time. Doctors recommended it, but I couldn't shake the sensation that someone watched me whenever I put a hand down my pants.

One thing was for sure. The man in front of me would never want to watch. He probably dated super-models. A petty and stupid thought and still I couldn't help but feel bitter. I'd never date. I'd probably die alone. A divorcee with a lot of cats who loved me.

I realized I couldn't stand in front of the guy slack jawed all day. "Thanks for coming to check on me, but as you can see, I'm fine, if embarrassed." I would have closed the door, but he stepped forward.

"I'm Jace, your neighbor." He glanced to the side, and through the trees, barely visible, I spotted a yellow cottage.

"Naomi." I didn't give him a last name because I'd yet to change it, but I'd begun the paperwork to take back my maiden name, Rousseaux. Automatically, I held out my hand.

He didn't shake it, probably on account the proper hand still held an axe.

The moment turned awkward. I tucked my hand behind my back. "You're living in the old Murphy place? I thought it burned down."

It happened well before I was born, so I wasn't clear on details, other than my grandmother warned me to never ever go near the place. According to her, it was haunted.

"I've owned it the last fifteen."

"And rebuilt, obviously."

"Obviously," he repeated. "What are you doing here?"

A valid question, given he'd not once seen me since he'd moved in.

"I inherited this place from my grandma."

"You're Rousseaux's granddaughter." He eyed me, disdain now clear in his gaze, and more than ever I wanted to shove the door closed. He was pushing the limits of my good manners.

"You've heard of my grandmother?"

"Who hasn't heard of the witch of the lake?"

I didn't even know I was about to slap him until he caught my wrist.

He arched a brow. "I wouldn't."

I yanked my hand free. "Then don't call my grandmother names."

"It wasn't said in disrespect."

"You're being facetious."

"Big words for a young lady."

My jaw almost hit the floor at his use of young, and then heated anger flooded me. He was flirting with me and not because he was attracted. I wasn't so dumb as to think he liked what he saw. He thought he could manipulate me. That I was some pathetic old woman who would coo and bow if he flattered me.

Ha. As if. "I know lots of big words, and little

ones, too. Like nice to meet you, but I'm done talking. Please leave."

"You're annoyed."

"Aren't you observant." My sarcasm emerged en pointe for once.

"Are you always this easily irritated?"

I sighed. "It's the crack of dawn, I was woken by a rat—"

"I thought it was a mouse."

"On second thought, given its size, it must have been a rat. After the morning I've had, I need coffee."

"I see." For some reason, he seemed amused.

Then to my surprise, he grabbed my hand with the one not holding a weapon and shook it, his grip warm and calloused. Firm and quick. He let me go and touched the brim of his ball cap. "It was interesting meeting you, Naomi Rousseaux. If you need anything, you know where to find me."

"Or I could just scream." A dumb joke that I immediately regretted.

His lips tilted slightly. "That works, too." He turned to leave, and it occurred to me he might have a few answers for me.

I blurted out, "Actually, before you go, do you know who's been minding the place?" Did I owe my neighbor thanks?

Rather than tell me, he sauntered off with a ridiculous, "The house took care of itself."

## 8

*THE HOUSE TOOK CARE OF ITSELF?* WHAT KIND OF idiot reply was that? Or was I misinterpreting? Could be he meant the trust took care of the house. That made more sense.

I spent the day settling in and just plain relaxing. I figured I owed myself a day of no driving, no worrying. The first part proved easy to avoid, the latter... I tried to keep myself busy instead.

A bucket under the kitchen sink had a scrubbing brush, an old can of Comet, and rags for cleaning. The place might look clean, but it wouldn't hurt to disinfect the bathroom and kitchen.

That, in turn, led to me sweeping the place and washing the floor. By the time I was done, I needed a shower. The water wasn't as hot as I'd have liked, but I turned my face into it anyhow. Then I soaped myself, doing the best I could to ignore my body. I knew there was a big push to love myself as I was. To see the stretch marks as signs of love because I'd given birth. The sagging breasts a sign of aging that everyone experienced. Magazines and the media were on a media blitz telling me that big was beautiful.

I didn't feel beautiful. My apron—the hideous name for my big belly—hung enough I had to lift it to wash under. Same with my breasts. Even though I'd lost some weight, the stretch marks on my upper thighs, breasts, and tummy would never fade. The loose skin would never become taut.

It shouldn't have mattered. I was in my forties. A woman of experience with the marks of it etched on my body. I want to embrace it, but I hated it. Other than eating better and exercising, I didn't know how to fix it.

My depression led to me overeating for dinner that night, having a second helping of the chicken salad I'd made with canned meat, mayonnaise, and some celery I'd caught on sale. At least it was low carb, but I was disappointed in myself. I couldn't let my old bad habits come rushing back.

The knock came just as I was about to settle on the couch and read the book I'd found in the desk. It was about the history of the area that I would have sworn wasn't there the day before.

*Knockity-knock.* I assumed it was my neighbor, returning to make me uncomfortable. Maybe instead of an axe, he'd have a chainsaw this time. Or a sledgehammer like that crazy woman in that Stephen King book.

To my surprise, when I swung the door open, I beheld Tricia.

Older than the last time I'd seen her but wearing it well. Like me, she'd put on pounds, but where I sagged in all the wrong places and did what I could to hide it, she flaunted her voluptuous hourglass figure. The purple wool knit sheath dress hugged her shape while a gray plaid shawl hung over her shoulders. Her tanned skin hid the signs of aging better than mine did, and she didn't have a single streak of gray in her long black hair braided to hang down her back in a thick rope.

For a moment we stood staring at each other, separated by a wall built of ugly words and hurt then a silence more devastating than I could have imagined.

Gazing upon her, I saw the good times. Recalled the days when I smiled and laughed. How she used to always be there for me. Like the first day of kindergarten when my mom forgot to pack me real food in my lunch and I had a bag full of shiny rocks, Tricia shared hers. When my mom died, and she stood in the pouring rain with me as I cried at her grave. How she'd biked home during third period to get me some pants because I wouldn't come out of the bathroom when my period came suddenly and stained my crotch. She'd not cared she got detention. She'd always been there for me.

And I'd abandoned her.

"Trish, I—I—" My throat thickened, and I couldn't spit out any of the words I wanted to say. How to apologize for not listening to her about Martin? How to say I was sorry that I'd left and never looked back. How could she ever forgive me?

Rather than speak, Trish's arms opened wide. A second later, we were hugging, and I sobbed. How had I ever thought my best friend had stopped being my best friend?

"I'm sorry," I blubbered.

"No, I'm sorry," she cried.

"I'm more sorry. I should have listened to you."

"No, it's my fault. He was your husband. I should have been more understanding."

We were a snotty mess of apologies. It was so Canadian I began to laugh.

She hiccupped as she said, "What's so funny?"

I only had to mutter, "Sorry, eh," for her to pause, and then she joined me in laughing. The joke an old one.

It came about because of a high school trip to the States, where we'd been billeted at an American student's house. We'd played into every single stereotype there was from claiming we lived in igloos to riding dog sleds to school. In those days, before the internet, we could get away with the prank. The memory of it had us both smiling as we pulled apart.

"It's good to see you," I said.

"Even better to see you," she exclaimed. "I've been trying to call."

"I lost my phone." I wasn't ready to admit what Martin had done.

"I'm pretty sure I have the right number." She pulled out a pink monstrosity, a smart phone encased in pink jewels with the occasional white one thrown in.

Before I could tell her that was impossible because only my kids and lawyers had it, she dialed, and my phone went off.

Frowning, I moved to grab it and saw "unknown number." I eyed her then the phone. "You're the one who keeps calling."

"Well, yeah. I was trying to see how you were doing."

"I didn't know it was you. We kept getting bad connections."

"No surprise given what's happening. I'm sure they're not happy you're back."

"Who's not happy?"

Tricia waved a hand. "Doesn't matter now. You're here. Just in time to help."

"Help with what?"

Rather than answer, she leaned down to pet the cat circling her ankles. "I see you got the present I sent."

I blinked. "Present?"

"The cat." She pointed to Grisou.

My brow creased more deeply. "What are you talking about? He's a stray I found outside my old place."

She nodded. "I knew he'd eventually find you."

I stared at her. "You can't have sent him. I adopted him in the States."

"Well, I did tell him you might be far, but he still agreed to find you."

It was becoming clear my friend had aged well only on the outside. Up in the belfry, she was completely batty. "Maybe you thought you sent a cat to me, but I doubt it's Grisou. We're talking an eighteen-hour drive from here. No way would an animal go that far." Not to mention the idea was ludicrous. The expression "herding cats" came about for a reason. They never did as they were told.

"It did take him longer than expected. I mean, five months, really?" She chastised my cat, who basically ignored her to groom his suddenly very dirty hind leg.

"How have you been?" I asked, rather than the more pressing question of, was she on meds, and if yes, had she taken them today?

"Preparing," she said.

"For?" I asked, having to move out of the way

as she fully entered and made herself comfortable on the couch.

"You, for one thing."

"You've been waiting a long time then," I joked weakly, sitting in a chair across from her.

"No kidding. It hasn't been easy being stuck here."

"You never left Cambden?"

"More like couldn't. Someone had to stay and try to keep those damned dark orcs from waking the lake monster."

## 9

---

IT SADDENED ME TO SEE MY FRIEND HAD GONE NUTS. Was this what small-town living had done to her? Or was she suffering from some kind of mental breakdown? When we were younger, I'd always seen her as the stronger of the two of us. Kind of scary that it seemed I'd survived the ordeal of my marriage better than she had boredom.

It was as if she read my mind. "I am not senile. There is so much you don't yet understand, but you will. Sooner rather than later, I hope. We don't have much time. Have you found her books yet?"

"What books?" Other than my Nancy Drew collection and the history of Cambden, including a chapter on Maddy the monster, I'd not seen any others. Then again, I hadn't snooped through every cupboard. I still struggled with the concept that this place was mine. Everywhere I looked I saw my grandma. I wasn't sure I'd ever feel at home.

"You know, *the books*. The ones she kept in her room."

"There are no books in Grandma's room."

"Did you look everywhere?"

"No, but the spots I did were empty."

A furrow on her brow, Tricia mumbled, "That's not possible. The house wouldn't have let anyone take them. They have to be here." She bounced off the couch and pounded up the stairs without even asking for permission.

Startled, it took me a second to follow. "Where are you going?"

"I'm going to find the books. I know they were…" Her voice trailed off.

I joined her in the attic bedroom as a new round of cursing began. One that managed to incorporate the F word in unique ways, interspersed with some words so crude I almost covered my ears.

"Tricia!" I exclaimed.

"What?"

"Your language."

She paused in her cussing to eye me. "What about it?"

"Can you tone it down?"

"Can I tone it down she says. Are you *bleeping* kidding me?"

I closed my ears to the intentional goading. "That kind of language is completely unnecessary."

"Actually, it's not strong enough to properly convey what I'm feeling. I need bigger and fouler words." Her arms waved as she exclaimed.

"Why? I still am trying to figure out why you're so upset." Because her level of rage made little sense to me.

"I'm upset because they're gone. The books that explained everything, the answers that were supposed to be waiting for you, are gone." She swept a hand to a room bare of knickknacks but for a candle sitting on a brass saucer.

"Maybe the person who acted as caretaker of this place took them. Which is fine, I might add. They did me a favor, so I won't begrudge them taking some old books." At least I assumed they must be old, given how long it had been since Grandma died.

"You don't just take *the books.*" There was that inflection again.

"What is special about these books?" I huffed, no longer able to contain my exasperation.

She blinked at me. "You really haven't the slightest clue, do you?"

"Clue about what? I wish you'd stop talking to me in riddles." I couldn't help my frustration, especially since it felt as if I should know of what she spoke. For a half-second, I thought I could even see them, a trio of old tomes. There one second, gone the next.

Her explanation emerged in a rush of words. "Your grandmother had some very old books that belonged to her grandmother, and the one before that. You were supposed to inherit them."

"I don't see the big deal. It's just books."

Trish gasped. "They're not just any books. They had knowledge in them that you need. Magical spells and instructions on how to deal with the coming crisis. And now they're gone!"

It sounded as if Tricia had read one too many fantasy novels. The kind where a young heroine found a magical object that changed her life.

I wasn't young. I wasn't a heroine. And I could change my own life, thank you.

"Maybe they'll turn up. I haven't explored every inch of this place yet."

"You could look for years and never find half its secrets. The house decides what you'll see. Apparently, it didn't see you as ready." Her lips turned down.

With her odd statements we veered again into loony territory. Despite my happiness at seeing her, it might be best for her to go. Maybe with a gentle reminder to take her meds. How would she react if I suggested she talk to her doctor about the dosage?

"So listen, Trish, it was really nice of you to stop by but—"

She interrupted me with a slash of her hands. "Don't patronize me. This can't be happening. Not now. We don't have much time. There was another sighting just last night."

I knew I shouldn't encourage the crazy, yet I couldn't help myself. "Sighting of what?"

But she kept going rather than replying. "I know how it sounds, and I wouldn't have believed it either, but then people started going missing. We're up to more than a dozen now. They never did find Thomas's other shoe."

I couldn't help the rounded O of my lips as I gasped in shock. What kind of danger had I put myself in? "There's a serial killer on the loose?"

"I wouldn't say loose. I've yet to hear reports of her coming onto land, but stay away from the water."

Understanding hit me. We didn't have a female serial killer but a bad case of people drowning. "Don't worry. I don't like to swim."

I didn't even own a suit anymore. Although, if I kept dropping pounds, maybe I would. If my mommy tummy ever shrank enough. I'd be wearing long shirts the rest of my life. Not the biggest deal. I could remove all the mirrors in the house so I didn't see it.

Tricia was still babbling nonsense, but I tuned into one word that stuck out.

"Did you say Maddy? As in the lake monster?"

"Haven't you been listening?" Trish stopped pacing and gesticulating to stare at me.

"No." I was honest, brutally so. "Because you're talking crazy. There is no lake monster."

"Yes, there is," she retorted saucily. "But she shouldn't be awake already. It's too early in the cycle."

This was getting sad. My poor friend. I pulled her into a hug and whispered, "I'm happy to see you, Trish, I really am, but you're freaking me out. I really think you should get some help."

She shoved me away and glared. "Well, that was some judgmental shit. I need help? More like *you* need help."

How dare she get mad when I just had her well-being at heart. "I'm not the one talking crazy about a lake monster eating people."

"I never said she ate them. No one knows what Maddy wants with humans. Could be she collects them like dolls. Maybe she turns them into her servants. Maybe it's not Maddy taking people at all but something else."

"Maddy doesn't exist," I yelled.

"Here less than a week and acting like a know-it-all. Haven't changed at all, have you?" She snorted and turned away from me.

Grisou chose that moment to hop up onto the bed.

Tricia wagged a finger at him. "Haven't you told her anything?"

It was hard to call someone crazy for talking to my cat—especially since I did it. However, this reunion had devolved into something strange. "My cat doesn't speak."

"Only because you don't know how to listen. Which I don't understand. You're her granddaughter. The last heir of her blood."

"Actually, not true. I have kids, remember?"

"Of course, I remember. I send them something every birthday."

True, she used to until the kids moved out. But my kids had then chosen to distance themselves from family. "If you want, I'll tell Wendy and Geoffrey hi from you."

Tricia waved a hand of dismissal. "Why would I need you to do that? I speak to them both at least once a week."

It had to be a lie. Neither of my kids ever spoke to me that often. Although Wendy was starting to since the separation.

"That girl Geoff is dating is quite lovely. And Wendy reminds me of you at that age."

Now I knew she lied. Geoff wasn't seeing anyone. Surely, he would have told me.

What if he hadn't?

I had to prove to myself she was lying, hence I blurted out, "Wendy is loving San Diego."

"Are you quizzing me?" she said with a laugh. "Seriously?" She shook her head. "We both know she's in Seattle and hates all the rain. Geoff is house shopping with Helena, and while he hasn't popped the question, he's been eyeballing rings. Wendy is worried about you because she thinks her dad might go postal and pull a murder-suicide stunt."

"She did not say that about Martin," I stated, and yet I could so easily picture Wendy saying it. There was no love lost between the pair.

"You really are oblivious, aren't you?" She tsked as she once more shook her head. "No wonder it took so long for the cat here to find you. And now it might be too late."

My chin lifted at her words because they were the opposite of my new mantra. "It's never too late to start over." Then, in case she didn't know, "Martin and I are getting a divorce."

"About time."

"He was cheating on me."

Trish's lips turned down. "I know."

"Oh. I guess you also know my house burned down and I've got nothing left. Nothing but this house and my cat."

"And whose fault is that?" Her pert reply had me bristling.

"I thought you came here to apologize."

"For what? I told you he was a no-good scoundrel, and you ignored me. You then proceeded to pretend I didn't exist. If anyone should apologize, it's you."

She was right, and yet a part of me was loathe to admit guilt. "I was dealing with stuff. Still am."

"Oh, for goddess's sake." Trish blew out a breath of exasperation. "While you're enjoying your midlife crisis, there are bad things happening. People are in danger."

"I'm sorry if they are, but that has nothing to do with me."

"We'll see about that." Tricia abruptly left me, skipping down the stairs while I could only follow once more, barely arriving in time for her to slip on her shoes and open the door.

"You're leaving?" Despite having asked, it still took me aback.

"For now. I'll be back." She perused me head to toe. "With dye, scissors, and my sewing machine. Really, Omi One Cannoli, what happened to being a fashion setter?"

She'd used the name she had for me as kids, styled after the very wise Obi Wan, and I suddenly felt horrible that it was our first face-to-face meeting in ages and I'd been…mean. No matter her mental issues, Tricia would always be my friend. Currently my only friend in the world.

This time when I hugged her it was gentle and heartfelt as I whispered, "It's nice to see you."

"You won't say that once I pluck those brows," she taunted with a laugh as she left with one final warning. "Stay away from the lake."

## 10

THE LURE OF THE LAKE PROVED TOO TEMPTING TO resist despite the advice to stay away from it. Within minutes of Tricia leaving, I had put on shoes, slipped on a sweater, and walked down the slight sloping yard to the lake's shore. For some reason, I'd avoided it since my arrival. Weird because I'd spent so many happy hours in these waters.

Twilight had fallen, that strange time of day where the last remnants of daylight fought against shadows and ultimately lost. When the familiar turned mysterious. Ominous even. Despite having spent decades forgetting most of the old stories my grandma told, they returned to me in a rush. Tales of warriors battling to the death, their bodies burned after the fight and set adrift on rafts to sink into the lake. She told me if they ever dredged the bottom, they'd find those old bones. But then she proceeded to explain how unlikely it was given how deep the lake went. Deep enough you couldn't dive to the bottom and touch it. So deep that if any weeds grew, they never got tall enough to tickle your feet when you swam.

It had to be deep given the monster that supposedly slept at the very bottom of the expanse. Maddy, or so they called her these days. Grandma liked to use the olden name.

Maed'doulain'a. I could never curl my tongue around the consonants the same way. Grandma had fancy names for a lot of things. But when I asked her about these people she told stories about, asked about their background, she always turned sad.

"They are family and legend. In a place we can no longer reach. A place lost to us, the last of the *cailleach*." A word she never explained, and back then, I didn't have the internet to tell me the answer.

At the time, I'd never thought to wonder at the oddity of her claiming some heroes in a story as relatives. Why not? When I was a young girl, it was fun to imagine myself special, the descendent of someone mighty. However, they were just stories, like the one about the lake monster. Everyone knew monsters didn't exist. Unless human ones counted.

The path down to the water was only a suggestion with a few flat rocks marking the way. I still recalled the younger me running ahead, the sun filtering through trees that used to be much shorter. Laughing when grandma yelled at me to watch out for imps. She also told me to never feed fairies and to steer clear from deals with those she called the two-faced people.

Funny how only now did I realize how seriously my grandma believed in those things. I better understood my father's issues with her manner of teaching. Had my grandma lived in the real world at all, or had she, like Tricia, chosen a version full of fantasy creatures?

The thought they might be alike only served to feed my guilt over how I'd treated Tricia. She had reached out to me, and I'd been a bitch.

I'd have to apologize, a realization that galled even as it felt right. I'd loved my grandma because of her crazy nature. I couldn't do any less for Tricia.

The last rays of the sun colored the surface of the lake as I stood on the edge. The unwary who waded too far quickly sank when it dropped off sharply. Given no one had ever measured the bottom I could see how the legends began.

A sharp breeze stroked across my face, enough to cause the lake to ripple, the small waves lapping the stony shore. The dock I used to fish off of jutted about twenty or so feet out onto the water, its wood faded, possibly even rotted. I'd know better once I gave it a closer look.

The rowboat with the tiny motor at the back

was missing. Probably sank or floated off a long time ago. If I was going to stick around, I wouldn't mind getting a canoe or a kayak, and I'd invest in a good lifejacket. I knew all about lake safety. My grandmother drilled it into me at a young age. Along with stories of Maddy.

It wasn't just grandma who told me stories about the lake monster. Everyone in town knew the legendary creature's name. Maddy had existed as far back as anyone could remember, the story passed down among the people, great-grandparents who were told by their greats and so forth. They spoke of a creature massive enough to eat a cow whole but who really preferred the taste of humans. She only came around every hundred years, feasting on those who dared to breach the waters she called home. When she wasn't terrorizing and feeding, she hibernated far beneath.

Lots of people had claimed to see her. None had actual proof unless you counted blurry pictures with what may or may not be a hump on the water. In many respects, Maddy was our version of the Loch Ness monster, talked about as if she truly existed, and yet there was no evidence.

I'd certainly never seen her, and despite the stories, Grandma never kept me out of the lake. She told me to not worry. Maddy was supposed to sleep for decades yet.

According to Tricia, I should worry. Hard to

believe with the pink and purple rays of the setting sun staining the surface. As a young girl, I'd never heard of any tragedies ever happening on the lake. No boating accidents or drownings. Yet there was no mistaking Tricia's vehemence and insistence that people were being affected.

Monsters weren't real. Not the kind that ate people, at any rate. The kind that reveled in telling someone they were fat and stupid? Tried to dump them without any regard? That kind of monster lived and breathed. Such a shame.

Three months since that turning point and I remained bitter. I tried not to be. After all, I was happier without Martin. Didn't want him back. Yet, a tiny part of me was angry. He'd acted as if I was at fault for everything. As if I was the reason our marriage failed. And on top of that, he made me question everything. After all, if Martin had never loved me, then perhaps neither did the kids.

What of my dad? Never really the hugging type, had he only tolerated me being around because he had to? My mom had left me. Walked out one day while I was at school and moved in with her boyfriend.

But that wasn't a bad thing at first, given she and my dad mostly stopped fighting. Then, one day, the visits stopped. I blamed my dad for keeping me away from her. When school let out early one day, I mustered the nerve to ride a bus to her place, found someone else living there.

She'd just moved out and not bothered to tell me. She died shortly thereafter in an accident, but she'd left me first. It might have been why I didn't fight more when my dad moved us away. Then my dad disappeared without a trace while on a trip.

Mom and Dad were gone, Grandma and husband, too. Even my kids had left.

Obviously, the problem was me.

Doubt was a vicious thing. It made me overanalyze everything in my life. Every word spoken to me. Every expression. When that cashier frowned, was she showing disapproval of me? When I heard laughter, was it at my expense? Had I misinterpreted everything in my life?

Did I know anything at all?

"Argh!" My frustration bubbled out, and it felt good to yell it. The sound of my annoyance carried over the water and grew in tenor, louder and louder.

I could have sworn I heard an echoing of my cry, but it returned to me warped and somehow mocking, the timber of it lower then higher. Someone taunting my vent.

The water stilled. The waves that lapped slowed until the surface of the lake became a smooth sheen just as the night claimed the land. The lack of sunlight made it harder, but I still could see to a certain extent. Even though the stars were far, they provided a little light, and I saw glints on the water as they reflected. But they proved misleading because the glints appeared to rise in a swell. My imagination creating something that wasn't there. I turned away from it.

*Lake monsters aren't real.*

The moon was only the barest of crescents, yet it, too, shed some illumination, in the open at least. I'd have a hard time making my way back even through the thin line of trees. As a child, I'd thought it wildly exciting to navigate my way, especially since Grandma made it a game. She'd ensure all the lights in the cottage were out and then dared me to find her as quickly as I could.

*"How am I supposed to find you?" I'd asked. "It's too dark."*

*"Only for your eyes. You have other senses. You need to tune into them. Trust what you feel."*

*Not exactly the most precise of instructions for a child, but Grandma wouldn't say more. Rather, she disappeared, and I remembered the fear in those first few moments.*

*I'd stood there listening to the sounds that were familiar by day and imagined them as something else because it was night.*

*"Grandma?"*

*She'd not replied, and I wasn't even sure she was close by. I had to find her.*

*I ran a few steps and hit a tree. Face first. My nose took the brunt, and as I reeled, my eyes welled with tears. But I didn't cry.*

*Tears for acting foolish wouldn't get any sympathy. In my family, only truly sad things got commiseration.*

*I recovered from my first mishap and took more care with my walking. I closed my eyes even though it was already too dark to see. Taking a lesson from Luke Skywalker, I looked with my other senses. Listened, not just to the noise of leaves rustling but their direction, how close they sounded. I began to navigate around the pitfalls. I aimed for the soft creak, barely noticeable, but I knew that noise. The weathervane atop the cottage. It was never completely still or quiet. Even on wind-less days.*

*The more I immersed myself inside myself, the more I discerned, including the various scents. Forest, wildlife, the hint of smoke from a chimney.*

*And then, a scent unique to my grandma. I paused and opened my eyes.*

*She beamed at me. "That was most excellent,* ma petite minou. *Hot cocoa?"*

The cocoa was always made from scratch, and just thinking about it made me crave it.

While I didn't have anything to make a hot chocolate, I could use a nice tea, and I'd brew myself a cup the moment I got back inside the cottage. Once I found it, that was. With the darkness complete, I had only a vague idea of its direction.

Perhaps I could use my tuning—as grandma

called it—to find my way. If I still knew how. It had been a long time since I'd played those kinds of games. Especially once my dad found out and had a blowout with my grandmother.

*"Don't you fill her head with your mumbo jumbo,"* he'd hollered.

*"If I don't teach her, who will?"*

*"No one. That's the whole point. She's going to be normal. Not a mess like her mother."*

Normal. To my dad, that meant moving us far enough away that I rarely saw my grandma. It involved not believing in lake monsters or fireflies that were fairies. I went to school. I learned. I forgot the things my grandma wanted to teach me. I forgot how to see the world through her eyes.

Sighing, I stared out over the water. Ah, to return to the days of my youth when everything was possible. A time when I might have believed the water had risen in a hump that flowed toward shore instead of just the shadows playing a trick on me. I wasn't a child anymore to believe in fantasy.

Turning away from the water, I headed for the cottage, the distance short, especially in broad daylight. However, now I couldn't see the house, not even any lights that surely should be shining in at least one window. The trees were only thinly popu-lated here, and yet they blocked my view as surely as if a curtain had been dropped.

I didn't have far to go. I simply needed to follow

the path at my feet. A trail I couldn't see when I looked down. It turned my steps into a shuffle as I spread my hands out in front of me, a game of Blind Man's Bluff except I didn't have any giggles to lead me in the right direction. I didn't hear a single thing except for my panicked breath.

My hand slapped into bark, and I yelped before I recovered and kept my palm on the rough bark. I moved past it, hand stretched to the next trunk then the one after. Any moment I expected to see light. Surely, I'd walked far enough, and yet in every direction I peered, all I saw was more darkness.

A chill settled with the lack of sunlight and a cold that surely frosted my breath. I couldn't see it, but I felt it cooling my exposed skin.

What a stupid idea coming outside at night. Never again, I vowed, even as a part of me whimpered, convinced I would wander these dark woods forever until I died of exposure and starvation. My epithet, once they found my weathered bones, would read, *Should have brought a flashlight.*

I stumbled, lost my grip on the tree, and hit the ground, my palms breaking the fall. The detritus of the forest floor dug into my skin, and I clapped my hands together to remove the loose bits as I rose.

Why did I suck so much at basic survival?

*Splash.* The watery sound had me whirling. Why did it seem so close? Surely, I'd not circled back to the lake?

*Crack.*

The snap of a limb had me turning again. What was that? Just a random branch breaking? Or was something in the woods with me? A bear? Wolf? Rabid raccoon?

Something hunting me.

Watching…

It was so easy to let fear take over. It took only the barest effort to invite it in. It played on my weakness. It thrummed all my inner trepidations and made them real. As my breathing quickened and my terror ripened, I wanted the cottage. Wanted to sit in that big, fat comfy chair and rest my head on that silly lace doily that draped it. I wanted to sip on a cup of tea, wrapped in the afghan my grandma had knitted, safe behind the doors and windows.

However, I now had no idea in what direction the house lay. Straight ahead, or had I veered off my course?

And why was it so cold?

So much for a warm late summer. I shivered inside my sweater and hugged myself. The tip of my nose frosted, and my teeth chattered. Time to stop screwing around and imagining things that weren't there. Next time I wanted to prove a point to Tricia or anyone else, I should do it in broad daylight where it was easier to pretend everything was okay.

I couldn't feel around for trees and hold myself warm at the same time, so I took my chances and just picked a direction to walk. My toe stubbed a root soon after. Limping, I grumbled at the unkind forest doing its best to injure me. So much for feeling welcomed home.

Brrr. Had winter suddenly arrived? It seemed like every step I took got chillier.

It reminded me of the night of the fire. Of the ominous impression I got. This time the hair on my nape didn't rise, but it was getting colder.

A whispering noise filled the air, not a voice or words, and yet it felt like speech. A stream of papery consonants that whipped around me, lifting my hair despite the lack of breeze. Speaking to me.

I chose to slam my hands against my ears rather than listen. I closed my eyes, too, and I ran. Turning inward, I ignored everything outside of that room inside my mind. A room I knew quite well but hadn't used since Martin had left.

Articles claimed it was a method used by abuse victims to hide themselves from the things that hurt them. In this case, I found it gave me the courage to not freeze. While my conscious self hid, the subconscious drove my body. As it turned out, it was much more adept at it. My steps were nimble as I weaved, missing all the limbs and trunks waiting to impale me.

As if it were angry that I dared not succumb,

the cold deepened. It did its best to numb my limbs. It wanted me to stop running. Its insidious whisper told me I shouldn't fight.

It was the wrong thing to say.

"Go away. Leave me alone!" I yelled. "Arrrrrrr!"

The noise of my refusal echoed in my head as I ran and ran. Until I slammed into something that didn't move.

## 11

I BOUNCED, AND IT TOOK ME A MOMENT TO REALIZE I didn't fall. Mostly because a strong pair of hands gripped me. And the rock I'd slammed into? Not so much a rock as a solid chest.

I only realized I still yodeled because his voice penetrated the noise with a barked, "Enough of the caterwauling!"

Only then did I slam my lips shut and open my eyes. I beheld my neighbor, his brows pulled together in a mighty frown, his lips taut with anger.

I thought he was angry at me at first, but he stared past me to the forest at my back. I almost opened my mouth to tell him there was something in the woods. I almost told him about the cold monster that wanted to freeze me.

Then my brain kicked in.

One did not tell the neighbor about one's paranoid flights of fancy. I could just imagine what he'd think. None of it very flattering. At best, that I was some senile, middle aged, crazy lady who imagined monsters in the woods, which was probably the most accurate explanation.

I'd let panic win.

Before I could yank free of his grip, Jace released me and stalked toward the woods I'd just fled. The light of the fire burning in his yard allowed me to see his broad backside and the fact he pulled an axe from a stump as he passed by.

What was it with this guy and that axe? Did he sleep with it? He certainly held it as if it were an extension of his body as he stood between me and my house. Was he going to kill me?

Sanity reared its head and asked why he'd kill me. I realized that he'd taken the axe toward… what? I'd never actually seen anything. But I'd certainly acted as if I had a monster after me. Was it any wonder he went into full-on male swagger mode?

"Sorry about the whole screaming and running thing," I said with a laugh. "It's been a while since I've been outside at night without streetlamps, and I got a little freaked out."

"You shouldn't be here," he stated as he headed back toward me. The firelight cast his features into partial shadow, giving him a menacing appearance. Without his ball cap, his hair curled in layers around his head, but the strands that were silver by day appeared inky at night.

"Obviously, I shouldn't have wandered onto your property. I got a little lost on the way back to my place. I didn't mean to trespass." Was the guy really going to give me heck given he'd crossed over to my place earlier that day?

"I mean you shouldn't be here in Cambden, period. This place isn't safe right now. Especially not for someone like you. You need to leave. The sooner, the better."

"Excuse me? Someone like me?" What exactly was that even supposed to mean? It only served to make me bristle. "You can't tell me what to do."

"Then call it friendly advice. You don't belong here."

"And you do?"

For a moment, the light caught his eyes, and they flashed green like a jewel suddenly lit by fire. "More than you. I have a right to this land."

"Well, that's some load of crap right there, Mr. I've-lived-here-fifteen-years." The sassy dripped from my words.

"And you've been here less than a week," was his rebuttal.

"This place has been in my family for generations."

"Which is part of the problem."

My gaze widened. "Excuse me?"

"Witches are what started this mess."

"You need to stop with the insults. Just because you hate women—"

"Never said I hated women." He leaned closer. "I just don't like witches."

The implication was there. I kind of wished I had a broom—to smack him with. "Too bad. I am staying in that cottage whether you like it or not.

"Your stubbornness will get you killed."

"Threatening me now?" I said, my heart pounding, especially since he still held that axe.

"I am not… You know what, never mind. I've given you fair warning. What happens now is on you."

"Meaning what?"

"Meaning you'll probably meet the same fate as your grandmother." Said flatly and without emotion.

A very cruel statement.

My grandmother had apparently suffered from dementia or some other mental disorder that led to her wandering from her house and dying of exposure. Having just gotten lost myself, I could see how easily it might have happened. That didn't mean Jace could use it as a taunt and threat.

Seeing a long branch sticking out of his fire, I grabbed the edge and pulled free a burning brand. A makeshift torch that would light my way and act as a deterrent if he got too close.

"I'm going home, and given your dislike of me, let's make a point of not running into each other. I'll stay on my side of the property line. You stay on yours."

"Or else what?" he retorted.

"I'll call the police and tell them you're harassing me."

That brought deep laughter to his lips. "Harassing you how? By telling the truth?"

"By saying I'm going to die like my grandma. You can't threaten people like that."

"For the granddaughter of a mighty witch you're awfully disappointing."

This time I ignored the witch part to concentrate on the last. Another person who didn't think me worthy. I was acquiring a collection. It stung, a lot. It didn't matter he was a stranger. His words only served to pile upon my already broken sense of self-worth.

"I don't care what you think." Said more softly than I liked, but I made myself say it. I wouldn't let him have power over me. I owed him nothing. "Stay away from me." I waved the burning brand in front of me as I skirted him. I'd oriented myself off his house and knew which way to go.

"Don't worry. I plan to avoid you. I'm not in the mood to watch you fail."

The statement stung. It shouldn't have. I didn't

know this man. But his words fed even more fuel to the slow-burning feelings of inadequacy.

Torch in hand, I fled, the dancing flames enough light for me to navigate and, oddly enough, helped me see the lights in the cottage. I don't know how I'd missed seeing them before.

It didn't matter. Reaching the porch, I dunked the torch in a rain barrel under the eavestrough to snuff it.

Sizzle. It steamed as it went out, but I left it immersed. I'd pull it out in the morning to dry. For the moment, I just wanted inside.

I opened the door, and Grisou let out a yowl at the sight of me. He darted past to stand with bristled fur on the porch.

"Grisou, get inside," I rebuked.

He didn't fight me as I leaned down to scoop him up, but he did keep a wary gaze on the woods. With him tucked in my arms, I went into the house, and my shoulders immediately eased.

Only as I closed the door did I see the scratches in the wood. "Grisou! Did you do that?"

Except it couldn't have been him. The scratches were much too deep and high on the door. Odd I'd not noticed them before.

Putting my cat down, I locked the door, the latch noisy as I turned it as if it hadn't been used in a while. For all I knew it hadn't. But tonight, I felt a need to be locked in. I pulled all the curtains, lingering longest at the one that gave me a view of the strip of land between our respective houses.

I could see the glow of Jace's fire. See it clearly. Yet when I'd been in the woods, I'd been smothered in pure dark. Freezing in the cold. Which reminded me that during my walk back from his place the temperature was pleasant. Could one torch make that big of a difference?

Was the madness that struck my grandma and Tricia contagious? Would I succumb next?

I made myself a hot cup of tea with a dash of honey, the jar in the cupboard a nice surprise and one I would have sworn hadn't been there this morning. Just like the teapot suddenly appeared in the jumble of pots and pans. I'd really have to do a more careful catalogue of the place. Figure out what I needed so that I didn't waste my time or money when I drove into town.

I'd have to do it soon. Start leaving my resume with businesses in the hopes of getting a job. I needed something to give me money for car insurance, gas, food, plus I assumed there was some kind of utility bill for this place. Electricity never came for free. Although I might wait a little longer before notifying them of my presence. I wasn't in a hurry to receive a massive unpaid bill of twenty-some years.

Eyeing the electric lamp glowing softly by the chair, it did occur to me they would have shut me off long ago. Could it be there was some secret monetary fund keeping the cottage from falling into ruin and foreclosure? When I'd inherited the place, the lawyer said it was in a trust and to be kept in the family, but at the time, I was smothered in grief and didn't ask what it meant.

I really needed to find out and made a mental note to contact my lawyer and have her look into it. In the meantime, I grabbed my cup of tea and made my way to the big comfy chair. My chair now, but I remembered sitting on my grandma's lap, listening to stories.

Always with the stories. No wonder I kept imagining things. Setting my tea on the coaster of the side table, I eyed the history book of Cambden on the low-slung table between the chair and couch.

Given the scare I'd given myself, I probably shouldn't be reading about any more legends, but I had nothing else to read unless I planned to dig into some teen adventures with Nancy. I tugged the thick tome onto my lap and flipped it open past the first few chapters, slowing as I reached the one titled "Witches and Magic." A name jumped out at me.

My name. My maiden name, that is. Rousseaux. The name my mother bore and my grandmother. A name that apparently had roots since the beginning of this town. I'd questioned my dad once and once only. Why did I have my mother's last name rather than his?

His expression turned dark. Angry. And his reply? "Because."

Nothing more than that. Naturally, I wondered. My parents had been married. I'd seen the pictures, but I was too young to remember if my mother had used his last name. The math indicated they'd tied the knot before having me. My birth certificate had my father's and mother's names, but I remained a Rousseaux.

A family with a long history and, apparently, descended of witches, which made me wonder if I'd misinterpreted what Jace meant. In olden times, wise women and midwives were sometimes misunderstood due to superstition.

Fascinated by the idea, I began to read. It was dry and disturbing, mostly because the book didn't speak of the witches or indeed my ancestors in a very nice manner. It spoke of the fact that the Rousseaux family emigrated from France and settled in the area, becoming quickly known for their remedies and powers. Crossing them would bring a blight on crops, a pox on livestock.

According to the book, only once was there an attempt to burn the witches. The townsfolk decided they'd had enough of the Rousseaux witches and went after them. It ended up in the whole town burning to the ground and dozens of lives lost.

None of the Rousseauxs died, though. Apparently, my ancestors were badass. They continued to live in the area and even helped rebuild the town.

I had to wonder if Jace had read this book or one like it. He'd called my grandmother a witch. Which was ridiculous. I'd never seen her concocting any strange potions or mumbling any spells. Just regular run-of-the-mill kitchen stuff from recipe books that involved a pinch of this, a soupçon of that. She didn't dance naked in the moonlight—that I knew of. Or ride a broom while cackling maniacally.

Why call her a witch at all? Could it be because Jace believed these superstitious histories? He didn't seem the type. Then again, what did I know about the guy? He lived alone in the boonies, had no problem threatening a woman, acted like a complete jerk, and appeared rather attached to his big axe.

This time I didn't need Trish to tell me a guy was bad news. I could see it for myself.

Closing the book, I rose and stretched. Immediately, my cat took my warm spot and curled up on the chair. I gave him a quick pet as I glanced out the window. Lights glinted in the forest, winking in and out. The fireflies were busy tonight. I watched them dancing and flickering, allowing myself to imagine for a moment they truly were tiny winged fairies like my grandmother had claimed. Out partying in the dark, getting drunk on the nectar of flowers, dancing until dawn.

Suddenly they all winked out. The deep darkness outside made it seem as if the lighted living room floated in the absence of anything. The hairs on my arms suddenly rose, and my breath frosted.

Approaching the window, I could see the ice spreading on the surface in fragile patterns that expanded in delicate whorls. I pressed my fingers to the glass. Cold to the touch. The chill was beyond anything I could have imagined.

Obviously, an insulation issue. I might have to replace windows. Or at least this one. A glance to my left showed the other window frost free.

How strange. I leaned closer and blew hot air onto it, melting a patch. A circle cleared, and I pressed my face close enough to see outside.

Another visage stared back at me just as the window cracked!

## 1 2

A SCREAM ON MY LIPS, I AWOKE SUDDENLY, jerking in the chair, startling my cat and sending the book in my lap flying. My fingers dug into the plush armrests as I stared at the window.

It took a few seconds to realize I'd dreamt it all. There was no frost inside the house. A part of me wished I had the daring necessary to actually peek out the window to see if there was anyone out there, but that would involve getting close. My fear said no.

As if I had that kind of bravery. It didn't matter how many times I told myself there was nothing there. I couldn't bring myself to look. Instead, I scooped my cat, wanting the comfort of his warm body, and went to bed.

I didn't immediately sleep. Perhaps because I'd

just napped in the chair. A nap that lasted literally minutes. How did I know that?

Because I'd glanced at the clock l made from a recycled wooden wheel. I'd noted the time as just after nine p.m. My stint outside by the lakeshore had taken longer than I would have credited. Or could be I'd lost track while running around the forest yodeling. If that were the case, no wonder my neighbor was so annoyed. I'd hate it, too, if I lived beside a crazy person.

Please don't tell me I'd have to apologize.

Ugh. I sighed, staring up at the ceiling and finding comfort in glowing stars. I couldn't believe the stickers I'd put up there as a kid still worked. They provided a comfort that reminded me of a time when this room was my safe place. Or was it my grandma who made me feel that way? She used to be the one constant in my life, my safe harbor, and I'd forsaken her for a man who wasn't worthy.

How that must have hurt her.

I turned onto my side. The cat made a sound of protest as I almost squished him. I lay my hand on his furry body. It vibrated under my palm, the purring a soothing thing that canceled the noise in my head. Allowed me to finally turn every emotion and thought off so I could sleep.

It proved to be a restless slumber spent waking at every sound. Each time, Grisou nudged me and shoved his purring head into me until I calmed again. Poor thing would be sleeping all day given I'd disturbed his rest. Perhaps I should look into getting another cat or two so he could have a break from dealing with his neurotic human.

The next morning, despite bleary eyes and a body that wanted to crawl back into bed, I showered and dressed in my best outfit. It consisted of ill-fitting corduroys, a patterned blouse that if you squinted might be considered a match, and brown slip-on loafers that pinched my toes.

I really needed to get myself a few items that fit. I just hated spending the money I had before getting a job to replace it. Except, I might not get a job looking unkempt.

My hair was a frizzy mess with no shape and too many strands of gray. It had thinned, too, which broke my heart. I used to be so proud of my waist-length hair. Now, it was mid-back, thin, with split ends. When was the last time I cut it? Not being the fancy type, and liking my hair plain, I usually tended to grab it in two ponytails in the front and cut the ends off. I didn't regret the money I saved when times were lean, but looking in the mirror, the reflection didn't lie. I appeared old. The long hair didn't give me a youthful, hippy vibe. It had gotten too thin for that. Add some gray paint to my skin, maybe some smudged eyeliner, and I could probably pass for a zombie if I groaned and shambled just right.

A pity I'd fought with Trish. She's said something about scissors.

Since I couldn't do anything about it for the moment, I wound it into a knot at the back of my head. A stern look that matched the grave expression on my face.

Today I planned to go forth and job hunt. Hopefully somewhere in town because anything else and I'd have to commute, which meant paying for more gas.

Eyeing my cat, who had curled up on the bed, I grimaced. "How do I look?"

A good thing he couldn't speak, because he'd probably tell me my outfit didn't spell success. More like a child rummaged through a discard pile and told me what to wear. Perhaps while in town, I'd splurge on a pair of black pants and a solid-colored, respectable shirt. And running shoes! Comfy shoes would make everything better.

The only new thing I wore was underwear. I'd been given a three-pack after the fire and every night washed a pair by hand and hung them to dry. I should get more of those, too, and a bra that actually lifted my breasts to where they should be rather than sadly aiming for my belly button.

I'd been glad to breast feed my two kids. It formed a bond between me and the babes. It was a happy time, even with Martin, who had quite enjoyed my enlarged bustline. However, once the milk dried up, the boobs shrank. Then grew again as I gained weight, only to shrink once more as I started losing it.

I didn't lose quickly in my belly or butt. That would have been too kind. The first place I lost fat was my breasts, and they were sad, floppy things now when left unfettered. Which wasn't often.

Rather than indulge in a pity party that involved me finding junk food and diving mouth first into it, I left the house. The fuel gauge on my car indicated I had enough gas to make it to the main road and the station there. Or so I hoped as it sat solidly on the E for empty. I clutched the steering wheel tight, praying I'd not run out until I was at least in sight of the gas station.

I managed to make it right up to the pump before the engine sputtered and died.

I smiled. Lucky day. I didn't have to walk or push. I put an even twenty dollars into it. Not enough to go far, but it would get me to Main Street and back, while leaving enough for me to hit the next town if I failed in Cambden.

*Click.* I got it to twenty oh three, which meant inside they'd round it up to oh five since Canada didn't deal in pennies anymore. No more dirty, coppery coins that used to end up shiny if you let them soak in a cola for long enough.

I headed inside.

Ding-a-ling. My entrance was announced to the

clerk that manned the store. He barely looked at me. I, on the other hand, took everything in.

The store offered basics like cigarettes and chocolate bars. In the refrigerated section, there was soda and milk. On racks, rows of chips and sweets —bringing an immediate craving. How many times had I drowned my anxiety in junk food?

Farther back, I spotted more basic grocery items and, in a small glass-door fridge by the counter, worms for fishing. Or eating, if my protein situation got dire.

The fellow behind the counter was a guy about my age, his jaw grizzled, his clothes worn, kind of like his expression. He had a binder in front of him and appeared to be making notes. Only as I reached the counter did he look away from his accounting.

"Morning," he drawled, his voice low and kind of rough.

As I paid with a crumpled twenty and a nickel, I attempted a weak smile. "Beautiful weather we're having," When nervous, fall back on the social niceties. Weather, destination, and hockey being the considered-safe topics.

"It's all right. Bit cold last night." He had a deeper voice than expected.

"It was chilly." A nervous giggle left me.

The twenty and the coin went from his hand into the till, and he slammed it shut. Transaction done. I wanted to walk off and not disturb the guy more than I had. He'd already dismissed me, but if I wanted a short commute, this was the closet place I could find to work.

I managed a meek, "Excuse me for bugging you still, but are you hiring?"

"What?" His attention moved from the paperwork to me. The washed-out blue of his eyes had probably been quite arresting in his youth. Now the color made his eyes somewhat vacant in a face that showed the lines of a hard life. Grooves in his forehead, crows' feet by his eyes. A hint of gray in the brown of his scruffy jaw and longish hair.

"I asked if you were hiring. Because if you are, I'd like to submit my resume." Which I'd left in the car but could easily run out and get.

He blinked. "There's no point in you applying. We tend to hire only local."

"I'm local," I immediately stated. "I live here."

"I ain't never seen you before," he said, leaning against the till, the angle of his body showing lean hips. Too lean, as if he didn't eat right.

"I just got here."

"Did you now." He eyed me more intently, his glance taking me in from the top of my head and stopping at my chest.

I flushed. I knew that I was supposed to say something and confront him about his behavior. I was a person, not a thing he could ogle. Yet, when he smiled at me, his teeth white if a little crooked, I felt a spurt of pleasure.

Hard to be mad at a man who'd looked at me and liked what he saw. "Well then I guess I should say welcome." He held out his hand, the fingers calloused. A working man, even if he stood behind a counter at the moment. "Name's Darryl."

"Hi. I'm Naomi." I clasped his hand and didn't know if I should pump it. I didn't recall the last time someone intentionally touched me. Unless a dentist appointment counted, but the dentist didn't give me butterflies.

Holy crap, I had tingles.

"Nice to meet you, Nay-ome-ee." He had a long drawn-out way of saying my name. "So you're looking for a job?"

I nodded. "Are you hiring?"

"Maybe. I might be losing my weekend kid. His parents just put their place up for sale."

"Really?" Weekends only wouldn't be enough, but a second job during the week would fill in the gap. "I've got a resume in my car." Which I kind of hoped he wouldn't ask for given it wasn't exactly professional to scratch out my old address and put in the new; however, a lack of a printer or a computer meant I did what I could.

"Does it have your number?" His query and smile let me know he might be using it.

Who cared if he looked a little worn out? I was

a little worn out, too. The pleasure of having someone see me as a woman was more than expected.

"I can give you my number now. That is, if you want it." I blurted it without thought, and then was immediately terrified. Was I ready to date? I'd resigned myself to the idea of being single. Maybe I should spend some time alone. I needed to figure out stuff about myself.

"I'd like that. He pulled a pack of cigarettes from his pocket and snared a pen. A smoking man. I wasn't sure how I felt about that. Would he quit? Maybe I would start smoking.

"So where are you living?" he asked as he opened the lid of his pack and handed me the pen.

As I scribbled my number, forgetting it for a second, I muttered, "My grandma's place. My place now, actually. She died, and I inherited." Which was probably more info than I needed to give. I finished my number and slid the pack toward him.

He tucked it back into his pocket. "Who was your grandma?"

"Adele Rousseaux."

"Oh shit." He appeared horrified and recoiled. "I didn't know you were her granddaughter."

"You knew my grandma?" Kind of obvious he did. I wondered why she engendered such an intense reaction.

"Everyone knows your family." Gone was the

teasing smile. He tapped at the cash register, and the drawer popped open. The same twenty I'd given him and a nickel were thrust at me.

A frown pulled at my brow, and I didn't take the money. "What are you doing?"

"I didn't realize you were a Rousseaux."

Both my brows lifted with incredulity. "Is this your way of saying my business is no good?"

"I'd never turn a Rousseaux away, just like I'd never make you pay."

"But you have to charge me. I gassed my car."

"Not the whole way. Let me finish it for you." Darryl hustled himself outside, and I stared dumbly as he pulled the hose back from the pump and added more gas to my tank.

I didn't understand what was happening. Was he flirting with me somehow? Except he seemed more nervous. I'd almost say scared.

So much for attracting him. With one mention of my family, I suddenly had the plague.

Going outside, I stood by as he finished gassing my car. He even wiped down the windshield before asking, "Do you need anything else? The milk in the fridge has still got a few days left. Want some chips? Cigarettes?" He thrust the pack I'd written my number on at me.

I stared at it dumbly. "Why are you trying to give me stuff?"

"You know why."

"Actually, I don't. Can you please explain it to me?"

Darryl finally looked me in the eye, but he wasn't trying to seduce me anymore. He was stiff as he said, "It's been like this for as long as a Rousseaux has been around. Your family doesn't pay for anything inside the town limits."

"But why?"

"Because." He shrugged.

"There has to be a reason," I insisted.

"Because bad things happen to those who get on the wrong side of your family."

The reply left me momentarily dumbstruck. "I would never do anything to you. Or anyone." The very idea was shocking, but he obviously believed it. What had my grandmother done?

"I'm not taking that chance."

"Too bad because I can't just let you give me stuff." Tempting as it was.

He opened the driver side door and said quite firmly, "You take whatever you need. No charge."

As I went to sit, I noted the twenty and the nickel on the driver's seat. I grabbed them, meaning to give them back, only he'd returned to the store.

He was nuts. He couldn't just let me drive off with a full tank of gas, or was this a ploy? Perhaps he and the cop in town were in cahoots and, the moment I left, he'd call his buddy, who would pull me over and accuse me of stealing the gas. Then they'd haul me off to jail to…

I halted that impossible fantasy. I wasn't the type to inspire elaborate plots so they could abuse me.

If he wanted me to have the gas and keep the money, then so be it. I could buy groceries with it. Shoes. A bottle of wine that I'd hate. I never did acquire a taste for it.

The twenty in my hand crumpled as I fisted it. I couldn't keep it. It wasn't right.

I marched into the store and tried to ignore the fact he retreated from me behind the counter. I tossed the wadded bill onto the surface and snapped, "I'll bring the rest by as soon as I get a job. I will not accept your misplaced charity."

I turned around and stalked back out.

He called after me, "This isn't over."

"Oh, yes, it is," I hollered.

I'd gas somewhere else if necessary. I jumped into my car and locked the door. I had this irrational fear he'd come racing after me, like the fellow in Terminator who starts running and catches up.

No one came tearing after me in the rearview waving that damned twenty. My nerves didn't care. I clutched the steering wheel and shook. What had just happened? It made no sense to me that he'd want to give me gas. And food. And stuff. People didn't do that. At least, not in my experience. Could this be some small-town quirk? A family getting benefits like free gas and groceries? But why? Surely anything my grandma had done to earn it died with her. Why extend it to me?

I left the gas station behind me. Its location being on the outskirts of Cambden, it wasn't long before the town appeared, sparse at first. Like the lone pizza place, the light dim in the window this time of the morning, but still open for business. I wondered if they'd offer something low carb like the place I'd found back in my old town. Although I'd yet to figure out how getting a pizza with absolutely no crust, just sauce, toppings, and cheese, cost more, which wasn't really a pizza anymore either given I had to eat it with a fork. You'd think taking out the dough would give some savings, but no. It was an extra two dollars. But for the times I just couldn't face cooking for myself, it did the trick.

I'd read in one of my dieting groups that you could just order a regular pizza and eat the toppings off it. I had two problems with that. The first being that it was a waste. The second was I didn't know if I'd have the will power to ignore that nice crust. Dip it in some butter or garlic dressing and mmm, mmm. No wonder I'd gotten so fat. It was truly unfair that the yummiest tasting things were so bad for me.

As I entered the heart of town, buildings dotted both sides of the road. I pulled into the first parking lot I saw for the grocery store, which could have fit in the deli section of the giant-sized one I'd left behind. Exiting the car, I grabbed a handful of my leftover resumes—with their lovely blacked-out address—and eschewed the grocery store. I'd apply there last and get some food at the same time.

Crossing the street, I eyed the first store. The faded sign read, Read with Me. A bookstore. The door was locked, the window dirty, and a peek through it showed it derelict. The shelves left behind still held a few paperbacks. There were a few even on the floor. How sad. I wanted to rescue those books and tell them they were still loved.

The next store, advertising flowers, had the same shuttered appearance, but it sported a new sold sign. The establishment just past it was the hardware store, and I almost fell over as the door actually opened. I stepped cautiously inside and was reassured to see the clutter you'd expect, tools and housewares, even some chunks of wood, the kind with the bark still on it, taking up space. Live edge as they called it, the newest thing to hit the interior design circuit. I was surprised to see it here. Then again, some might drive to get what they considered a more authentic piece.

A loud "Hullo!" boomed at me from somewhere in the vastly cluttered space, and it took a moment to notice the fellow who shouted it, given he was on a ladder, light bulb in hand. He waved. "I'll be with you in a second."

I lost sight of the man as he climbed down behind the stacks of wares. He truly had a bit of everything inside. Kind of reassuring to see at least one business never went out of style.

He appeared, an older man, probably in his sixties, maybe even seventies. He had white hair, thin on top, trimmed fairly short. His skin held a dark tan and the grooves of age. He was thin, and his pants were loose, meaning he probably needed the suspenders clipped to them.

"Well hello there, young lady." He beamed at me.

I appreciated the sentiment and thankfully didn't get butterflies. I'd hate to think every man who spoke to me gave me a thrill. "Hi."

"What can I help you with?"

"I'm looking for a job." I thrust one of my sheets at him.

"A job?" He stared at me then the resume. "I'm afraid I only hire local. You should look closer to home."

The same thing Darryl had said to me. "But this is home," I replied. "I live by the lake."

The man shook his head. "You really shouldn't lie, honey. See, I know everyone on this lake. I been here my whole life, and I ain't never seen you."

He wouldn't have because, as a child and even a teen, I'd had no reason to go into a hardware store. As a matter of fact, I had never actually shopped in town because it was too far to walk or bike. Usually, when my grandmother took me for a drive, she travelled to the next town over. As for my dad, he was always in a hurry to leave. I had to wonder now how much of that was intentional.

"I don't think we ever met, but you probably knew my grandmother, Adele Rousseaux?" I tossed her name out there determined to find out if Darryl's reaction was a one-off thing.

I might as well have tossed a grenade.

"You're a Rousseaux!" This time there was no mistaking the fear in the gaze. The resume fluttered to the counter. "What do you need? Building supplies? I can have a load delivered to the house."

"I just want to apply for a job," I repeated.

He shook his head violently. "I can't do that. You need money?" He opened the till and pulled out some bills, thrusting them at me.

"I want to earn it, not take it from you." I recoiled as if they were snakes. In a sense they were poison to me. Taking those would be like stealing. Why did my grandmother's name engender such a reaction?

"It's all right. Really." He waved the bills at me, and I fled, my feet moving quickly, half expecting he'd chase after.

He was the most extreme. The few other places still open for business were more subtle. They heard my name, and sorry there was no job available, but hey, if I needed something…

I took nothing.

I reached the end of the storefronts on the east side, more of them abandoned than inhabited. More than a few sporting sold signs.

Despite the few dollars left in my pocket, the small café with its blinking sign, Maddy's Family Diner, and a sea serpent that undulated each time the lights flashed, beckoned me. I needed a coffee, and when I entered, I also eyed the freshly baked pie covered by a glass dome on the counter.

I wanted that pie. With ice cream on top. A big piece. It would taste so good.

I chose a booth in the back corner with a view of the street. Not that there was much action. I'd seen two cars go down it the entire time I was out there pounding the sidewalk.

"Hey there, *cherie*, what can I get you?" The waitress arrived, dressed in a faded pink shirt with a sea monster embroidered on it. Her nametag read Marjorie. She appeared about my age, but less tired looking. Her blonde hair had been curled and hair sprayed into bouffant obedience. Her makeup, while thorough, gave her a pleasant appearance. The blue eye shadow actually suited her, as did the bright lipstick.

Rather than fall back onto excuses and bad habits, I behaved. "Coffee for starters, then two scrambled eggs, nothing added to them, and a side of bacon."

"White or brown toast?" she asked.

I shook my head. "No toast, and I can't have hash browns." A reminder that almost made me sob because I bet this place had the crunchy deep-fried kind that I loved.

"Ah, you want a low-carb special. Got it."

I might have gaped. "How did you know?"

"It's gotten real popular lately. I know a few people who are on it and doing great. Here's your coffee." She served me some hot brew, somehow managing to slide a little plastic pitcher of cream onto the table to go with it and packets of substitute sugar. The zero-carb stevia kind I could use.

The coffee tasted sweet and creamy. I'd gotten used to the aftertaste and now didn't notice it at all. For my eggs, I allowed myself a small dollop of real ketchup, trying not to think of all the sugar in it.

I still had all my resumes. Not one damned person would take one, insisting if I needed anything, I could just have it.

Why? I just wished someone would explain how it was that, despite being dead more than two decades, everyone turned a bit loony when I mentioned my grandmother. It made me think once more of Jace and his calling her a witch.

Did the entire town believe Grandmother to be

a witch? Did fear of a dead woman have them offering me stuff?

Just who was my grandma?

Or did this have to do with the history book? It didn't paint the Rousseauxs in a flattering light.

Marjorie came by and refilled my coffee and took my cleaned plate. "Want some pie or anything else, *cherie*?" she asked.

"I'm fine, thanks. Just the bill please."

"Looking for a job?" The waitress indicated my resumes, which I'd dropped on the table.

"Yeah, but the pickings are slim."

"Have you tried the hardware store across the way? I think they're hiring."

"I did, but the guy working the counter wouldn't let me apply."

"What the hell? Why not? I know he's been looking. I swear, if that old codger is pulling his macho bullshit, I will tear him a new one," Marjorie grumbled with a glare out the front window.

I blinked. "Uh, no, my being a woman had nothing to do with it. He knew my grandmother."

"Was she a thief? Does he think you'll be just like her?" She jumped on a possibility that I could have accepted.

I shook my head. "Apparently she had some sort of reputation in town."

Marjorie sobered. "You must be Rousseaux's granddaughter. I heard you were back."

"How?" Today was my first outing.

She must have read my expression. "Oh, *cherie*. This is a small town with little to excite it. If you came expecting privacy…" She shrugged.

"I can handle nosy people. What I'd like is for them to not freak when they hear my last name," I grumbled.

"Not easy being a celebrity."

"More like a pariah."

She laughed, the sound light and bright. "It's obviously been a while since you've visited."

"Try more than twenty years."

Her brows arched. "That is a long time. What brings you back?"

"A combination of things." I wasn't about to get into my divorce and current financial situation with a stranger.

"Well, it's nice to meet you. I'm Marjorie." She held out a hand, and I eyed it almost suspiciously.

When I shook, it was quick and brisk. "Naomi. And just so you know, I'm paying for breakfast." It emerged almost defensively.

"I should hope so. I need to balance the till at the end of the day." Her smile dimpled her cheek.

It was almost a relief to find out she wasn't impressed by my name. "I don't suppose you know why no one will take my money?"

She glanced over her shoulder, and her voice

lowered as she dipped close to say, "I do, but I can't say nothing here."

"How cloak and dagger." My attempt at a clever response.

"Lots of superstitious folks in these parts. But if you want to know, we can meet somewhere."

"Like where?" I asked.

"You going to be at your place tonight?"

I nodded.

"I'll pop by after work if you want."

Socialize with a stranger? I looked at her, the first person to not get some strange vibe going on after finding out what family I belonged to. A normal person.

"I'd like that." It almost surprised me to know I meant it. "Do you want dinner?"

"I probably won't make it until after eight-ish. We usually shut down around seven."

"That's fine. I can delay dinner. Any allergies?"

Her lips curved. "Nope. I'll bring dessert."

I didn't mention the fact I couldn't eat any. Let her bring whatever she liked. I had dinner plans with someone. I wouldn't do anything to ruin them.

"See you tonight."

"And I'll see what I can do about getting you hired." She swiped a resume from the pile on the table.

I felt a need to say, "I know I don't have much work experience, but…"

"*Cherie*, it's taking orders, serving, and then cleaning up. It's hard on the feet and back, but it's a paycheck. How do you feel about working part-time?"

"I'll take anything," I exclaimed.

"Then you can start tomorrow."

"Just like that? I thought you had to talk to someone about it."

"Don't worry about Orville. I'll handle him." She winked. "Be here at four o'clock. I could use another set of hands for the Friday dinner rush."

"Sure thing." My head bobbed in agreement. "Let me just get the bill." I reached for my wallet.

Her hair didn't move an inch as she shook her head. "Good news, *cherie*, employees eat for free." She winked and sauntered away with a saucy, "See you tonight."

I might have protested, but she'd hired me, and she was coming over. I had to get ready. Despite what she said about the food being free, I left a large tip.

At the grocery store, I didn't say a word to anyone. Just grabbed some necessities and paid for them quickly, the bored cashier running my stuff through and not ever actually looking me in the face.

I was feeling pretty good by the time I got back to the cottage. Emerging from the car with my two bags of groceries, I noticed a box on the porch.

Inside were some cookies, chips, juice, and that damned twenty-dollar bill from the gas station that I thought I'd escaped.

Darryl had been by. And I might have been more peeved if I'd not seen the tiny bundle of daisies placed on top. He didn't sell flowers in his store. Nor did they have any in town.

He'd picked flowers for me. There were those tingles again.

## 13

INSIDE THE CHINA BUFFET, I FOUND A CRYSTAL VASE. I'd have sworn I'd not seen the first time I peeked inside. I really needed to work on my powers of observation.

The flowers were a little wilted. I didn't care as I added water to the container, placed them within, fluffed them so they fanned out, and set them on the table.

I couldn't remember the last time someone got me flowers. Certainly not my husband in at least more than a decade. To his credit, in the beginning, he sometimes remembered. Then he stopped caring, or I stopped caring. Not that it mattered at this point. We were both at fault in a sense. Relationships required work, and we'd both failed.

I could accept some of the blame for where we ended up. I also needed to learn from it. Pretty flowers now didn't mean Darryl would turn out to be a nice guy down the road.

I needed to discover more about myself before I worried about that kind of commitment.

Work wouldn't start until tomorrow, and I felt a need to dust before company came over. Oh my God, company. When was the last time I'd entertained someone?

Everything had to be perfect. My anxiety insisted. I used a damp cloth for wiping the almost nonexistent dust, and at the same time, I got to explore the house top to bottom.

Tricia had been so adamant there were books. Books that she claimed were heirlooms passed down from generation to generation. At the time, I'd scoffed at her, and yet, the more I thought about it, the more I remembered, and I was pretty sure I knew which books she meant.

Odd how I'd forgotten. Especially given how often I'd seen my grandmother perusing them, flipping through pages yellowed with age. There were three of them in total, the exterior hues of the thick leather covers differentiating between them. One was a faded burgundy etched in flaked gold leaf. Another in dark blue with black lettering, the black barely visible. And the third a motley patch of various colors with no words at all.

I'd never read them. Grandma had offered; however, at the time, I'd not yet discovered the joy of escape in reading. That came later. Back then I was more about the fun and games to be had outside the house. Chasing down frogs. Fishing in the lake. Building a fort for my pretend fairy army.

Even in winter I was happiest in the snow, building snowmen and making snow angels, earning my rosy cheeks and hot cocoa—a recipe in that book with the patched cover. All of Grandma's special drinks for me came out of that old grimoire. That was her name for it. My father called it chicanery. Grandma's recipes added another reason why he tried to forbid my visits.

*"Don't you dare feed her any of your home remedies," my father threatened.*

*"We had a bargain," my grandmother had said.*

A strange reply at the time, and it hadn't gotten any clearer with age. As I recalled, Grandmother kept plying me with drinks, meaning I had to lie to my father.

*"Don't worry, Dad. I stuck to drinking water."*

I hadn't seen the harm. To me, the concoctions were tasty, like hot smoothies, spicy and a little sweet. It wasn't as if anything ever happened after I drank them. I didn't shrink like Alice or see smiling Cheshire Cats.

Were the books here, or had someone taken them? Could be an old grimoire of recipes had some value. Weren't the pharmaceutical companies interested in old wives' remedies? Could they be worth some money?

I started my search upstairs in Grandma's room, going through every drawer first then peeking under the furniture and in the closet. I repeated my actions on the main floor. I found all kinds of things. Linens that were hand stitched with fragile lace. Pictures in frames, old sepia prints of strangers. Dishes and more dishes, most mismatched, many of them chipped, piled inside the giant wood buffet and more hiding in the panty. Knitting needles and a basket waiting for some yarn. More pots and wooden stirring spoons than a person surely needed. Which made me think of Jace next door calling Grandma a witch.

If anything, my grandma was a wise woman. Pity it hadn't rubbed off on me. I had to wonder, if she'd lived, would I have remained in a terrible marriage for so long? Doubtful. She would have told me to get out much sooner than I did. Kind of like Tricia had.

Would I have turned my back on my grandma if she'd said the same thing?

I wanted to think I'd have listened, but I'd been so stubborn when I was a teen living with her. Rude and chafing at the restrictions put on me. As I got older, she kept treating me like a child, expecting me to believe in fairytales.

She never stopped me from pursuing my dream

of going to college, even as she saw me off with the saddest expression. As if she knew I wouldn't return.

Even then she knew. I think that partly explained why I acted so stubborn about Martin. Convinced myself he was what I wanted. A part of me must have known Grandma would hate him, because the few times I went to visit, I left him behind, and I kept my stays short.

Grandma never complained. Not once.

I should have known something was wrong. Should have seen it. Maybe I did but ignored it.

Grandma died, and I was too late.

Grief hit me hard, and Martin was there to give me a shoulder to lean on. He held me as I shook at the funeral. He kicked out his roommate and had me move out of my dorm and into the apartment he leased. He took care of me. Had someone told me then how miserable I'd be, I'd have probably told them off. We were soulmates. We were in love. A pity love didn't always last. Sometimes it faded or it changed into something ugly.

When my first search of the cottage didn't reveal the books, I went a little deeper. I pulled the drawers out of the tracks and searched the inside of the dresser. I found a tiny box tucked in the lining between the bottom two drawers and opened it to see a strange ring. Inside the box spring, through a tiny slit, I pulled out an envelope with a single sheet of paper and an intricate drawing on it.

I traced it with my finger and imagined the line heated. There was something about it that seemed magical, if fanciful. I put it aside.

Couch cushions littered the floor, and all I found was thirty-seven cents. The sheets were all pulled out and shaken, revealing only a single photograph of my grandma, looking younger than I did now, maybe in her twenties, pretending to dance with a broom. The black and white image showed her mouth wide open in laughter, her head thrown back, full of joy. There was a man watching her that I knew to be my grandfather. He'd died before I was born. A hunting accident I'd been told.

When I peered closer, I noticed someone else on the other side of the bonfire, not that I could see the flames. Old-style instant cameras had a hard time capturing the image. If I didn't know better, I'd have said the half-turned face in the picture was that of my neighbor. Impossible of course, given Jace appeared younger than me. Perhaps he was related to someone in the area.

By the time I'd emptied everything and crawled around more than my old knees liked, I'd yet to find one book, let alone three. Kind of disappointing but not exactly surprising. Other things had gone missing, like Grandma's big brass bed and that cute little vanity with the many drawers filled with colorful powders that I was forbidden from touching

*"When you're older,"* Grandma used to say.

I was older now, but it was too late.

Flopping onto a beanbag, I tilted my head back and stared at the sloped ceiling. The converted attic had been adapted to follow the peaks with the insultation placed between the beams that braced the pitch and notched pine on top. Everything was painted white, but from this angle, I could see a faint tracing on the ceiling. Patterns similar to that on the doors and windows. My, the carver had been busy.

My head flopped sideways, and I noted the door to the bathroom, which took up the entire end of the attic to my left, about fifteen feet in length. Much of that space was given over to the massive claw foot tub. A soaking tub that took forever to fill.

I glanced to the other side and eyed the off-center door to the closet. A closet that wasn't as big as the bathroom and yet the wall ran the same length.

Strange.

Intrigued, I rose and entered the closet. There were no clothes hanging, just empty hangers and plain plaster met my gaze. Not a single seam to be seen, nor a hook to pull and reveal a door. I actually groped the wall in search of a nodule or something that might depress and unlock a secret mechanism.

The wall remained intact. I knocked on it. As if I knew what it would sound like if there were a hollow space behind.

*Tap. Tap. Tap. Tock.*

I blinked and knocked again.

*Tock. Tock.*

No doubt that it sounded different in that spot. Standing back with my hands on my hips, I stared intently.

The painted plaster appeared unblemished. Could it be someone had covered over a door? But why?

For a moment, I imagined busting through and finding a room full of treasure. I even debated hunting down an axe in the shed, and I might have gone Jack Nicholson—*The Shining* version—on the wall if I hadn't heard a knock.

Most likely it was Marjorie, the waitress I'd met that morning. I'd not expected her so soon, though, if at all. She'd said I'd see her closer to eight. Maybe she'd gotten off early.

I eyed my dirty garments with chagrin. Would she care? There was no time to change, and if I dawdled, she might leave.

Heading downstairs, I heard tires spinning on gravel, and by the time I wrenched open the door, the car, a rusted gold-colored hatchback that had gone out of production before the turn of the century, was already heading out. A glance down showed a grocery bag.

I had a feeling I knew what I'd find. I crouched and pulled the plastic open to see a note. *Sorry, didn't know it was you.* It was clipped to the money I'd paid for my stuff that morning in the grocery store and, under it, a huge ham.

Like literally, a head-sized ham. Way too much for me, but I doubted they'd take it back. So I did the only thing a person could do when they had too much food—and worried the expected guest wouldn't appear.

I invited more people over.

## 14

I DIDN'T KNOW MANY PEOPLE, AND FOR THE FEW I did know, I had no phone numbers. Google wasn't very helpful when it came to searching for a next-door neighbor named Jace. I instead got the link for some romance novel about a hot recluse and his quirky neighbor, which I bookmarked for reading later. Tricia wasn't listed either.

Stumped, I eyed the stove. I'd already put the ham in the oven and cranked the heat after slathering the whole thing with a sugar-free syrup. I'd found the recipe on the internet, along with one for mashed cauliflower that supposedly would fool people into thinking it was potatoes. I highly doubted it, but maybe I could fool my own taste buds. However, would I really inflict that kind of culinary torture on other people? I wanted this to be an apology dinner, not a hey, this chick must hate you because she's feeding you fake but healthy stuff event.

At least Darryl had left me carb-laden cookies, which I could throw at people if dinner turned out to be an epic fail. Assuming anyone even showed up. Maybe Marjorie would forget or not come. As to having anyone else over, that required me inviting them.

Given I knew I already owed Jace an apology, I chose to handle him first

Last night had gotten ugly quick, and in the light of day, I could see how I'd jumped to many wrong conclusions. No wonder he'd been peeved. The man had literally done nothing to me other than tell me I should go. Given he'd found me running around in the dark screaming my head off, it was probably sound advice.

I mustered my courage and stalked over to my neighbor's place in my clean outfit of baggy jean overalls and an oversized sweatshirt. Again, not my finest look, as it was a bit tight over my belly. Still, I wasn't here to seduce him but feed him. They did say the path to a man's heart was through his tummy.

Wait, I wasn't looking for a heart, just a neighbor that didn't stare daggers at me or hope I fell and drowned in the lake.

I knocked on his door and waited. It was almost a relief when he didn't answer. It meant I could tuck the note I'd written in the crack under the door. A simple missive that said, *Sorry about last night. Let me apologize by giving you a homecooked dinner and a special dessert. ~ Naomi*

Only after the note was out of reach did it occur to me how he might construe it. Would he think this was some kind of romantic thing? In that case, he'd ignore it, but what if he showed up? What if he made some moves on me thinking that by special dessert I meant sex?

Reality set in. Gorgeous guy wanting to get naked with me?

Not happening.

Besides, I wasn't done with my invites. He could hardly expect any kind of bodily fluid exchange if there was someone else present. The realization Trish could act as a buffer made it easy to get into my car and drive to where she grew up. She had lived just outside of town, in a converted mobile home with a dirt yard that even the weeds avoided, a perpetually broken car on blocks, and a drunken mother who'd been found more than once passed out on the floor just inside the door.

The problem with being gone more than two decades? Nothing was the same anymore. Where Trish's house had once sat on cinderblocks was now a fenced-in junkyard.

Leaning against my steering wheel, I wondered how the heck I'd find her. I could call my daughter and ask for her number, but that might open a can of worms I wasn't ready for. Such as me asking why Winnie was so chummy with my ex-best friend instead of me.

I didn't want to wreck what we had started building by bringing my jealousy and insecurities into play. So instead, I drove home, my plans for a dinner to say "I'm sorry" ruined before I'd even started.

Except, once I pulled into my driveway, who did I see sitting on my porch with my cat in her lap?

"Tricia!" I exited my car. "I was just looking for you."

"I know. Grisou told me."

This time, rather than get all judgy about the crazy, I pretended I didn't hear it. If I could love my grandma with all her nutty stories and beliefs, then I could do the same for my friend. Besides, who was I to talk? I'd freaked out about a nonexistent monster in the woods the night before.

"I'm making a ham," I announced rather than ask what else my cat had supposedly told her.

"It smells delicious. I brought some green beans from the garden and butterscotch ice cream. They're in the fridge."

I could use the veggies but held my tongue rather than tell her I couldn't eat the ice cream. Not her fault I was on a diet. "I'm glad you came back."

"As if there was any doubt I would."

"Actually, I wouldn't have blamed you after the way I treated you." It was hard to admit I'd been a bitch. My cheeks heated, and I wanted to stare at the ground, but I had to own my actions even if it was uncomfortable.

"Pshaw." She snorted. "You think I'm nuts, which is fine. If I were in your shoes, I'd probably think the same. I never realized just how little your grandmother told you."

"She told me plenty," I admitted, joining her on the porch in the other rocker. Where had they come from? They'd not been there this morning when I left.

"Your grandma might have talked plenty, but you didn't believe any of it."

"And you do?" I scoffed.

"There are things in this world that seem fantastical. Things that people can't comprehend or accept, so they must be hidden."

"Let me guess, you know about these things."

"I don't just know; I'm a guardian." Her lips turned down. "Which I'll admit sounded a lot loftier a position when I was young. How naïve I was back then. How flattered because only a privileged few are ever allowed to see beyond the veil."

"I hate to tell you, I'm not one of those people." Pity. It might have been nice to escape mundane reality for one where I could actually speak with my cat.

"Are you sure?" she asked. "After all, you did come back."

"Because my house burned down."

"The Fates work in mysterious ways."

"You going to tell me fate made sure my husband cheated on and dumped me?"

"Sometimes the path to our future is convoluted."

I snorted. "And twenty years too late. We're old ladies now, Trish."

"Old!" she exclaimed. "How do you figure that? More like halfway there."

"I'm surprised to hear you say that. Look at our families." At least in mine, they all died fairly young. Even Grandma. She couldn't have been more than sixty when she passed.

"Accidents don't count."

"I'm still pretty clumsy," I admitted.

"Remember how you used to trip over that one step going into the cafeteria almost every day?" Trish snickered.

"I do." I also recalled how much I'd hated the laughter that erupted each time. I got over an hour on the bus every morning and afternoon for my peers to mock me.

"That was a long time ago," she replied softly.

"Yeah." I reached out and grabbed her hand. Squeezed it. "I've missed you."

"I missed you more," she stated.

"Tell me what you've been doing since we last saw each other."

"Other than trying to hold back those orcs and the forces of darkness? Filing and phone calls."

It turned out she worked for the town's municipal office, mailing out notices to the residents, paying the town bills, and keeping the mayor—who happened to be Mr. Peterson of the hardware store—on track for the tasks he had to perform.

"Although I don't know how much longer he can afford to keep me. People keep leaving Cambden."

"Relocating to the city?"

She shrugged. "Some of them are, I guess. The young folk mostly. Can't really blame them. There's nothing here since the mill shut down."

"What, when did that happen?"

"About ten years ago. The wood mill needed too many upgrades to pass environmental regulations, so it closed its doors and took away the one source of work that kept the town alive."

"Do you know who's been buying up the property in town?" I asked, remembering the letters I'd received and the sold signs in many of the Main Street windows.

At first, I thought she wouldn't answer, because she hesitated. "It's not a person but a company bidding for them."

"Let me guess. Airgeadsféar." I recalled the name from the letter.

"How did you know?"

"Because they sent me an offer for the cottage."

"And you said no?" Her eyes went wide.

"Yeah. A good thing, too, since I needed a place to live after the fire."

"Actually, it's bad," she muttered. "I didn't realize they'd gone after you."

"What's that supposed to mean?"

"Have you heard from them since you got here?"

I shook my head.

"If you do, let me know."

"Why?"

She rocked, the creak of the chair a sign of her agitation. "Because bad things happen to those who don't accept the deals."

"You can't tell me they're strong-arming people for worthless property." I snorted. "I can assure you that hasn't happened. They sent me a few letters, which I ignored."

"Since you didn't reply, they'll send an agent to speak to you in person." She sounded certain.

"Meaning I should expect a goon to threaten me?"

"Don't make light of this. The D'Argent family doesn't play around."

"Never heard of them."

"Have you met your neighbor?" She jerked her head in the direction of Jace's place.

"He's a D'Argent?"

She nodded.

"Oh." He'd never told me his last name, I now had to wonder if it was on purpose. "Why is Jace buying up property around the lake?"

Instead of replying, she popped out of the chair. "Look at the time. It's getting dark so early now. We should probably get started on the side dishes."

She rebuffed my questions about why this Airgeadsféar, with the freaky company logo, was buying up the town. Nor would she even speculate on the reason why.

I had a few ideas. Maybe they wanted to revive the mill because the market was shifting. Maybe something big was about to come this way and property would suddenly quadruple in value.

I did find it interesting that my neighbor wasn't the simple backwoods guy I'd taken him for. If he was buying up property, that made him a business-man. A hot one who dressed in plaid and worn jeans and carried an axe.

Brilliant me, I'd invited him over for dessert.

*Groan.*

As we set the table for dinner, there was a knock at the door. Instantly, my cheeks heated.

"Can you get that?" I asked, not ready to see my

neighbor yet. Perhaps if Tricia answered, then he'd understand I'd not meant the note as a booty call.

Was it even called a booty call anymore? I wasn't ready to date, so why was it I kept looking at men in terms of eligibility and do-ability? I eyed the flowers on the table. They still made me happy, droopy petals and all.

Could be I just liked remembering I was alive. Or as Trish said, only halfway there.

I had a sudden urge to listen to Bon Jovi and me without an active Spotify account. A pity my cassette tapes hadn't survived.

Trish answered the door, and it turned out my worry was misplaced. Marjorie stood at the door, looking flustered. It turned out she and Tricia knew each other.

"Jojo?" Trish exclaimed. "What are you doing here?"

Marjorie pursed her lips. "I could ask you the same."

"I told you I was having dinner with a friend."

"Well, so am I," Marjorie hotly retorted.

"Who?" Tricia asked.

"Me. I invited her," I replied, moving to say hello. I couldn't believe she'd come. I began to feel a bit panicked. Old friend meet new one. Already tension bristled between them. Maybe I shouldn't have been so quick to tender so many invitations.

"Come in," I offered. "I wasn't expecting to see you for at least another half-hour."

"The restaurant closed early because of a kitchen fire."

"Oh no. Is everyone all right?" The polite thing to say rather than the selfish, *Do I still have a job?*

She nodded. "We're all fine. It was a grease fire. Happens all the time on account Orville doesn't clean out the traps as often as he should."

"I'm glad you're okay." I meant it. I might have only met her this morning, but I rather liked the waitress, and not just because she was the only one to treat me normal.

Trish's gaze bounced between me and Marjorie. "Let me guess. You met Jojo at the diner."

I nodded. "I had brunch there."

At the admission, Tricia arched a brow at Marjorie. "You let her pay?"

"Did not. I told her it was free."

"She did," I said. "Which is why I left a large tip."

"And you took it?" Trish groaned. "You're lucky it was just a little fire."

"Trish," I interrupted, "the fire isn't because I left some money."

"Shows how little you know. Jojo was told what would happen."

"And it still doesn't make sense," Marjorie exclaimed.

"Do you know why the folks in town won't let me pay for anything? And why is it such a problem? So what if I left a tip? She earned it."

Tricia's face still appeared stony. "She knows that accepting it can kill her."

"Ugh," Marjorie groaned. "And this is why I want to move. Five years I've been listening to this superstitious crap."

"You haven't lived here your whole life?" I asked.

She shook her head. "I'm married to Orville's brother. Not for much longer, I hope. I filed for divorce."

"What happened?" I knew I was prying, and yet, I felt an instant kinship to Marjorie.

"My husband, Milo, ran off with some floozy a few months ago."

"You have my condolences." I knew how that betrayal felt. "Same thing kind of happened to me, except in my case, he flaunted it."

"His loss." She shrugged. "In any case, I'm over it. Milo wasn't all that great as a husband. I stuck around mostly because it was easier than starting over."

"Because do-overs suck." Look at mine, which kept crashing and burning before it got off to a start.

"That is the wrong attitude to have. Like I told Jojo, you have to own your life. Own what happens to you. A reboot on your life will only suck if you let it suck." Tricia imparted her words of wisdom.

I grimaced. "You make it sound easy. It's not easy."

"Which is why it's good you're home where you can figure things out."

"And fight dark orcs?" I teased.

"Oh, don't ever fight them," she exclaimed. "They'll twist off your head and drink from you like a fountain."

Marjorie laughed. "Trish likes to exaggerate."

"No, I don't."

The teasing went on, and it occurred to me that here we were, three middle-aged women, having a bonding moment. It was kind of cool. It demanded something like wine, which I didn't have. Or beer. My glance went to the buffet and the decanter of dark liquid. Probably booze that had gone bad. Or did alcohol just get more potent with age?

Guess we'd find out. In no time, I'd poured us three shot glasses of the fluid. Which, I'll admit, I eyed the most dubiously.

"To being single and not alone." I held up my glass.

"To making out like a bandit who gets everything in the divorce," Marjorie declared with her glass in the air.

"To replacing plastic with the real thing." Trish winked before tossing her toast into the mix.

We clinked to our toasts and tossed the liquor back. Then proceeded to cough and sputter. At least Trish and I did. Marjorie snickered and held up a full glass.

"Cheater," I wheezed.

"I don't drink."

"Smart girl. It's awful." Trish's face went through a whole parade of expressions.

It actually wasn't bad once you got past that initial urge to spew it right back out. By our third, we weren't even choking anymore.

I sat in Grandma's chair while Marjorie and Trish took over the couch, the former having grabbed herself a glass of water, the latter looking a little glazed by the antique brew.

"I probably should have said something before... I have bad news." Marjorie bit her lower lip.

I sighed. "Let me guess. Your boss said I couldn't have the job."

"I'm so sorry," Marjorie gushed. "Orville got so mad at me when he found out I kept the money. Says I'm paying for the fire damage since I caused it." Her nose wrinkled.

"How was it your fault if he's the cook?"

"According to him, I shouldn't have accepted it, and he ordered me to give it back." She held out the five-dollar bill, but I shook my head.

"I'm not taking it back. He has no right to tell you who can tip you or not."

"Actually, Omi," Tricia said, interrupting, "he's right. She can't keep it."

"Why the heck not?" I exclaimed. "Marjorie doesn't owe me free service. Which reminds me, do you know why everyone in this town insists on giving me everything without payment once they find out who Grandma was?"

"Because they have to."

"Have to why?"

"Because you're a Rousseaux," Trish said, as if that answered everything.

"Yes, I am, and I have no idea why people keep acting crazy around me."

"It's because of the curse."

## 15

"A CURSE?" I REPEATED.

Tricia nodded as if it was the most logical thing, so I looked to Marjorie, who clamped her lips.

I frowned. "Seriously? You're going to say something like that then stop talking? I deserve an explanation."

"It's silly," Marjorie said. "Small-town superstitions."

Tricia interrupted. "You know it's more than that."

"Maybe. Maybe not. Part of the reason why I took the tip was because I planned to mock Orville about his belief in old wives' tales, only the fire happened. Needless to say, he immediately claimed it was because I'd ignored his warning and sparked the curse."

"Is this a good time to say I told you so?" Tricia taunted.

"Perhaps there's some validity in this particular tale."

"Don't tell me you believe this malarkey." I eyed them. Intelligent grown women putting stock in superstition.

"Talk to anyone in Cambden, and they'll have the same reply. The Rousseaux family placed a curse on this town a long time ago. The Rousseauxs get anything they want within the town property line for free. Those that don't comply tend to experience an untimely accident," Tricia explained, matter-of-factly.

"That's nuts. You're talking as if people believe my grandma was a witch."

"Not just your grandma, everyone in your family," Marjorie offered, which only made me scowl.

"I'm not a witch." I drank my fourth shot, suddenly more sober than I liked.

"Don't be so sure." An ominous reply from Tricia.

"What's that supposed to mean?" I asked.

"Being a witch is hereditary in most cases. You don't just suddenly decide to become one. It requires the right kind of bloodline. At least that's how it was explained to me," Trish said in a tapering voice as I stared at her.

"Even if it's not some kind of family gene, it

doesn't matter." Marjorie leaned forward. "Everyone in town *thinks* you are. I knew about you before you showed up at the diner. Word has been buzzing since your arrival. Some people say it's good you're here. Some say it's bad."

"That's insane. My arrival hasn't changed anything. I just want to live quietly. It's the townsfolk acting all crazy trying to give me stuff. I offered to pay."

"And they can't accept," Trish repeated. "The curse is still potent even after all this time."

"How do I break it then?" If I couldn't talk them out of this nonsense, maybe I could do a fake exorcism.

"The curse will end when the Rousseaux family line does, I assume." Trish wasn't too helpful.

As for Marjorie: "A few people at the diner claimed your arrival is a good thing. After years of the Rousseauxs being given stuff, this is where you give something back."

"I have nothing to give, though." If the town expected me to be their philanthropist, then they'd be disappointed.

"It's said you'll keep the darkness from us." Tricia's statement sent a chill through me. Why did she look so serious saying it?

I didn't like the dark. "Who said?"

"It's part of the prophecy."

"A prophecy?" I snorted. "I can't believe that in this day and age people believe in such crap."

"Oh, they do," Marjorie said with an exaggerated tone. "Because they're superstitious. They think if they break the pact that they'll suffer horribly or die."

"And they'd be correct." Trish appeared so earnest as she leaned close to me. "It's not mumbo jumbo, no matter what you think. Cambden isn't like other places."

"You mean modern and living in this century." I couldn't help the sarcasm.

"I'm sorry if we can't all be perfect and bitchy like you city folk," Tricia drawled.

"Actually, Tricia is right. There is something different about Cambden. I never used to be scared of the dark until I moved here. And even then, it wasn't until about two years ago that I started locking my doors," Marjorie admitted, hugging herself and huddling in her corner of the couch.

"What happened two years ago?" My curiosity was piqued.

"That's when the first person went missing," Marjorie said softly.

Trish nodded. "I'm still convinced Patty's disappearance is linked to the awakening of the lake."

Their answers had me blinking. "Is this about the serial killer again?"

"What serial killer?" Marjorie asked.

Before I could open my mouth, Tricia replied, "Rather than accept it's Maddy, woken before her time, Omi thinks there's someone behind all the disappearances."

"Naomi might be right," Marjorie defended. "I'll be honest; at times I've wondered, too. But in most of the cases, the people moved on. Look at my husband. Sleeping in my bed one minute and running off with some woman the next."

"He didn't run off," Tricia mumbled.

"Then explain the message I got," Marjorie hotly retorted.

At my questioning gaze, Tricia explained. "The people who disappear seem to do so legitimately. In the case of Marjorie's husband, he ran off with someone who was passing through town. The McGraw family, all five of them, are presumed dead in a house fire. The Stevenson brothers drowned in a fishing incident. Then there was Peggy-Sue who ran off to the city. A few of the younger ones supposedly did that as well."

I frowned. "Sounds plausible to me."

"It's all very plausible if it were true." Tricia rose from her chair and paced. "In the case of the fire, no bodies were ever found. No bodies for the drowning victims either. All the runaways have only ever left a single note or message. Nothing since. Like Marjorie's husband." She eyed the waitress.

"Neither you nor Orville ever heard from Milo again, did you?"

"No. Good riddance, the cheating bastard," Marjorie grumbled.

"People move on. Doesn't mean there's anything nefarious behind it." I couldn't even believe we were still discussing this. Then again, it beat being by myself, contemplating the merits of getting more cats or whether or not my next-door neighbor would appear, expecting me for dessert.

"Don't you get it? These stories, they're not real," Tricia insisted.

I'll admit I found myself confused. "Are you saying people haven't disappeared?"

"They have, but it's Maddy's fault. She's the one getting rid of them."

"You think an imaginary monster is killing people?" I snorted. "Come on, you can't tell me you believe that."

"She's real," Trish insisted while Marjorie remained oddly silent, once more chewing her lower lip.

*Beep.* Saved by the bell, the one for the ham that was. The conversation stalled as I pulled it from the oven and let it rest with foil on top while I pureed the cauliflower, adding cheese when it looked more like soup. The green beans were quickly sautéed in garlic and butter.

We worked together as a team. Marjorie setting

the table without being asked. Tricia moving around me in the kitchen, helping me plate the food and serve it. As she prepared a fourth serving, I opened my mouth to tell her it was one too many when—

*Knock. Knock.*

I stared at the door.

Oh shit. He'd come. And I was a mess. I glanced down at myself and my still hideous clothes covered in spatters of cauliflower. I was pretty sure I had some in my hair. I really needed to do something about my wardrobe. Although, given I'd already lost my new job, it might have to wait.

Or I could take advantage of superstitious fools and go shopping at the local secondhand boutique on their dime.

"You going to answer that?" Tricia nudged me from behind as she passed with a plate piled twice as high as the others.

Feeling butterflies that made me want to puke, I answered the door. He was as tall as I recalled. Just as stony faced, too. Jace glanced at me, and then past me.

"I didn't realize this was a party," were his rumbled words.

My cheeks heated. Oh my gawd. He had gotten the wrong idea. I didn't know if I should be flattered or mortified.

"Come in. We're just about to eat." It was the

only thing I could say for the moment. Anything else might have resulted in me stammering and trying to explain he'd misinterpreted my note. Or maybe, I was once more misreading the situation. Could be he didn't think any such thing and I was flattering myself that he'd even look at me in that kind of way.

Did I need to strip and cry in front of a mirror again? The reality was no man would want me looking like this. Except for maybe imperfect Darryl. I eyed the flowers over my shoulder.

Jace noticed them, too. "Someone courting you?"

"Of course not," I hastily stammered. "I might be separated from my husband, but I'm still technically married." I really shouldn't be thinking about getting involved at all until the situation with Martin was resolved.

"You looking to reconcile?" he asked.

"Never!" Spoken a tad more vehemently than deserved.

"How long were you married?"

"Too long!" Tricia declared. "The guy is an asshat with an emphasis on ass. She's better off without him."

I couldn't argue with that. Despite a few panicky moments, I was happier and about to sit down to dinner with, if not friends, then at least real people. There would be conversation. Maybe some laughter. For once, I didn't panic at the idea of socializing but looked forward to it.

"Shall we eat?" I declared.

"Heck yes. I am starving," Tricia declared.

"This is way better than crappy frozen dinners," was Marjorie's addition.

"You work in a restaurant," I blurted out, baffled by her reply.

"Exactly. Day in and out I see and smell the same stuff." Marjorie shuddered. "It's a treat to have an actual home-cooked meal."

I almost winced. She'd yet to taste the cauliflower potatoes.

Trish was already digging in as Jace seated himself.

As I went to sit down, there was another knock. Trish's lips pursed.

"I'd hoped I was wrong," she muttered as she rose from her chair and stalked back to the stove.

Whereas I frowned. Who could it be?

Heading for the entrance, I opened the door to see Darryl, clean-shaven and freshly showered, his hair still damp. He wore a jean jacket over a T-shirt tucked into jeans.

"Darryl. How unexpected." Understatement. Yet, despite the surprise, I smiled.

"Did you get the package I left?"

"I did, thank you." But I did wonder why he'd

popped in. Despite the flowers, I'd gotten the impression he wanted to steer clear of me.

"What are you doing here?" Jace barked from behind me. The statement emerged rude and territorial.

Even an old gal like me could feel the testosterone in the air, but I lacked the gullibility to think this was about me. The men eyed each other, and only an idiot wouldn't see the history between them. The dislike.

Darryl rose in my esteem, as he didn't slouch under Jace's hard gaze. "I'm here to see the lady."

He called me a lady. It made me wish I'd changed out of my food-stained clothes.

"As you can see, we're having dinner."

Implying Darryl should leave, and yet, this was my house, and Darryl had come to see me.

I put my hand on his arm. "Would you like to come in and join us? There's more than enough to go around."

Darryl's lips split into a smile. His appearance taking on a more youthful cast. How had I ever thought him plain? "I'd love that."

It was a tense dinner, and I thanked the fact Tricia and Marjorie were there to keep the conversation flowing, because Jace spent most of it glowering while Darryl exclaimed over the delicious meal.

He lied. The fake-tatoes were gross, the ham too salty, although the green beans were delicious.

As for the pie Marjorie brought in from the car? A low-carb almond-crust thing with some kind of cheesecake filling. I had some of it but abstained from the high sugar ice cream.

Not that I needed anything as I fed on the strange atmosphere. I'd gone from being alone to having four people at my dinner table. A good thing we'd scrounged up a fifth chair from the storage area under the stairs that I never even suspected existed until Tricia showed me.

How many more secrets did this house hold?

When it came time to relax after dinner, we actually managed to squeeze into the living room, with Jace taking the big chair and Tricia sprawling on the carpet in front of the woodstove, petting my cat. Marjorie had one corner of the couch, and with Darryl in the other, that left the middle for me. A fact that narrowed Jace's gaze.

I wanted to believe it was jealousy. My ego craved it. Instead, I got a dose of reality.

Darryl, whose thigh pressed against mine and whose fingers lightly touched my shoulder, given he'd draped his arm on the couch, said, "So, Jace, have you told Naomi yet that the only reason you're sucking up to her is to buy her property?"

## 16

---

Darryl's query was met with a moment of silence before Jace snapped, "Shut your mouth. You don't know what you're talking about."

"I will not be quiet. You've been snatching up property all around town. Care to tell us why?"

It was better than a tense tennis match. My gaze, and those of the other women, bounced between the men as they faced off.

"I don't have to tell you shit," Jace snarled.

Tricia came to his defense. "Jace isn't the only one who's been on a buying spree. Rumor has it you snagged a few, too."

Wait, Darryl was also buying up property? It surprised me, mostly because I'd made assumptions about him. Not very nice ones apparently. Why wouldn't he be interested in buying up more businesses? After all, he had a vested interest in the town.

"Yeah, I have. Places around my gas station so I can't be squeezed out. But he's the one going aggressively after the waterfront properties. Rumor has it he just snagged the Wanderbilts' place. So what's the scoop? Why do you need all that land? Know something we don't?"

"It's none of your business." Jace stood, towering over us all, a looming presence. Menacing even. I didn't even realize I'd tucked closer to Darryl until his hand squeezed my upper arm.

Darryl drawled, "I've lived here my whole life. I'd say that gives me a right to know what your plan is."

The curl on Jace's upper lip proved impressive. "I don't owe you anything. And if we're going to talk about truth telling, then why not start with the fact that you're married."

"Separated," Darryl said through clenched teeth. "And I'd be divorced if I knew where Sue-Ann went."

"Have you told Naomi why Sue left?" Jace asked. "About the fact the cops had to show up more than once because you were out of control?"

The accusation had me rising from the couch, moving away from Darryl. Instinctive and, yes, as an afterthought, mean. However, it was hard to regret my choice because, by the way a nerve ticked in Darryl's cheek, I knew there was some truth to what Jace said.

"I would have told her. It's not like it was a secret." His gaze met mine. "I was a drunk. And a mean one. I never hit Sue, but I could be nasty with my words."

"You got banned from a few bars last I heard. Got arrested how many times for drunk and disorderly?" Jace appeared to be taking pleasure in relating all of Darryl's sins.

Help came from Marjorie. "Stop attacking him. You know Darryl's not like that anymore."

"I've been clean for eight hundred and four days now," Darryl declared.

"And I'm going to add that if we're piling on Darryl for having made mistakes, then I guess that means I'm next. I've been drink free for only a month now." Marjorie's gaze met mine. "I didn't take Milo's leaving very well at first."

My dinner party had turned into a disaster. Because of one man. Luckily he didn't need to be told he'd overstayed his welcome. Jace headed for the front door, barking, "Thanks for the food."

I hastened to follow but ended up having to chase him outside, where he'd already made it off the porch. "Jace!"

For a second, I thought he'd keep stomping. Instead, he halted and pivoted. "What?"

I tucked my hands behind my back so he

wouldn't see them trembling. This man had the ability to make me nervous. "I'm sorry things got tense inside."

His brows rose. "You're sorry? I'm the one who caused it."

It surprised me to hear him admit it. I took a few steps so that I didn't feel as if I were shouting. "Why?"

He scraped a hand through his hair, the silver waves of it fluttering. "Because I don't like Darryl."

"I'd say that feeling was mutual."

"Watch yourself around him."

Funny he should say that, given he was the one who roused my trepidation the most. "I will." Then because he hadn't yet run off—or grabbed an axe— I hastened to add, "I know thus far our meetings have been somewhat…" I lacked a word.

He supplied it. "Mangled?" His lips held the ghost of a smile.

"That's one way of putting it. But, given we're neighbors, I'd really like us to not be fighting."

"Who says we are?" He took a step back toward the porch. "Listen, about what I said about you not belonging here…" He paused. "It wasn't meant to be mean. Just that there's a lot going on right now."

"Did you say it in the hopes I'd run away and sell you my property?" The query slipped out, and the apology on his face slid away.

"I don't want to buy your place."

"The letters I got from your company say otherwise."

"What letters?" He sounded genuinely surprised.

Before I could reply, Tricia was at the door. "Hey, you coming back in? I found some games under the stairs. How long since you've played Operation?" She held up the box and rattled it.

"Give me a second."

Turned out I didn't need it because, when I looked back, Jace was gone.

THE MORNING AFTER MY DINNER PARTY—WHICH ended up finishing on laughter as we all failed miserably at saving the red-nosed man on the operating table—I lay in bed staring at the ceiling. In the morning light, I couldn't see the glow in the dark stickers. Not that I was paying attention to anything as my mind whirled.

Jace's evasions last night had only made me wonder more about why his company would be buying property. The highway had already been rerouted. The mill was a decrepit ruin that wouldn't make a comeback without millions being spent. The lake, while nice, wouldn't suddenly turn into a tourist hot spot. I could discern no reason why anyone would invest here. So why was Jace so tight lipped about it? And why the surprise I'd received an offer? It implied more than one person swung deals in his company.

Then I had to wonder about Darryl's motive in bringing it so baldly into the open. It seemed cheeky that he'd throw accusations given his abusive alcoholic past. Jace wasn't the only one hiding stuff, but I would admit to being impressed that Darryl had done something about it.

Marjorie had made a good point. If I was going to judge Darryl on the past, then I needed to judge myself, too. It wasn't just alcohol that made a person bad. Actions counted, too. If I wanted forgiveness and a second chance, then I should be ready to extend the same thing to Darryl. As for Jace…that man confused me. I still didn't even know if I liked him. He came across as a tad too grumpy and a plain ol' misogynist for my liking.

Getting out of bed, I wondered what I should do with my day. Given I'd struck out in Cambden, I'd have to search farther afield for a much-needed job. Glancing at the stairs on my way to the coffee pot reminded me I'd yet to find an axe, which meant the closet upstairs remained intact. For the moment. I'd gone over every inch of the space, looking for cracks. I'd groped it more than I'd groped anything in the last decade. Nothing budged. Yet I was more and more convinced something hid behind that wall. At times I even imagined the wall as some kind of illusion. Ridiculous really.

If things hadn't gotten weird with Jace, I might have asked to borrow his axe. Perhaps I still would. Maybe he'd offer to help. I could bring him upstairs and show him my problem. He'd take off that shirt and swing that axe while I watched. And when he opened the space, revealing the hidden treasure within, I'd thank him by throwing myself on the bed and telling him to have his way with me. I'd strip, he'd cringe as I showed him my less-than-stellar physique, and I'd probably never get naked again.

On second thought, best if I didn't bother him and ruin the tenuous peace we'd forged. Especially since I surely imagined any kind of interest on his part. Darryl on the other hand… He definitely had a thing for me. I just didn't know if I was ready to pursue it. After all, ignoring our marital status for the moment, we both lived in the same small town. What if I said what the heck and we slept together? What if it didn't work out? I'd have to gas my car in the next town over because I surely couldn't ever face him again.

What if he was less than impressed with loose skin and flabby boobs? Not so long ago, I might have scoffed those that had plastic surgery to correct issues, but now… Now I kind of wished I had the money to fix a few things.

Halfway there with a body that had already quit.

*Knock. Knock.*

For a house in the country, I was getting an awful lot of visitors. More than I'd had living in suburbia surrounded by people.

A smile stretched my lips as I saw Tricia when I opened the door.

"Hey, Trish. What's up?"

"Wondering if you'd recovered from last night."

My lips twisted into a wry smile. "It was rather intense for a bit."

"Only because your macho neighbor made it that way. I don't know what got into Jace."

"I don't think he and Darryl like each other."

Trish snorted. "Ya think? It doesn't help they both have the hots for you."

"They do not!" My cheeks flamed.

"Please. I'm surprised they didn't whip out their things and get into a pissing match." She mimed spraying a firehose.

I laughed even as I exclaimed, "Trish!"

"What? It's true."

"Maybe Darryl has a thing." It felt silly to even say it out loud. "But Jace most definitely doesn't."

"If you say so," Tricia sang. "Which one do you like better?"

"Neither. I'm not ready to date."

"Who said anything about dating? You need to get laid." She then proceeded to make the boom-chica-wow-wow noise. The one most often associated with horrible porn.

"Stop that!" The heat in my cheeks increased to the point I'd surely erupt into flames.

"Satisfying your bodily needs is as necessary as a proper diet and exercise."

"I'd rather not talk about it."

"Prude." Tricia rolled her eyes.

"I'm sure you didn't just come over to see how many times you could embarrass me."

"You're right. I didn't, although you have to admit I am on a roll." Her grin widened. "However, I'm actually here for something more important than that. You and I are going shopping for clothes."

For an instant I almost said yes. I longed for something that fit me better, maybe flattered my very few positive attributes. But then I recalled the job situation. "I can't. I have no money." I hung my head, utterly ashamed.

Whereas Tricia laughed. "What are you talking about?"

"Until the divorce is final, I just get a bit of alimony. And I already spent most of the current month's allowance making the trip up here." I shrugged. "I'm kind of tapped until I get a job."

"You know they won't charge you in town."

I shifted, uncomfortable at the reminder.

"Knowing doesn't mean I should take advantage. It doesn't feel right."

"You can't stay dressed like this." Her hand waved at me. "Good thing I brought you a few things. But you need more. Get changed." She thrust the bag she'd been holding at me.

"What is this?"

"Stuff that would look better on you than me."

Inside the bag was a long skirt, a few tops, and even a pair of sandals that were a bit short in the heel but nice after having my toes crammed in the loafers. I emerged from the bedroom and twirled.

"Tada."

"Better. But we still need to go shopping."

I shook my head. "I can't. I told you, I'm broke."

"Borrow from the emergency fund."

"I don't have one."

"Not yours." At my blank look, Tricia exclaimed, "Did your grandma not ever show it to you?"

Which led to the discovery of yet another hidey-hole that Trish knew about, but I didn't. It hurt to see how much my grandma had revealed to my friend and not me.

The cookie jar behind the fake panel under the counter held bills. Most of them were old but still good. A good thing money never went out of style. I clutched a fistful and frowned.

"Why was she hiding money?"

"Your grandma didn't trust banks."

Or me, apparently. "Maybe I should hold on to this, just in case."

"In case of what?" Tricia asked.

"What if I don't find a job?"

"You'll find a job. But only if we do something about your hair and clothes."

"What happened to you cutting it for me?"

"I'm good, but not that good."

I winced. "It's not that bad."

"When was the last time you actually had someone cut and style your hair?"

A part of me wanted to squirm at her query.

She hmphed. "That's what I thought. We need the pros to help. And a second opinion."

Which was why we ended up grabbing Marjorie on our way. She climbed into the back of Tricia's Corolla exclaiming, "Thanks for the invite. I thought I was going to have to tidy the house today since the diner is closed for cleaning."

"Is it going to be shut down for long?"

"Nah. Orville figures we'll be open by Monday or Tuesday. He's using the shutdown as a chance to also get the seat covers fixed."

"Why? Did he run out of duct tape?" Tricia said with a snicker.

"Actually, it was the investor's idea that Orville do it to spruce up the place."

"Investor?" I asked. "Who bought the diner?" Could it be Jace?

"No idea. I just found out about it today, and Orville won't say much other than he sold the diner but on the condition he still ran it."

"When did that happen?" Trish divided her attention between the road and the rearview mirror.

"Recently from what I understand. And I don't think the diner is the only thing that changed ownership, or didn't you notice the renovations that started at Mr. Peterson's hardware store?"

Knowing Jace had bought property made me wonder if he was behind it. Had he embarked on a mission to spruce up the town? Perhaps turn it into one of those cutesy tourist towns? I hoped not. I might just have to move if they put up a sign as you entered showing happy families camping by the lake with a smiling monster swimming in it.

Then again, would that be so bad? I could embrace my supposed witch heritage and open up a shop where the tourists could buy amulets and charms to ward off evil spirits. I could make a fortune playing on my reputation.

It was just as wrong as taking from the town. I couldn't lie. Not yet. But if I got desperate…

The mall the next town over was gone, which led to a spot of nostalgia as I recalled the food court with its orange and green cafeteria chairs. Grandma used to drop me and Tricia off at least once a month with a bit of money to spend. We roamed the mall for hours, shared sodas, and people watched. Giggled and gossiped.

"Do you remember that store we used to go to?"

That was all I had to say for Tricia to exclaim, "Holy crap, are you talking about that one with only plaid stuff? I still have one of those skirts. I just can't fit my ass into it."

"Seriously?" I giggled. "That is so vintage."

"Ugh. You did not just call one of my favorite outfit old." She grimaced.

I bit my lower lip. "We are old." For once saying it didn't make me wince. So what if I was old and they'd replaced my mall with a strip plaza dotted with several big box stores?

Walmart was the only one in my budget. It didn't take long before I had some bulging bags and money left over. A good thing since the beauty salon cost me a fortune. However, even I had to grudgingly admit they knew their stuff.

I emerged with a sleek style that fell to just past my boobs. I could pull it back if needed, blow dry it straight, or go au natural. They'd added some highlights to my hair, silver ones that embraced my age rather than hid it, giving me a striking effect when I looked in the mirror. The new me looked sophisticated and as if she had her shit together.

I'd almost cried when they waxed my brows and

took care of my upper lip. I really should do an Ancestry kit and see where my luscious pelt of body fur came from.

But that wasn't the only torture. I swear the beautician took pleasure in plucking my three chin hairs. I almost got her back during the pedicure when a ticklish sole resulted in my foot twitching, narrowly missing her face.

I tipped her generously when I saw the end product. I didn't stare at myself for long on account of the tears filling my eyes.

Instantly, arms went around me.

Trish mocked me a little. "Stop crying. You'll get snot on your new shirt."

I sniffled instead. "Thank you."

"For what? Reminding you that it's okay to pamper yourself?"

"I'd forgotten what it was like to feel good about myself," I admitted.

Marjorie hugged me. "It took me a while and several bottles of cheap whiskey after Milo left to remember to still love me."

"But I'm not sad Martin is gone." I really wasn't. What I mourned was the loss of everything else. And that needed to stop.

I couldn't change the past. And yes, what happened to me sucked. Like majorly sucked. However, I didn't have to let it define me.

The woman in the mirror at the salon could

handle this world with her head held high. I couldn't let fear stand in my way. I also needed to stop hating myself.

Yes, I remained overweight, but I would keep working on losing it. I'd make the healthier choices. I'd take care of me.

Bye, bye frumpy Naomi. A spark of mischief made me say, "I look like a hot cougar."

That drew the expected laughter.

"You know what, though, we *are* hot cougars." Tricia winked at Marjorie. "We are also looking much too fine to just go home and veg on the couch."

"Are you thinking what I'm thinking?" Marjorie asked.

"Bulldrafts!"

"What the hell is bull drafts?" I asked.

"A bar," said Marjorie.

"But you don't drink."

She shook her head. "Don't worry, I am not planning to start."

"But being around it…" I didn't mean to cast doubt, but a friend should look out for someone recovering. Or was I meddling in things I shouldn't? I now wondered if I should have kept my mouth shut.

To my relief, Marjorie didn't look offended. "Don't worry about it. I am done drinking. I don't even like the taste, so I can't even remember why I thought it was a good way to drown my sorrows. Besides, who needs booze when I'll be getting my high from dancing?"

Dancing? Panic suffused me. "I don't think—"

Tricia interrupted. "That's the point. No thinking."

"I can't dance," I admitted. The last time had been at my wedding. Martin wasn't the type to boogie. Meaning I didn't dance either. I hadn't the slightest clue how. It was pathetic.

"It's not hard. Just let your hips do the wiggling. And remember, no one cares how you dance."

Except for me. What if I embarrassed myself? I'd be that person they made fun of in memes. I'd probably end up on the internet looking stupid and old and—

A sharp pinch drew a yelp from me. "Ouch! What was that for?" I glared at Trish.

"Dude, I can read your mind."

"Dude?" Marjorie snickered. "That is seriously eighties."

Which led to a discussion on the best and worse things of the eighties. Tight jeans and hair teased into puffy bangs made the top of that list. Jelly shoes and shoulder pads were at the bottom.

"I miss my crimper," I admitted in a moment of nostalgia.

"Stick your finger in a light socket for the same effect." Tricia had often teased my attempts to look cool. I was awkward as a teen. Gawky and lacking any sense of style. At the cottage, with Grandma, appearances didn't matter, but in high school, appearance was everything.

"I still have my jean jacket," Marjorie admitted.

Tricia nodded in approval. "Jean jackets are cool. They never go out of style."

"I miss mine. I even had it bedazzled."

That drew laughter as I was soundly informed denim should never be covered in sparkles.

Ever.

We had dinner at a fast food chain that provided a flame-broiled burger on a lettuce bed, along with a side salad, for me.

Trish ate her fries and eyed the healthy choice. "I could never give up carbs."

"I didn't want to. I had to." But seeing the benefits made it easy. Weight loss. More energy. Joints less achy. I felt younger and more vibrant than I had in a while.

"You going to get as skinny as Jojo?" Trish asked.

"If you're implying I'm too thin—" my new friend said with an indignant huff.

"Never. You look good, and you know it." Trish laughed and winked.

Whereas I actually pondered what my reply would have been. I'd not really thought that far ahead. I'd started eating better to kind of show

Martin that I wasn't the fat cow he named me. But the truth was I didn't care what he thought. I had to do this for me.

If I looked at my life as only being halfway there, then that meant I had just as many years left to make new memories. Healthy choices meant being able to actually enjoy the decades left to me.

Decades. I could do the things I'd always wanted.

What did I want to do?

"I smell panic," Trish muttered.

"Do you guys have things you want to do?"

"Do you mean like a bucket list? I sure do," Marjorie declared.

"What's on it?" I asked.

"I want to go see the Grand Canyon because it's pretty. Eat one of those famous Halifax donairs they're always talking about."

Travel? A cool idea. I thought of the pretty pictures I'd seen of Greece, but the idea of flying, finding a hotel, and being somewhere I didn't know by myself scared me.

Hello, panic, my constant friend.

"Your bucket list should be things that make you excited. Or scare you. A thing you want to conquer," Marjorie added, completely enthused.

Whereas I was daunted. "I don't know. I've experienced so little. Where would I start?"

Tricia was the one who said, "Start small." Small being going to a bar.

The idea shouldn't have made me anxious. Yet, I sweated in the front seat. Would everyone see what an uncomfortable dork I was? How pretentious to think anyone would even give a second thought about me.

The parking lot of the bar already had a bunch of cars and pickups parked. Too many.

Panic kept fluttering. "Maybe this isn't a good idea."

"Tell me, what's the worst that can happen if we walk in?" Marjorie asked.

My mind raced with possibilities.

What if this was a biker bar, or outlaws came in to have a few and a fight broke out and—

That happened on television or in books. Not a few miles outside of Cambden.

I would be too old.

Dressed wrong.

The music would be too loud.

Wait, I didn't mind loud music. It was Martin that hated it.

Tricia expected me to dance.

But I was a big girl who could say no.

I'd feel uncomfortable and out of place.

My friends would be with me.

I wouldn't be alone. "Let's do this." I got out of the car before I changed my mind.

The second we stepped out of the Corolla I could hear the steady thump of bass from the music playing inside. I immediately felt the urge to tap my toe.

My new canvas shoes didn't make any noise on the pavement compared to Marjorie's heeled ankle boots. A very cute look to go with her distressed jeans. She dressed young. Or was it I let my style veer to something old? A certain expectation of what a woman my age should wear?

I glanced down at my sensible slacks and then the blouse I'd left hanging loose, the puffiness of it hiding my tummy. Some people called it a muffin top. Mine was a whole cake.

I saw people younger than us going inside. My step slowed as my gaze narrowed in on the woman strutting between two guys, her body thin and wearing something tight to showcase it. My inadequacies all began shouting at once.

"I changed my mind. Maybe this isn't a good idea." Trepidation froze my limbs.

They wouldn't let me back down.

"Live a little, Omi." Tricia grabbed my arm and pulled.

"This is bullying," I declared, even as I followed.

"It's for your own good," Marjorie declared. "Nothing bad will happen. You'll see."

"Just don't get drunk and you won't be hugging the porcelain god later."

"The what?" I blinked. "Never mind. I am not drinking."

I fought the panic as we reached the doors. What was the worst that could happen? It wasn't as if going into a bar would kill me.

I hoped.

The music rolled over us in a loud percussive wave as we entered. To my relief, despite what I'd seen outside, the age of the patrons ranged from the barely legal to old enough to be my father. At least we wouldn't look out of place with the vast majority appearing in their thirties to fifties.

For a small Canadian town, there was plenty of diversity everywhere I looked. Style, too. Cowboy hats to bobbing, flashing eye stalks on a headband.

We lucked out and found a high-top table surrounded by four stools. The surface was sticky, so I sat straight on my seat and tried not to touch it.

Then felt like the biggest snob. Why couldn't I just relax like every one else?

Marjorie grimaced. "I am going to find something to wipe this with." She headed off to the bar, returning with drinks and napkins, the latter of which she wiped over the condensation on the glasses then used on the table. Seeing her attack the sticky spots made me feel oddly better.

While Marjorie had ordered herself something virgin, she decided Tricia and I needed a drink with a higher alcohol content and little to no carbs, which turned out to be tequila. I'd never done tequila shots. By the third one, with salt poured into my palm for licking and a wedge of lemon for after, I was glowing.

I'd finally relaxed enough to truly take in my environment. The Bulldraft was old. The building hideous I'd wager by daylight, but vibrant at night with its bright neon sign. Inside, a giant bar formed a square in the center with a dance floor edged by tables and chairs to the left and a ring with a mechanical bull surrounded by more seats to the right.

The place was packed. Saturday night in the boonies. I was pretty sure everyone in this town and a few surrounding ones had shown up.

Almost everyone. A glance around hadn't shown either Jace or Darryl, but I saw other men, some who held my gaze and smiled.

At me.

Each time I blushed and pretended interest in the lemon on the napkin. A fourth tequila shot was placed in front of me.

"I didn't order this," I said, trying to hand it back.

The waitress waved me off and shouted, "Courtesy of the gent at the bar."

Tricia uttered a drawn-out, "Oooh, look at you getting a drink bought for you."

A glance over my shoulder showed a bunch of

guys sitting at the long counter but only one tipping his glass in my direction. An older guy, his hair pure silver, his features the leathery tan that came from being outside. He wore a dark jacket, light shirt, and a bolero. Not something you saw often in Canada.

I smiled apprehensively, and when his widened in reply as if I'd given some signal, I panicked and turned away.

Trish cackled. She'd also received a shot, as had Marjorie, although she pushed hers toward Tricia.

"You can have mine."

Double-fisted, Trish lifted them and yelled, "Bottoms up!"

Not used to drinking, I probably should have paced myself. Yet I downed it. A warm glow spread through my body. I felt limber and hot. My foot kept tapping to the pulsing beat of the music. I even swayed a bit in my seat. When Marjorie hopped to her feet and said, "Let's dance!" I was too drunk to protest.

On the dance floor, bodies gyrated. I moved sinuously with them. My body undulated in a way I'd not attempted since my teens. I shook and shimmied. I flung my head around and laughed.

It was hot. Sweaty. Fun.

Bodies brushed against mine, sometimes suggestively. But I didn't take offense because everyone was doing it. Sometimes Marjorie was the one waggling her butt against me. Trish did a shake of her boobs that I matched and had us both laughing uncontrollably.

So when hands palmed my hips and someone began to dance in time to my movements, I thought nothing of it. Although I did feel.

I felt a sweet tingle and a breathless anticipation. I felt desirable. And horny. Not that I planned to act on it. It was just nice to feel as if I'd shed all my trouble. To once more feel alive and vibrant.

When the song slowed, those hands twirled me and I opened my mouth to tell the person thank you, only to blink as I saw the man from the bar before me. "Hi."

His lips curved. "Hey." He didn't seem as old as I'd thought now that he was close to me. Sure, his hair was gray, but his face was only lightly lined. His shoulders were still broad, and he smelled good. I almost leaned in to nuzzle him.

Woah. That was some good tequila. It took some effort to remember not to randomly sniff strangers.

While his hand remained firmly on my waist, he didn't try to get too fresh with me. There was a bit of space between our bodies. We moved slowly in time to the beat of the song, an eighties ballad about love.

A more appropriate one would have been about

lust. I blamed the booze for the fact I moved closer to the man. A stranger.

The possibilities unfolded quickly in my mind. Making out with him somewhere in a dark corner just to see how it felt. If I didn't tell him my name or give my number, he wouldn't be able to find me.

But what if he lived nearby and we ran into each other?

Assuming he would even make out with someone like me.

He pulled me into him, the space between our bodies gone, the hardness of his erection pressing into me. I almost gasped because there was no denying it. He desired me.

It made me bold, and I raised my gaze to his. "I'm Naomi.

"Kane."

We weren't strangers anymore. I tucked in closer, practically rubbing myself on him. I'd forgotten all about by body-image issues, the fact I was in the midst of a messy divorce, and even my friends. I wanted to get closer.

Our slow dancing brought us to the edge of the dancefloor and a door marked exit that had been propped open. I didn't even think to argue as he tugged me outside, navigating us through the fog of cigarette smoke as people huddled outdoors puffing on their little white sticks. Some had adopted the newer e-cigarette, the metal cylinders glowing all kinds of colors.

We left that cancerous cloud behind and didn't stop moving until we reached the edge of the parking lot. Only then did he lean against a luxury car that I'd bet he owned. It suited him, long and sleek. Elegant, too.

A faint mist appeared to be forming past the edge of the parking lot. The air held a chill to it.

I shivered.

"Are you cold?" Rather than offer me his jacket, he drew me close, tucked me into his chest, his arms banded around my body. The action fired my blood, and also sparked a little bit of worry.

What was I doing out here? I didn't know this man. What did he want?

I figured that out when his mouth touched mine.

Oh. He stole the breath from me as he kissed me thoroughly, deeply, making my toes curl. It was so different this embrace from a man other than Martin. For a second I felt guilty. I was still technically a married woman.

And then I felt even more guilt as I thought of Darryl and even Jace.

Then a bit of panic as I wondered, was I a slut? My trepidation had me almost pulling away.

Almost.

A faint voice murmured to me.

*Relax. Enjoy it.*

This was a meaningless kiss. I'd never see this guy again. Why not enjoy it? Enjoy the mastery of the kiss. The breathless nature of it.

Literally. It was as if I were starved for oxygen. My knees grew weak. My senses dimmed. I felt cold and hot at once. Then...

The next thing I knew I was in the back seat of a car. My head in someone's lap.

"There's the party girl!" Trish exclaimed, aiming to sound buoyant, and yet I heard a hint of desperation in the tone.

"What happened?" I asked groggily.

"Someone had a bit too much to drink and thought it was a good idea to make out with a stranger in the parking lot."

My cheeks flamed. "You saw?"

"Good thing we followed because you were so out of it. At least the guy was good enough to back off when we told him you were drunk."

"Drunk and dumb." I rubbed a hand on my forehead.

"Not dumb. Horny," Trish corrected.

"Was he a good kisser?" Marjorie asked from the driver's seat.

"Yes? I think so." He'd definitely made my knees weak. But as for pleasurable? I didn't really remember much of it.

"No more tequila for you," Trish teased, and I

wondered at the look she gave Marjorie in the rearview.

Marjorie dropped me off first. The ladies putting me to bed despite my protests I was fine.

In reality, I wasn't. I wobbled when I stood. The room spun when I lay down.

Grisou hissed at me, not liking the scent of booze. I didn't like the feel of it either. I did end up hugging a porcelain toilet and saying oh my God by the time I was done.

I crawled to bed. I was never drinking again.

Closing my eyes, I fell asleep and dropped into a nightmare where I was once more in the living room, seeing the frost covering the window. But this time, when I pressed my hand against it, the face I saw was Kane's. And when he opened his mouth wide?

I got sucked into an abyss!

I FELL OUT OF BED AND HIT THE FLOOR WITH A thump. It took me a moment to orient myself. My mouth was pasty, my limbs weak and trembly.

Having spent twenty-some years not drinking, my sudden foray into alcohol meant I had an honest-to-goodness hangover. I didn't enjoy it one bit. It took every ounce of strength to get to my feet and stagger to the kitchen. The coffee maker took some coordination, and I spilled more than a handful of the ground beans trying to get them into the filter. Then I collapsed in a chair as it brewed.

I held my head in my hands as it gurgled away. Soon I held a steaming mug in my hands and managed to totter to the big comfy chair, where I sipped my caffeine jolt and tried to not blush at what I'd done.

Harder not to be embarrassed by what I might

have done if my friends hadn't intervened. Was the alcohol to blame for my complete lack of inhibition? Was I suddenly so desperate for male attention I would make out with any old stranger? Or was it simply nice to realize that, despite everything, I remained a woman with needs who could desire and be desired?

*Knock. Knock.* I glared at the door.

First, it was much too early for anyone to visit, never mind the clock read ten a.m. My body insisted it had to be earlier. Second, the door was much too far from the chair. Third, I didn't want anyone to see me like this. I glanced down. At least my friends had stripped me and put me in pajamas.

I sipped my coffee and decided to ignore the visitor, only I'd apparently forgotten to lock the door, because it opened. Shocked, I spewed my coffee before I realized it was Marjorie.

She beamed. "There's the party girl. How are you feeling?"

"Like death," I admitted.

"Which is a great reminder as to why I stopped drinking." She laughed. "I'll bet you're wondering why I'm here."

Not really, but hey, maybe I'd care after a second cup. Okay, I actually did care. Marjorie was making every attempt to be my friend. And I appreciated it.

"Why are you here?" And please don't let it involve tequila.

"So I was cleaning my house this morning"—I wanted to make the sign of a cross against her excessive energy—"when I found this."

She whipped out a rectangular piece of cardboard from her purse as if it were the biggest find of the century. I had no idea why.

"What is it?"

"It's a business card."

"I see that, but why is it important?"

"Because I found it in *his* things."

His, as in her missing husband. I snagged it and read the company name. "It's a law firm."

"The bastard was planning to divorce me and yet turned cowardly and ran instead!"

"You don't know that for sure." I flipped the card to see if it detailed their specialty and froze at the symbol. The card fluttered to the floor, and I had to force myself to pick it up. It was the same weird symbol I'd seen on that offer for my grandma's cottage. Jace's company, Airgeadsféar.

"What else would it be for?" She snatched it back and waved it around. "He was talking to a lawyer. As if he had anything to be unhappy about." She glared at the offending rectangle of thick paper.

"Men are scum." Seemed like the right thing to say, and she beamed.

"Exactly." Marjorie bustled into my kitchen and made herself at home, pouring a coffee then grabbing some eggs from the fridge. Initially the sight made me queasy, but after she fried an egg and served it to me with some slices of cheese and a hunk of leftover ham she also fried in the pan, I ate it with gusto.

Slowly but surely, I recovered.

"You look human again," said Marjorie with a laugh.

"I can't believe how badly I was hung over," I exclaimed as leaned back in the kitchen chair.

"Yeah, that's crazy." Her tone had something in it. A hint of censor?

I glanced at her, only she'd grabbed our plates and headed for the sink. I'd said the wrong thing.

"I'm sorry. Here I am talking about that which should not be named like the most insensitive jerk."

She turned a startled gaze on me. "What are you talking about? I'm fine. I told you the drinking doesn't bother me."

"But something is," I said, hoping I hadn't said the wrong thing again.

This time I proved right. Her lips went into a straight line, and she turned to the sink as she ran the water. "You were really out of it."

"Like I said, a drinking lightweight."

"It was four tequila shots, hardly enough to get

you drunk even if you don't have experience. Trust me, I know."

"Maybe I had a bad reaction."

"Maybe."

As I stared at her, I had a strange revelation. "You think he roofied me?" When she didn't reply, I started to laugh. "Why on earth would any man roofie me, of all people?"

"What else explains your behavior? You have to admit it was out of character."

"Meaning what?"

"Meaning I don't think you would have gone off with a stranger unless you weren't feeling like yourself."

"I wasn't feeling like myself," I admitted. "But just because I decided to make out with a stranger doesn't mean he drugged me." Please no. I'd hate to think I'd mistaken almost rape for attraction. "Besides, he never had a chance. We went from the dancefloor to this car."

"Could have been in that shot he sent over."

"Trish was fine," I countered.

"He probably knew better than to go after Trish," she mused aloud.

The words stung. "Meaning I'm stupid?"

Marjorie eyed me with shock. "That's not what I said. Just that his tricks wouldn't work on Trish."

"But I'm stupid and ugly and gullible, which is

why he fooled me." Tears pricked my eyes as I realized how Marjorie saw me: pathetic.

"Oh, *cherie*." She went to hug me, but I stepped aside.

I didn't need her pity.

"You're not any of those things. How is it you don't see yourself the way we see you?"

"I don't know what you think you see," I said on a bitter sob, "but I know what I am. An overweight, old, almost-divorcee with nothing to show for my life."

"What about your amazing kids?"

"They're doing better now that they've gotten away from me." The truth hurt.

"You mean since they got away from Martin."

"Whatever." I hugged myself and wouldn't look at her.

"Naomi." She said my name softly. "I know we've just met, but I hope you believe me when I say I want to be your friend."

"Why?" I eyed her, feeling the fragility of my spirit as I hugged myself.

"Because you have a sharp wit."

I snorted. "A nice way of saying I'm sarcastic."

"Maybe a little." Her lips curved. "But that's not a bad thing. I like it. You're intelligent."

"Book smart, not people smart," I corrected.

"And I'm neither," she said with a self-deprecating shrug. "Does this mean you don't like talking to me?"

"Don't be stupid. Of course, I do. And you're just as smart—probably even smarter—than me."

"How do you figure that? I never knew my husband wanted a divorce." The card waggled again.

"I was so humiliated when I found out Martin cheated." Gutted. Wrenched apart as a woman to know he'd touched someone else.

"I wanted to hunt them down and cut off body parts," Marjorie admitted.

"But you didn't."

"Because he wasn't worth doing jail time over." Her white teeth gleamed. "Besides, I'm dating someone much better than him now."

"Really?" My eyes widened. "But you're still married."

"Separated."

"Why does it feel taboo?" I asked. "I don't want Martin back. I can't wait until the divorce is done, but when I was dancing with Kane last night…" I paused. "I couldn't help but freak out a bit."

"Milo and I weren't married as long as you, so I can only imagine. But I will say, that's normal. I felt it, too, at first, even though I was angry. You get used to someone. You think you know them, and even if there's shitty moments, they're your moments. You can't just forget it all as if it never happened or never mattered."

"According to him, I didn't matter."

"Wrong. You did. But then people change. Sometimes forever is only a few years."

"Not in the movies it's not." The kind of books I read and films I watched implied a long happily ever after.

"Some people are lucky enough to find that love early in life and hold on to it. Others need a few tries to get it right," Marjorie said with a shrug.

"You think you met Mr. Right?" I asked.

"Mr. Right?" She laughed. "I don't know if I'd say that."

"I don't think I'm ready to be looking yet." And then immediately realized how it sounded. As if she'd moved on too quickly.

"You don't have to look. When the time is right, it will just happen."

Would it just happen?

I wanted to believe Marjorie. But after Kane, the man who might have drugged me, I had to wonder. Was I just going to be a perpetual victim in life? How did I stop the cycle?

Marjorie left to give Orville help with the diner so they could open in the morning, but she'd forgotten the lawyer's card beside her coffee cup. I eyed it with distaste. I couldn't have said why I found the symbol on it so repugnant. A part of me was tempted to burn it. What if Marjorie needed it, though?

Instead I sealed it in an envelope. I'd give it to her next time I saw her. Then, because I couldn't stand to have it in the house, I put it in my car on the passenger seat.

Out of sight, out of mind.

Not quite. Seeing the symbol gave me an idea. A strange one that I blamed on the lingering fog of my hangover. I recalled the drawing I'd found on a piece of paper with no apparent use or value, yet it was hidden away. Why?

Now, I wasn't a person who believed in magic. Or ghosts. Or anything weird, even if my panic did sometimes overwhelm and attempt to persuade me otherwise. However, I couldn't help a strange urge to march upstairs, slap that piece of paper on the wall, and do some mumbo-jumbo routine where I pretended I was a witch with the power to open secret doors.

Except I didn't know what to say.

I held the paper to the wall, and my mind went blank. Say something. Anything.

"Open sesame."

Nothing.

"Door open."

Still nothing. I tried a more direct approach.

"Va-va-voom!"

Nada.

"A la peanut butter sandwich." Nonsense that also didn't work.

Who knows how many stupid things I would have said had it not been for the knock on my front door? Another visitor? Who could it be?

Marjorie had left and headed to work. Perhaps her boss sent her away?

Could be Tricia. I was surprised she'd not texted me yet.

Could be my neighbor again. Or Darryl.

I hoped not in both those last cases. I might have gotten a makeover, but after a night of partying, I needed a solid twelve hours of sleep and another shower before I'd look remotely human again.

*Knock. Knock.*

Was I really complaining about people coming to see me? Either they accepted me as I was or... too bad. I could only be me. Still, I did attempt to smooth my hair and was glad I'd at least managed to find a bra.

I flung open the door, only to gape in surprise and stutter, "What are you doing here?"

## 19

IT WASN'T ANY OF THE GUYS I'D RECENTLY BEEN lusting after standing on the porch, nor one of my female friends, but my youngest child. She wore an oversized sweater, the yarn pulled in several places, over khakis that didn't quite cover the ankles of her black unlaced boots. Her hair was pulled back into a ponytail, and she had a knapsack slung over a shoulder. A dark compact car sat parked behind mine.

"Winnie?" No helping the surprise in that word. "What are you doing here?"

"Thought I'd pop in on you. Make sure you're doing okay." She said it as if it were the most natural thing in the world.

Not for us, so I eyed her more closely and noticed the redness of her eyes and the bags under them. My daughter was upset.

"I'm fine, but you don't look okay."

For a moment, she appeared stoic. "I'm peachy keen." A second later, her face crumpled. "Actually, I'm not. He dumped me."

"Who did?" Hello, mother of the year. I never even knew Wendy was seeing anyone.

"Erik. My professor." The words emerged in a gush. "We've been dating since my second year of college and then kept seeing each other even after I dropped out. He told me he loved me and that I meant everything to him."

My heart sank. "I take it he's had a change of heart?"

"More like *she* changed it for him," she said with vehemence.

"She, who?"

"His *wife*," Wendy spat as if it were a foul word.

"He's married? Winnie!" I couldn't help my shock.

"Don't say it like that. It's not my fault. He said he didn't love her but he couldn't leave on account she was sick."

I wanted to close my eyes as she admitted to falling for the oldest scam in the book. "Oh, Winnie. Why didn't you tell me before about this man?"

Her chin lifted despite the wobble. "Because I knew this was how you'd react."

"You mean because you knew I'd tell you to stay away from a married man?"

"I don't need you judging me." Her lower lip trembled.

It might be the wrong thing to say, but I was her mom. I couldn't help it. "What did you expect, getting involved with not only a teacher but a married one?"

"He said he loved me. That he would leave her for me the moment he could. But I got tired of waiting, and when I pushed him on it, he dumped me."

In that moment, I could have kept being her judgmental mom, but...that wasn't what my girl needed. I opened my arms and said, "What a jerk. He obviously had no idea how special you are."

She flung herself at me, and I hugged her. Hugged her like I'd not hugged her in forever.

Was it wrong to be glad that the married man-whore set Wendy free and she chose to come to me? I was her first choice. If I had the money, I'd have sent him thank-you flowers.

She sniffled in my arms. "Once I quit my job at the college café, I couldn't stay. So I left. And here I am."

Here she was. Which suddenly made me wonder... "What's your plan?"

"I figured I'd stay with you for a bit. That is, if you'll have me." In that moment she sounded uncertain, and I dove on her, my clasping of her hand clumsy but heartfelt.

"Of course, you can stay. As long as you want. I'd like the company." I liked even more the second chance I was getting to make things right.

"Awesome. I'll get my stuff."

By stuff, she meant the entire backseat of her two-door car, a sturdy Honda hatchback full to the brim with boxes and bags. This was more than a few days' worth. This was my daughter starting over.

I helped her carry the stuff in, piling it by the entrance, only to realize she needed a room. There were only two, and I'd technically claimed the one on the main floor, leaving the attic available. Would I really give up the extra space plus the use of my own bathroom with that amazing tub?

"I'll move my stuff out of the main floor bedroom and up to Grandma's room." I really needed to start thinking of it as mine.

Wendy eyed the ceiling. "Thanks. I don't think I could sleep up there. From the outside, the windows look like eyes. Kind of freaky. This whole place is weird."

Her words put me on the defensive. "I love this house."

"I didn't say I didn't like it, just that it's strange. I thought I was in the wrong place because you can't see a thing and then, boom, it's suddenly there."

"Grandma liked her privacy." Come to think of it, we never really had visitors. Not while I was there anyhow. Times had changed. Now I was like a train station with people coming and going all the time. I kind of liked it.

"I think Great-Granny liked the boonies a bit too much if you ask me," Wendy grumbled. "I drove back and forth a few times before finding the driveway."

"You're here now, at least." I carried a medley box of books and clothes to the bedroom. Once I set them down, I quickly grabbed the clothes I'd mostly dumped on a chair and rammed them back into the garbage bag that acted as my suitcase.

My daughter grimaced, not at the room but my antics.

"What are you wearing?"

"Donations. From after the fire." The pajama from the old stash of stuff. I'd wanted to wash my new clothes first before wearing them. I'd already run everything through a wash, and now it was drying.

"Donations. You mean you haven't gone shopping yet?" She sounded quite incredulous.

"I have. I just haven't had the time to replace everything. And who cares? It's pajamas."

She winced. "You're wearing plaid bottoms and

a patterned rose top. It's hurting my eyes."

"Sorry. Next time I'll be sure to wear my negligee."

"Mom!" she exclaimed, only to immediately giggle. "Seriously, it wouldn't kill you to get some matching pjs."

"I will once I get a job."

"Didn't you get any money from the fire?"

"There was no insurance."

"Let me guess, *Martin*," and yes, she gave it a nasty inflection, "cancelled it and then wouldn't give you any cash to help out after it happened."

"I didn't expect him to."

"You should."

"He pays me alimony." Again, why did I defend him? She only said the same things I'd thought and been angry about.

"He barely gives you anything and only because the courts said he has to. We both know he'd leave you high and dry if he could."

She saw the situation better than expected, and she was on my side, which I wanted to cheer, yet the part of me that had been a wife for over twenty years still felt obliged to say, "What's happening is between us. He's still your father, Winnie."

"He donated sperm. Doesn't mean he knows how to be a dad."

"He had no idea how to be husband either." The words slipped out of my mouth, and I almost apologized for them. Then again, why should I? It was the truth. He was a shitty husband.

Winnie laughed. "About time you admitted it."

"Let's not talk about him."

"You're right; he's not worth the breath. Let's get my stuff in the closet, and you can show me around."

We got her things stowed in her new room and a few shirts hung on hangers and tucked into drawers. Wendy then insisted on helping me move into Grandma's room, which was feeling less and less weird.

Of course, the whole helping thing didn't last long. As she pulled the clothing from the plastic bag I'd used to pack my donations, she grimaced. "Mom, please tell me you haven't worn this."

"This" being a knitted sweater in a lovely shade of reddish brown, a black bear with fiery red eyes and teeth woven into it. Someone had a sense of humor when they knitted it.

"It's warm and snuggly for chilly nights," was my faint reply.

"And this?" She held up green legging-type pants with elastic stirrups on the heels.

"I'll have you know that stirrup pants were the height of fashion in the eighties."

"It's not the eighties, and you are not a jockey." More clothes went flying, and I quickly realized her intent.

"I can't throw those out."

"You can and will, because I will not let you wear them," my daughter insisted.

"Fine, but we should donate them."

"How can you be so cruel?" my daughter lamented.

Eyeing the pile of discards, she had a point. Besides, where would I drop them? There weren't any thrift shops in town. "I have a better idea."

Which was why that night we sat around the firepit in the yard on the porch chairs we'd dragged onto the lawn. The pile of clothes proved very flammable, and my daughter was gleeful as she added to the blaze, digging out pictures of her ex and tossing them onto the fire. Presents, too.

Over our laughter, I never heard we had company until Jace's deep voice interrupted. "Looks like you could use some marshmallows."

"Well, hello there. Who are you?" Wendy asked with a flirty smile.

It was probably immature of me to feel jealous that my daughter ogled Jace. He was probably closer in age to her than me, not that I knew the exact date of his birth.

"Jace. I live next door." He jerked a thumb at the forest.

"This is my daughter, Wendy." It only occurred after I said that I'd just proven once more just how much older than him I was.

"Nice to meet you." Winnie held out her hand and he leaned in to shake it.

"I saw the fire and came to make sure things were all right."

"As you can see, we're fine." I didn't need him here reminding me of how foolish I was to think he might be eyeing me with any kind of interest. I'd not seen him since my makeover. Did he even notice I'd cut my hair?

"Would you like a drink?" Wendy offered. "I've got iced tea in the fridge."

"That would be nice."

"Let me grab it. I'll be back in a second." She winked, which made me realize she was flirting with him.

Could I blame her for being attracted? Despite being a jerk most of the time, he was still quite handsome.

When Winnie ran into the house for more drinks, I did warn him, petty as it was. "Just so you know, she's recovering from a breakup."

"Why tell me?" Jace asked with a lazy drawl.

"In case you're thinking of getting involved. You know what they say about the rebound guy." Did he recognize the pathetic attempt to turn his interest away from Wendy for what it was?

"Actually, I don't know, nor am I interested. Your daughter is nice, but I prefer my women more mature."

"Oh." Not sure there was a reply for that.

"You cut your hair."

I hoped the darkness hid my blush. "I did."

"It looks nice."

I heated in more places than just my cheeks.

A heat that was doused as he also added, "You appear…tired." The pause was obvious. He meant I looked like crap.

"I had a bit too much fun last night."

His gaze narrowed. "Did something happen?"

I wasn't about to admit I got drunk and made out with a stranger. "Just too much alcohol and dancing. This old body isn't as fit as it should be."

"You're not old." The statement was a soft purr.

Okay, I wasn't imagining stuff. He was flirting. And then suddenly he wasn't.

He rose abruptly from the chair I'd dragged to the fire—pulled from the shed that didn't have an axe or a sledgehammer.

He eyed the woods before he barked, "Get inside."

"What? Why?" Standing, I shivered as a chill descended in the air, a wave of intense cold that seemed to dampen the flames of the fire.

"It's here."

"What's here?"

"Danger. Stay close to the flames. It doesn't like fire."

My eyes widened. "Is it a bear?" Bears ate

people. I was a person. So was my daughter. She'd not yet come back from the house. "I need to check on Winnie."

"Naomi, don't—"

Too late.

I ran for the back door, the flickering fire at my back casting shadows that leaped and jumped. My breath misted with every step, and I heard Jace mumbling behind me, the words an incoherent mess of consonants. I didn't care.

What if my girl was in danger? Never mind she was probably safer than I was at the moment. I wouldn't let her face danger alone.

I slammed open the back door and noticed the empty kitchen with the glasses of iced tea sitting on the counter. Where was Winnie?

I heard the murmur of voices. My gaze went to the front door, where my daughter was talking to someone. I took a step, then another, a strange languor filling my limbs. Winnie laughed, and there was a deeper masculine reply. It seemed familiar, and the reason why chilled me a second later. Because I knew that voice. That face.

Kane. The man from the bar.

"What are you doing here?" I asked, astonished he'd tracked me down.

"Do you know this guy?" Winnie glanced at me over her shoulder.

"Yeah, he's—"

"Leaving!" barked Jace, who'd apparently followed me inside.

Rather than mind my rude neighbor, Kane glanced at me. "Won't you invite me in?"

For some reason the very idea was repugnant. I didn't need my cat standing at Winnie's feet, hissing and yowling, to say, "I don't think that's a good idea."

"And here I thought we had a good time last night." The way he phrased it held innuendo.

Shame heated my face as two sets of eyes focused on me. The middle-aged slut. Or so I felt in that moment.

"What's he talking about?" Jace asked.

"We met at the bar. And danced."

"We did more than that." A reminder that sent a frisson across my skin and rounded my daughter's mouth.

"Mom!"

I cringed. "It's not what you think." Only partially, but I wasn't about to admit what I'd done.

Kane's gaze veered to Wendy. "Is this your daughter?" I didn't like the way he eyed her.

Heck, I didn't like the fact he'd shown up on my doorstep.

"You haven't said why you're here."

"Our evening ended abruptly last night."

"Because I was drunk and out of it." I didn't accuse him. Not yet.

"Your friends are very protective. Regardless, I wanted to see you again."

"You will leave, right now." Jace sounded angry.

It made no sense. Why the level of anger? It wasn't as if he had a right to be jealous, or did he know Kane? He certainly acted as if he did and obviously didn't like him. Then again, he hated Darryl, too.

"While I am flattered you sought me out, last night was—" I wanted to say a mistake, and yet that would be a lie. I enjoyed the kiss. Even now, despite Kane's stalking, he remained very handsome. Strong and virile. I wouldn't deny there was something exciting about his interest in me.

Then I recalled the possibility he'd drugged me. That wasn't sexy.

"I'd like to take you to dinner. No alcohol this time." He smiled. Wide and engaging. His interest made no sense.

I resisted his allure. "I think you should go."

"If you insist. But we will meet again."

Ominous sounding and I expected trouble, yet Kane left, getting into a dark sedan that barely made a sound as it drove away.

Only then did Winnie exclaim, "Who was that guy?"

I didn't know what to say, so imagine my surprise when Jace declared, "My brother."

## 20

WELL, THIS WAS AWKWARD. I'D MADE OUT WITH Jace's brother. Not that he knew that specifically. Not yet. But I wondered how long before Kane let it slip. After all, I imagined, given they were related, they'd see each other again.

Or not.

Jace didn't seem too fond of his sibling.

Should I be proactive and tell him about the kiss? The very idea made me want to throw up. Especially since Winnie eyed me in a way that made me want to apologize for not living up to her expectation of what a mom should be.

Moms didn't make out with strangers in bars.

But I was more than a mother. I was also a woman. If I wanted to kiss random men, I would. Next time, though—assuming there was a next time

—I'd make sure they weren't related to someone I knew.

"When did you encounter my brother?" Jace asked, the query tight and controlled.

"Last night at the bar," I mumbled.

"Oh really. And did you *talk*?" There was an inflection on the word that stung.

Guilt suffused me, and as it did, I wondered at it. After all, Jace was simply an acquaintance. I wouldn't even call him a friend. How dare he have an opinion at all on whom I chose to spend my time with? He had no claim on me. I could do whatever I liked with whomever I liked.

He wanted to know what happened? Fine. I'd tell him.

Squaring my shoulders and throwing out a defiant chin, I said, "Kane bought me a drink. We danced. Made out a little."

"Mom!" This time Winnie squeaked my name.

I slanted her an annoyed look. "Oh, don't be such a prude about it. I kissed a man. It's not the first time." Although I could count on one hand the number of boys I'd locked lips with.

"You're my mom."

"I am, and I'm not dead. So you better get used to the idea, as I imagine I'll kiss more than one man given I'm single again." If separated counted for Martin, then surely it counted for me as well.

"You will not kiss anyone. It's gross," Winnie huffed.

"Exactly how do you think you got here?" was my exasperated retort.

"Immaculate conception," she rumbled, not even trying to hide her discontent.

Jace chose to speak up. "She is right. You should not be kissing Kane."

That drew my ire to him. The man who thought he could tell me what to do. "You don't get a say in this."

"My brother is not who he seems."

"Exactly how do you know how I perceive him?"

"You think he is attractive and charming."

He was. He also gave off a creep vibe without the tequila and the strobing lights. "So what if I do like him? It's none of your business."

"I am making it my business. You don't know him. Who he really is."

I arched a brow. "Are you calling me a bad judge of character?" Which was technically true, but how dare he point it out.

"My brother is a devourer of souls."

"That seems kind of harsh." Not to mention poetic in a dark, disturbing way.

"I am telling you so that you understand why it's important you stay far from him." Jace looked entirely too serious, and annoyed. I wanted to even say jealous, but that might be pushing it.

I jabbed a finger in his direction. "I'm going to take a wild guess and say you and your brother don't get along."

"Total understatement," muttered my daughter.

"He's my half-brother, and it's more than just disliking each other. He is not a good person."

"And you are?" A teasing yet curious question. Jace had so many different faces and a masculine side that he couldn't rein in. I'd been married to a man who didn't think I should have an opinion. Who told me what to do. I didn't need someone to take his place.

"You shouldn't trust me either."

"Exactly who are you, anyhow?" Winnie asked. She eyed me. "I mean, this has been fascinating and all, but I came here to see my mom and then you randomly show up just before your brother does?"

"I told you, I live next door."

"This isn't the first time he's wandered over," I added.

"Is that why he thinks he can act all macho like?" Wendy pursed her lips. "Are you trying to get into Mom's pants?"

"Wendy Melanie Dunrobin!" All three names emerged in a horrified rush of air.

"I think it's a valid question. Look at him telling you to stay away from his brother." Winnie swayed from side to side as she ranted. "Look at me, I'm a big bad guy who is going to tell a woman what to do."

"I'm trying to protect your mother."

"He just has a weird way of showing it," I mumbled. "The other day he wanted me to leave town."

Jace tossed me a dark look. "So that you wouldn't draw the attention of Kane or the others."

"What others?" Wendy ping-ponged her gaze between us. "Is this some sick game for you and your brother? Are there more of you? Preying on someone vulnerable who is going through a tough time." Her voice raised in pitch. "My mom doesn't need a guy to tell her what to do. She doesn't need a man period because she is strong."

Wait, what? I blinked at my daughter's words.

"Beautiful and sexy—"

Okay, this obviously wasn't about me.

"—Decent mom." Not a ringing endorsement, but I'd take it. "And she has been handling the shit she's been going through like a champ."

Aaaaaw.

"Which means she doesn't need you screwing that up!" Winnie stood on tiptoe right in front of him. Red-faced and ranting, mad not at Jace so much as she was peeved at men in general. Poor Jace got the brunt of it, but I wasn't about to step in front of Winnie. Let her get the anger out. Much of what she said was true.

I would make my own decisions. Good or bad.

He crossed his arms and inclined his head. "Are you done with your caterwauling?"

"No!"

I came to his rescue, sort of. "I think it's time you left."

He didn't even argue. "I agree. Stay inside. Lock the doors. Don't come out until dawn."

More crazy orders. Which I might have spurned, only I still remembered what had happened the last time I went wandering around in the dark.

"But the fire…" I sputtered.

"I'll handle it. Don't open the door for anyone."

"Gotcha. Get going." Winnie shooed him out, slammed the door, and locked it. As she turned, the anger on her face turned to a wide smile. Then she giggled.

I blinked at her. "What's so funny?"

"You've got two guys fighting over you."

## 21

"I MOST CERTAINLY DO NOT!" I'D HUFFED IT THEN, and I still believed it now, three hours later, as I lay awake in bed, staring at the ceiling.

It didn't have the glow of the dark constellations in my room. I wondered if I could buy a set, as I missed the familiar shapes. Blankets rustled as I turned onto my side. The closet door was a faint outline with the scant moonlight delineating the shadowy frame.

I'd still not smashed through the wall to see what hid alongside it. Too many distractions and still no axe. Probably smarter if I didn't start demolishing walls. Perhaps that area was enclosed for a reason. Could be a utility room, which made little sense given the electrical panel was off the kitchen and there was a crawlspace under the cottage that handled the water pump for the well.

The hot water tank was tucked into a closet in the main floor bathroom. I didn't have a furnace, only the woodstoves and a few baseboard electric heaters.

Maybe it was an old fireplace, covered over. Although wouldn't it have been better to repair it than lose space to the woodstove installed?

As I stared at the wall, shadows shifted on the surface, reaching and grasping. I knew it was just the branches outside, swaying in the wind, and yet to my imaginative mind, it appeared more like sharp fingers.

What was odd, though, were the lines. Dark and straight intersecting lines, as if the shadows formed a door. Obviously, my imagination at work. The equivalent of staring at fluffy clouds and seeing animals.

I rose from my bed, wearing only a long T-shirt and panties. On bare feet, I moved to the wall, scared and chanting to myself.

*There's nothing there. Nothing there.*

So far, so good. I stood in front of the rectangular outline. Up close, the shadows appeared as deep grooves. The edges of something. An opening even.

Impossible. I'd groped this wall thoroughly. There were no crevices.

*They're not there.* I placed my hand on the dark line. Felt the indent against my flesh.

I yanked my hand away as if I'd been burned. This wasn't real. I must be dreaming.

*Touch it again.* It was as if I heard a voice urging me.

With my hand halfway to the wall, I hesitated, hovered. I couldn't have explained my trepidation. Shadows and plaster couldn't hurt me. If something weird happened, I'd know I was dreaming.

I placed my palm firmly on the line. Pursed my lips as I felt the crack. A little shove didn't shift anything. My gaze drifted down, and I saw a knob, a ball of shadow about waist high.

This was totally a dream.

I wrapped my hand around the knob, and I gasped at the jolt that went through me. I sucked in a breath. I swear my hair stood on end. All of it, pubes included.

The sensation faded along with the door, wall, whatever you wanted to call it. It disappeared, and I finally saw what hid behind it.

A replica of the chair downstairs, right down to the lace doily on the headrest. Sitting beside it a pie plate table, the top of it round with raised edges on a pedestal. The surface held three books.

*The* books. I couldn't help the inflection as I noted them. Just as I remembered.

The top one was a faded wine color, the cover showing a design in gold leaf. The title of it simple: Recipes. A flip of the cover showed the paper yellow and old, but not as brittle as expected when I leafed through it. The names of some of the recipes were snort worthy.

*The Husband's Curse,* which—according to the fancy handwriting—caused erectile dysfunction. There was a note at the bottom that was underlined. *Husband's Boon.* Which essentially modified the concoction to make him super virile.

Useful, but I didn't understand the one for *Repair of the Soul.* It had ingredients such as the blood of a lover and the feathers from some kind of bird I'd never heard of. There was even a poem to chant.

I closed the book and set it aside to peek at the dark blue leather-bound volume below it. There was a spot on it that was attached to a band that wrapped around the book and kept it shut. Since I didn't want to force it, I placed it atop the recipe book and eyed the third.

The motley-covered book was last, and while it didn't have a title, it had a tree of some sort on the cover. The branches many and varied, as were the roots stretching below it. I expected a family tree when I opened it. Perhaps a listing of the Rousseaux clan. But only blank pages existed. Yellowed and many. Not one of them holding a single word or image.

Disappointing. Then again, what had I expected? Tricia had made these books seem important. I guess I'd expected more. And I kept forgetting this was a dream, which totally explained the spells and blankness.

I yawned.

Which was ironic given I was technically asleep. I left the books on the table and went back to bed. When I woke in the morning, there would be no table and chair. No hidden room.

And I was getting an axe.

I fell asleep immediately, and when I woke, I thought I still dreamed. That or I was going crazy because, in the corner, where there used to be a wall, was a reading nook with a doily-covered chair and lots of books on the shelf, plus the three on the little side table.

What I didn't see was a wall. At all.

Or a closet, for that matter. Instead, I saw a huge wardrobe that, when opened, revealed my clothes. It was as if the closet never existed. I turned slowly in the newly uncovered space. Was I still dreaming?

I pinched myself.

"Owww."

Rather than ponder the impossible missing closet, I headed downstairs and was surprised to see Winnie had beaten me to the kitchen. She slid a mug toward me.

"Rough night?" she asked.

"Weird night. Remember my closet?"

"What closet?"

I blinked at Winnie. "What do you mean, what closet? The one you helped me put my clothes into. The one opposite the bathroom."

"Mom, you don't have a closet."

"I do, too. I mean I did. Now there's some huge wooden thing and a chair."

"And books, too. What about it? You trying to say you want to get rid of those and put a closet in instead?"

"No." I stared at her. Was she playing some kind of joke? Or did she really not recall?

"Are you getting senile in your old age?" Winnie laughed, but I didn't.

I could have sworn there was a closet.

Just like I would have sworn I'd never seen the little porcelain eggcup she pulled from the cupboard. I'd gone through those cupboards thoroughly. It hadn't been there. Maybe she'd pulled it from her things.

I sat down heavily in a chair. "How did you sleep?"

"Awesome, but those stickers on the ceiling have to go. They freaked me right out."

I wanted to protest. Those were mine. How could she hate them?

Was I really going to have a fit over some old stickers?

"You do whatever you like to the room. It's yours for as long as you need it."

I'd finally said the right thing because she beamed. "Really?"

"Yes, really."

I should have been job hunting that morning and taken Winnie with me to find one, too. Instead, I got the ladder out of the shed and held it while Winnie perched a few rungs up and scraped the stickers from the ceiling. It hurt to watch them flaking off. I wondered if I could glue them on the ceiling upstairs. Don't judge. I winced each time one fluttered to the floor.

When that was done, we ran into town and tried to buy some plaster and paint. We weren't allowed to pay, so I tossed two twenties in their charity jar to save the ducks. We left with a bucket of light purple for Winnie's walls. As for me? I got some glow-in-the-dark paint. I had an idea for my room.

As we drove by the diner, I thought about stopping in. I wanted to say hi to Marjorie, but I also wanted to boycott it given the owner didn't want to hire me. He was lucky I wasn't actually a witch, or I'd put a real curse on the place.

Back at the cottage, Winnie insisted on handling her room, so I brought my purchase upstairs then went back for the ladder. I hadn't been able to find constellation stickers, but the paint, Mr. Peterson assured me, would glow at night. Perched on the ladder, I could see the same sigils and etchings that adorned the doors and windows also embedded into the beams of the ceiling. I filled them in with paint, the brush tracing the signs, mesmerizing me to the point I would have sworn I saw light trails. The pattern illuminated and glowed a soft blue, not green as expected.

The more of the symbols I painted, the more light I created, and I noticed a soft hum. Like a buzz but not of any insects. It had an electrical feel to it.

If I touched the signs I'd painted, would they shock me?

"Mom, what are you doing?"

I blinked and noticed I'd stopped using the paintbrush and was dipping my fingers into paint and then sliding it in and out of the carved grooves.

"I don't like the dark," was my reply as I clambered down the ladder.

"Since when?"

"I've always been afraid."

"How did I not know this?" she asked.

"Because I never let you or your brother know. I didn't want you to be scared like me."

"Seriously?"

I shrugged. "I'm also afraid of thunderstorms and rodents."

"I had a hamster when I was in elementary school."

Which we kept hidden from Martin. A good thing he rarely went into the basement.

"I was terrified it would escape."

"To do what?"

"Eat my face in my sleep."

Wendy stared at me a moment before laughing. "Oh my God. I had no idea. How many other things did you pretend for us?"

"A few. I was determined to raise you to be brave."

"You did good, Mom." She took my hands, not minding the fact they were covered in paint. "But you know, you don't have to keep pretending for me."

I couldn't meet her gaze and stared at my feet. "I can't make any promises." In my head, moms had to act a certain way. Behave and dress in a specific fashion.

"Were you faking it with Dad, too?"

The question threw me for a loop, and my first impulse almost had me opening my mouth to claim everything was fine until Martin left me. Except that would be a lie. And she knew it. I could tell by the way she stared at me.

The sigh I uttered was heavy. "It didn't start out that way. Your father didn't used to be that angry all the time."

"What happened?"

I frowned. "I don't know. Life. Work. The stress of making ends meet."

"Lots of people deal with those things. They don't turn into dicks."

"I'm sure your father never meant to. It just kind of happened." And I'd allowed it. I'd make excuses for his outbursts rather than put my foot down and demand he apologize. I'd placated him rather than deal with his quick temper. I'd crushed every ounce of my spirit and every mean word I wanted to yell, trying to keep the peace. But that wasn't the worst of it.

I'd not stepped in when he turned that raging voice on the children. Luckily, he'd never hit them, but that didn't excuse my actions—or lack thereof. I should have protected Winnie and Geoff from Martin's anger. Words could bruise even more deeply than fists.

"Don't make excuses for him, Mom."

"I'm not. I honestly don't know why he is so angry all the time. I swear, he wasn't like that when we met. He was kind and thoughtful. He made me laugh. When Grandma died, he was the one who kept me going."

"Wish I could have known that guy." Winnie grimaced.

"Me, too," was my soft reply. "Maybe now that he's doing his own thing, he'll be happier."

The remark earned me a snort. "Okay, Mom.

Sure. Do you know he's not called me once since he left you?"

"I…" I paused. "I didn't know. I'm sorry."

"Don't apologize. What he does or doesn't do isn't your fault."

"I know, but twenty years of habit is hard to break."

"You need a Martin patch. Or maybe a hot neighbor." She waggled her brows.

I laughed. "While I appreciate your faith that I could be a woman of interest for Jace, he's much too young for me, and I'm not ready."

"Says the woman making out with guys in bars."

"It was one time. I was drunk." I winced as I said it. "Okay, that's a bad excuse."

"Do you know how often it happens at college? Girls going to parties and having a few too many. Throwing themselves at guys and then having buyer's regret in the morning."

"Did you—" I couldn't even finish that sentence.

"Mom! I am not talking to you about my sex life. Although…if you really want to know…"

I shook my head violently. "No. I'm good. No need."

Winnie chuckled. "Are you sure? Maybe I can help you bring your terms up to date."

"I don't need any help." I did, however, want to

sink into the floor with heated embarrassment even as I was humming inside with happiness at this conversation. This was the kind of relationship I'd always wanted with Winnie. Something open and honest, where we could say anything. Be not just mother and daughter but friends.

"Want help finishing up in here?" she asked, pointing to my sloppy can of paint.

"I am done, actually. I just need to clean up." I held up my hands with a rueful grin.

Winnie chuckled. "I'll make us some grilled cheese sandwiches while you scrub."

My daughter left, and I was smiling as I folded the ladder and brought it downstairs. I returned and eyed the ceiling, not truly able to see the effect of my work yet, but I was excited about tonight. I reached to grab the paint can, still half full, only I somehow managed to tilt it over instead.

"Oh no." I ran for the bathroom and a towel to mop up the mess, only by the time I returned, the paint wasn't in the expected puddle but sitting inside the grooves of the floors. Scrubbing at it didn't do a thing to help, so I leaned back on my haunches and sighed.

Things might get interesting tonight when all that paint began to glow. I might be visiting the hardware store again for something to cover it.

"Lunch is ready," Winnie yelled from downstairs.

As I stood, the lines in the floor began to glow blue, racing out from my feet and spinning in a series of circles that were interconnected. Within those round spaces, more sigils, the shape of them rising in a nimbus that made all the hair on my body rise.

"Are you coming?"

Winnie's yell snapped my attention, and the glow was gone. My room was normal. But I was beginning to think something was wrong with me. Sane people didn't see things. I needed help.

Since I couldn't afford a pro, I went looking for my new friends.

## 2 2

---

It only occurred to me as I sat behind the steering wheel of my car that I had no idea where Marjorie or Tricia lived. I did, however, know where they worked.

Tricia was easy to find, as she was located in the only downtown municipal building. The term downtown seemed too grand for the number of buildings, even if we counted the ones boarded over. It surprised me to see the defunct bookstore's front door was propped open and a pickup truck loaded with lumber was parked in front of it.

Another renovation? I really had to wonder at the revitalization of a dead town. What did these investors know that the townsfolk didn't?

It bothered me more than it should have. I barely knew this town. My grandmother had done a decent job of keeping me away from it. I had to wonder why.

Odd how I never wondered before how I'd managed to live as a teen for years in the cottage but didn't know the streets or buildings like I did the mall the next town over. It had to be because of the witch thing, and the free gifts. What I just couldn't fathom was why my grandmother never told me about it. I mean she regaled me with stories about fairies and monsters, of godlike men battling for good, but not that the people of Cambden thought we were some kind of spell-casting sorceresses.

It made me wonder how many folks would make the sign of the cross if I dressed as a powerful witch for Halloween and went trick or treating. Given how many of them owned shotguns? Probably not a good idea. But funny as heck.

The smile remained as I parked in the back of the town hall, which provided permits for everything indicated in the many bylaws, property information, including ownership and taxes, and dog and cat licenses. Having lived in suburbia with all the many branches of office required anytime anything had to be done, I appreciated the simplicity of the one stop for everything.

I turned off the engine and got out of my car, which I'd parked right beside Tricia's distinctive Pinto. Entering the building was like falling back in time. The sight and smell were seventies to eighties chic with a few minor attempts to modernize things. The old? Lots of thick, scrolled newel posts, which acted as columns, and smaller, scuffed ones that created separation of space. All were a dark brown, having long lost their shine.

The many columns went well with the wood paneling, which rippled and even showed splintered cracks, obviously well past its best-by date. I was impressed, however, with the linoleum floor that had survived the test of time. Black and white squares, with only the seams showing signs of wear and tear.

Better than the laminate flooring we'd tried in the house. The one that burned down. It scratched, it creaked, and I hated it, but it was cheaper than dealing with juice-stained carpet. The sippy cups of two decades ago weren't as leak proof as today's.

Tricia was sitting at a rusted metal desk. The computer atop it sported a giant screen, the kind that took some muscle to lift. She spoke on a phone, an honest-to-goodness landline, with an avocado green handset that had a curly black cord. There were a few chairs in front of her desk. I chose the one that looked the least uncomfortable as Tricia kept talking.

"No, Mr. Morrison, for the last time, we are not sacrificing any of Mrs. Basinette's goats to appease the lake monster."

My eyes widened.

Whereas Tricia rolled hers as she said, "I need to go now, Mr. Morrison. Talk to you tomorrow."

She hung up, and I exclaimed, "Was he serious about killing something?"

"Probably. But I should add that he's not too fond of his neighbor, Mrs. Basinette. He also never offers his own herds but those of others."

"And he calls you to suggest it?"

She nodded. "Every day since the Maddy sightings started. Yesterday his plan was to throw packets of gelatin into the lake and see if the monster would get so full eating it that it would go back to sleep."

"Surely you've told him the monster isn't real."

"Why would I lie to him?" Tricia wrinkled her nose.

Why indeed?

The phone rang insistently. She sighed. "Give me one second. Hello, Cambden Town Headquarters, Tricia speaking, can I help you?"

I almost snickered as she put on her "phone voice." I shouldn't laugh. I had one, too. A fake, fluttery, breathy way of speaking to the person on the other end. Martin was so good at it. Yelling about something one minute, answering his phone calm and collected the next. Until he hung up. Then he had the ability to resume yelling where he'd left off.

Tricia's forehead creased. "I see. Yes, we're

aware." She paused. "Have you contacted the police?"

My brows lifted.

Tricia drummed her fingers. "You need to call them and tell them what you told me." Another pause, then, "You take care, you hear me? No going out to the lake at night. And keep the rest of your herd penned far away." She hung up.

"What was that about?"

"One of the farmers on the south edge of the lake let his herd out into the lake pasture and lost two cows."

"Let me guess, he thinks it's the lake monster."

"You don't need to sound snotty about it. Especially since you'll feel stupid later when you discover it's real."

She seemed so normal and serious. She had more than one person calling her about it. Was it me who was wrong? Did Maddy truly exist?

"I'm sorry. It's just hard for me to believe."

"Which is weird because you used to totally believe until you went off to college."

I frowned. "I don't recall that."

"You don't recall a bunch of things, I suspect."

On a hunch, I said, "Do you remember the books we were looking for?"

"Your Grandma's? What about them?"

I bit my lip, suddenly reluctant to say anything. "I found them."

"Really?" Her eyes widened. "Where?"

As her phone rang again, it occurred to me that I'd interrupted her work. What made me so important it couldn't wait?

Tricia answered yet another call about Maddy. A news reporter that she blew off with a pert, "I don't know what you're talking about. Maddy is only a legend." Then she hung up and smiled at me. "Back to those books."

"We can talk about it later. I really should let you work. I'll call you later if you give me your number." Because she always came up number unknown for some reason.

"We're fine. People pop in to yap all the time."

"Yeah, but next time, maybe I'll visit you at home, after work. Where do you live?"

"My housing situation is complicated."

"Are you okay?" I asked. "Do you need a place to stay?" Sure, I now had Winnie in the extra bedroom, but we could figure something out.

"I'm fine." She waved a hand. "Give me your phone and I'll add my number."

I handed it over, and she keyed it in while I looked around. "You work here alone?"

"Most of the time. Unless the mayor decides to pop in. Which is rare."

"When's your lunch?"

She pulled a sign out of a drawer and propped it on the desk. *Back in an hour.*

"Lunch is anytime I like. Shall we hit the diner?"

"Sure." I still had some cash left over from the makeover and night out.

We walked to the restaurant, and she poked me for information. "You found the books."

"I did, in that hidden space beside the closet."

"What hidden space?" Tricia's nose wrinkled. "Was there a hidden compartment in the wardrobe?"

In that moment, I believed I was the one going crazy. How could she not remember the closet? She'd gone into it to search for the books.

"They were on the little pie plate table."

"But I looked there," Trish sputtered. "I can't believe the house hid them."

Nope, Trish was still the crazier one.

"Anyhow, I have them, but I don't know what good they do. One of them is blank, another locked."

Tricia's step faltered. "Blank and locked? That's not good. What of the third?"

"Some kind of recipe book, but the ingredients and stuff are nutty." If that was what my grandma dabbled in, no wonder she'd scared the superstitious in town.

Again, Trish stared at me. "You really don't remember."

"Remember what? And you're one to talk about

recollecting stuff. How is it I'm the only one who remembers Grandma's closet?"

"Because the house was only hiding stuff from you."

She said it so logically, and yet I was a rational woman. Houses didn't hide things. Although dryers did eat socks.

"Let's say the house is hiding things... why?" I exclaimed. "Why would it want to keep my grandma's books away from me?"

"Because you're obviously not ready."

"Ready for what?" I grumbled.

"I could be dramatic and say the apocalypse."

"If you think I'm supposed to save the world, then you're obviously on some really epic drugs, because I'm barely keeping myself together. I could never hope to be strong enough to handle the fate of others."

"It is adversity that strengthens us."

"I don't feel strong." Both a truth and a lie. Since my separation, there had been times when I felt on top of the world. But I'd also experienced some of my lowest points.

"You might not feel it now, but it's happening. You're taking back control of your life. Finding that inner strength that was always there and just needed a spark."

"Even if I were strong, I'm not a hero in any story." Heroes knew how to do the right thing.

Never put their whole foot and part of their leg in their mouths. Never hid from a fight.

"Not yet. But you should start to prepare."

"I'm not buying leather and dressing in it."

Tricia laughed. "Why would you do that? If you're going to fight to save this town, you should wear something light that dries quickly."

"We are not having a conversation about my outfit for the coming apocalypse."

"It's never too early to plan."

"You're crazy." I snorted. "But then again, so am I apparently, because I found the books in a hidden room beside a closet I clearly remember but that you and Winnie claim never existed. Obviously, it's a sign I'm going senile." They would place me in a home with a secure perimeter and people to make sure I wouldn't wander off and forget my way back.

"It has to some kind of illusion and forgetting spell," Trish mused aloud. "But targeted, obviously, since Wendy and I never saw anything amiss."

"What are you talking about?"

"Magic," Tricia exclaimed. "When we couldn't find the books, I suspected there was some kind of cloaking spell hiding them. I just wasn't sure if it was a leftover from your grandma or the house. To think they were under our noses the entire time."

"You keep talking like the house is…" I paused for the right word. "Alive."

"More like sentient and attuned to its inhabitants. Surely you've noticed how your home responds to your needs."

I had, and assumed I was imagining it. Admitting it? That was crazy. "Houses aren't sentient."

"You're right. Most aren't."

I paused on the sidewalk, and she kept going. I had to skip to catch up. "But you're saying mine is alive."

"Not alive in the way you'd define it. But yes." She opened the door to the diner, and we saw a few tables occupied, the buzz of conversation steady until we walked in.

A sudden dead silence ensued. I wanted to hunch my shoulders and slouch right back out. Everyone was looking at me.

What were they thinking? Would someone get mean about the fact I was a Rousseaux?

The history book said they'd tried to burn one of my ancestors. And failed.

I froze and yet stumbled as Trish grabbed my arm and hauled me after her. She waved her free hand. "Nothing to see here. Carry on."

It was almost magic in the sense that it worked. Gazes drifted away, talk resumed. The murmurs emerged quieter as we made our way to the booth in the back. It took a few minutes before a teenage girl, her hair drawn back in a ponytail and an annoyed expression on her face, appeared and slapped menus down.

Tricia frowned at her. "Hey, Beth. Where's your Aunt Marjorie?"

"Not here, obviously," said the very disgruntled teen. "Dad made me come in when she didn't show up for work this morning."

"That doesn't sound like her," Tricia murmured. She eyed Beth. "Shouldn't you be in school?"

"Yes. But until Marjorie comes back or Dad finds a replacement to take the shift, I'm stuck helping out." The angry teen stomped away, and Tricia leaned forward.

"I don't like this. Marjorie was planning to come in to work."

"Maybe she's sick."

"I'd know if she was sick," Tricia declared. "I'm going to call her."

The phone went to voicemail right away with no ringing in between.

"Maybe she's sleeping or having a shower."

"Maybe…" Tricia abruptly slid out of the booth. "I need to go check on some things."

"But what about lunch?"

"Stay and eat or poor Orville is going to think you're cursing him. I'll talk to you later." Trish rushed off, and I had a choice.

I could run because everyone was surely watching the pathetic pariah eating by herself, or actually stay and have a meal because I was hungry.

Pity no one was getting food today. The teen never returned to take my order. An argument broke out in the kitchen, and Beth stormed through the swinging door, tossing her apron on the counter, yelling, "I quit!"

"You can't quit. The lunch rush is coming!" yelled a man who could only be Orville. He stepped out of the kitchen, a big bear of a man wearing a scowl and a stained apron.

"You can't make me. I hate this diner. I hate this town. I'm going to live with Mom!" With that declaration, the teen slammed out.

Orville huffed.

A patron shouted an encouraging, "Bloody teenagers. It gets better, Orri."

"No, it won't," he muttered. Then louder, "I'm afraid I might have to shut down early."

The words led to many groans.

Before I knew I was going to do it, I stood. "I'll help."

A brown-eyed gaze passed over me. "Not you." So dismissive.

I moved closer. "Why not me? I'm not saying hire me. Just let me help out. I'm a friend of Marjorie's."

"Is that supposed to be a selling point? I know who you are."

"In that case, aren't you supposed to give me what I want?" I arched a brow.

"Why would you want to work here?"

"Why not? I'm not too good to get my hands dirty and put in a day's work."

A few people who'd stood to leave paused by the door and watched us argue.

Orville flicked a glance to them then to me. "You want to wait tables, then fine. But only for today."

As I slid on the discarded apron, everyone who'd stood sat down. And more came in.

The diner didn't stop. People kept arriving, meaning the seats were full and the kitchen humming. I encountered more than a few curious gazes, heard more than one whispered "witch." I made more tips than I would have imagined, as if everyone I served was afraid they might offend me, or thought I gave really great service.

Which I didn't.

I'd never waitressed before. It was hard. My whole body hurt by the time midafternoon hit.

My only reprieve was Orville's decision to close early. He ushered people out, even someone who tried to walk in, saying, "What do you mean you're closing for dinner?"

"Out of food. I gotta hit my suppliers. Come back tomorrow."

The door clicked as he locked it behind the disgruntled customer. Orville turned to face me. A big man, who I'd noticed wasn't thick with fat but muscle. He lugged things around as if they weighed nothing. And I was alone with him. He'd made no bones he didn't like me, not in so many words, but I still recalled his reluctance in letting me help.

Orville didn't say anything, so I ventured a timid, "Guess I'll go now. Here."

He eyed the wad of cash I thrust at him. "What is that?"

"Half of the tips." I wasn't giving him the whole thing. I'd earned my share. But he had as well by working hard in the kitchen.

"Keep it. You did good."

I must have imagined the praise. "Excuse me?"

"You heard me. You did good. Come back tomorrow."

"I'm sure Marjorie will be feeling better by then."

"I hope so," he said under his breath. "Either way, do you want a freaking job or not?"

With that kind offer, how could I refuse? "I'll have to work around my schedule at the gas station." I'd not forgotten Darryl's offer. And while a part of me hesitated in accepting it, I was too desperate to turn it down.

"That's fine. Thank you." Stiff words that I didn't get the impression he said often.

As I headed out of the diner, the cooling late afternoon air kissed my skin as I walked back to my car. Tricia's was parked on the other side of it. She'd obviously gone somewhere.

The door opened, and Trish popped out. "About time you showed up."

"I didn't know you were waiting for me."

"I wasn't going to, but I didn't know what else to do. You have to come with me to Marjorie's house."

"Is something wrong?"

"Yes, she's missing," she hissed. "After I left you at the diner, I had Danny—he's a cop I know in the area—drop by her house. She's gone."

"What do you mean gone?" For a moment, I thought she meant dead. She couldn't be dead. I'd just met the awesome and vibrant Marjorie.

"As in her car isn't in the driveway, she didn't leave a note, isn't answering her phone. She just vamoosed!" She flung a hand off into space.

"Well, that's rude. She didn't even say goodbye." I'll admit, my feelings were hurt.

"Jojo didn't leave voluntarily."

"What are you saying?"

"That I think Maddy took her."

"The imaginary lake monster?" I sighed. I was too tired for this. "I'm going home."

"Aren't you going to come with me to look for clues?"

"Sounds more like a job for the police. If she even went missing."

"She wouldn't leave without telling me."

"You can't be sure of that. Could be she decided it was time to start over in a new place."

"She did not have a midlife crisis." Tricia seemed adamant about it.

"How can you be sure?"

"Because I'd know."

"How would you know?"

For a second, she looked away and shifted her feet before saying softly, "Because we're seeing each other."

## 23

---

NOT THE ANSWER I EXPECTED, SO MY NEXT FEW questions were probably dumb at best and most likely ignorant. Not addressing it seemed even worse, so I blundered ahead.

"You're a lesbian? How can that be? You dated boys in high school." She'd been more popular in that respect than me.

"I prefer to think of myself as free spirited." Tricia's chin lifted. "I am attracted to a person's inner beauty."

"Have you always been, um, like this?" Immediately, I apologized. "That wasn't meant to sound like it's bad or anything. It's just…" I rolled my shoulders. "I never knew."

"Because I didn't want anyone to know. Can you imagine telling people back in the eighties and even nineties?"

I grimaced. "I can see your point." In our youth, being gay or bi was a big deal.

"The good news is times have changed. Things are getting better all the time. I don't have to hide who I'm dating anymore."

"You hid it from me."

Her head ducked. "Honestly, I wasn't sure how you'd take it. It's been awhile and…"

"I was a jerk," was my rueful interruption. "I am trying to be better."

"I know, which is why I told you."

"And you're dating Marjorie?" I asked to clarify.

"Yup."

I thought of the times we hung out together. "You never acted like you were a couple."

"Exactly how do couples act? Did you expect us to be making out in corners or going around arm in arm? Not everyone does that in public. And Marjorie is still leery about letting people know. Cambden is a small town. And she is kind of still married to Milo."

"But he ran off."

"People are dumb. She's worried they'll see her as the bad guy."

"Because they might assume he found out she likes women and left her," I said softly. "Ugh. I can see why she might hesitate. But still, I can't believe I didn't know. Not once did I get a couples vibe from the pair of you." I scowled.

Tricia laughed. "You're just bent because you never figured it out."

I could have held it in, but I was tired of not expressing how I felt. "I am kind of angry and hurt. You hid stuff from me. Made a fool of me."

Tricia didn't apologize. "We didn't tell you because we weren't sure how you'd feel about it."

A valid point since I wasn't sure how I felt about it, but also a slap. "You're my friends. Why does who you're sleeping with matter?"

"You're one to talk. Look at what you did for your husband."

A stark reminder that being with him had changed me.

"Well, I'm glad you told me so I can tell you I don't care." Again, with the wrong words. "And by that, I mean I think it's great you're together." It truly was because if they were happy and finding love in their forties, then I could, at the very least, find my happy spot, too.

"I am glad you approve," was Trish's sarcastic reply. "Now, go ahead and ask."

I wanted to say, "Ask what?" but the query she expected emerged on its own. "Were you..." I paused, utterly unsure of the right word to use. "Were you like this when we were young?" I couldn't help but think of the times we'd slept over and changed without regard.

"Is this your awkward way of asking if I ogled

your boobies when you stripped in front of me?" Her shoulders lifted and fell. "Then yes, maybe a little."

"Trish!" My cheeks flamed.

"Don't blame me. It's not entirely my fault. My hormones were going wild back then. It's why I went after guys way more than I should have."

"But you were attracted to girls."

She nodded. "It was confusing, especially since I couldn't talk to anyone about it. Back then we didn't have the internet and a zillion articles or access to support groups."

Her words put it into perspective for me. How hard it must be attracted to someone of the same sex in a culture that disapproved.

"Did you have a crush on me?" I ventured.

She nodded and laughed. "How could I not?"

"You never said anything." Or maybe I'd just not noticed?

"Say what? Hey Omi, I think you're hot, let's date. You would have run the other way."

I almost denied it, but she told the truth. I wouldn't have handled it very maturely. The whole wisdom coming with age? True. At least in my case.

"Sorry I couldn't be there for you." It was the best I could give her.

"You were, though, up until college. Then you met *him*." The distaste on her face was almost comical. "I think partly why I hated Martin so much was because I'd always imagined one day telling you how I felt. And then you came back all gushy from college with Martin this and Martin that." She lifted a shoulder. "I knew then I'd waited too long."

"And now?"

"I am not pining for you if that's what you're asking," she said with a snort. "I'm with Marjorie, and besides, you are so obviously hetero."

"What makes you say that?" I exclaimed. How could she know when I'd never even thought of it?

"Asks the woman with her own harem of men."

Heat made me flush. "I do not have a harem."

"Yet."

"Ever. I am not interested in dating." Not until I learned more about me and didn't hate what I saw in the mirror.

"So don't date, just screw."

"I don't do casual sex."

"Because you're too uptight. Gotcha."

"I am not— That's not why—" Flustered, I finally stammered, "I am not a whore."

"Taking charge of your needs and sexuality is not being a whore. That's a term men have labelled women despite being able to indulge freely themselves."

"I'm not interested in sex."

"Tell that to the tongue you had in your mouth the other night."

I blushed. "Marjorie thinks he roofied me."

"I guess that's one way of looking at how he uses his allure to snare people."

"Allure?" I scoffed. "At the very least I was drunk and not thinking right. It won't happen again."

"So you wouldn't kiss Darryl or Jace?" Tricia dared.

"No."

"Liar."

Not exactly, because I had no idea how I'd react. Old me would have never kissed a stranger in a bar. Who knew what I'd do next?

"I don't suppose we can continue this chat somewhere with a comfortable couch. After working on my feet all day, I need to sit down."

"What about Marjorie?"

"Are you sure she's gone? Maybe she had to run some errands or had to deal with some family crisis."

Tricia's lips pursed. "She would have called. And I've tried calling her, but it keeps going straight to voicemail."

"Her phone might be dead, or could be she lost it."

"It's not like her to disappear like this."

"I assume you didn't fight?"

She shook her head and gnawed her lower lip. "Everything was fine last time I saw her. I'm worried."

"Okay. I'll go with you to see what's going on at her place." The right thing to say despite my fatigue. "But we're taking both cars so I can go home right after you see everything is fine."

"Thanks, Omi."

We hopped into our cars, and when Trish peeled out, I followed. The route led us to the road circling the lake with waterfront properties on one side and forests and fields on the other, occasional houses dotting the landscape. When I saw the smoke, I had a feeling I knew whose house it belonged to.

Pulling into the gravel driveway, I parked alongside Tricia, who clutched the steering wheel, gaping. There was no point in getting out to look and see if Marjorie was still inside. No one could have survived the flames shooting from the house. Every window showed a tongue of fire. The roof smoked in several places.

The inferno exploded out of the house. One of the streaking missiles landed on the hood of Tricia's car, causing a massive dent.

"Trish!" I fell out of my car in my haste to check on her.

She sat with a stunned expression behind the wheel, staring at the can of paint that burned merrily from its spot on her hood.

I yanked open her door and pulled at her. "Come on, let's get you out before the car explodes or something." It happened in the movies.

She turned a glazed expression on me and said nothing.

"Come on." I leaned in and unbuckled her seatbelt before yanking her again. She followed me, still moving stiffly, in obvious shock. I dragged her to my car and shoved her into the passenger seat before sliding behind the wheel and driving us a safer distance away. Only once we'd parked again did I call the fire department.

Tricia had yet to say anything. Nor did she cry. She just stared, eyes wide and vacant.

"Trish." I spoke her name softly. When she didn't reply, I added reassurance, not only for her but me as well. "She wasn't inside." She couldn't be.

"We don't know that for sure. I should have checked earlier, but when Dave said no one was home..." Her voice broke. "I should have gone to check."

"She's fine. Probably had to go somewhere and forgot to call. You watch, any minute your phone will ring. Could be she's in a bad service zone or the battery died."

"She has dropped it in the toilet before."

Despite all the benign possibilities, we couldn't help but worry. The sirens soon overpowered the stillness of the night, the wailing ringing in our ears. Firemen poured from the truck, and Tricia was the one to try and weakly pretend we weren't sick to our stomachs wondering if Marjorie was all right.

"Think we got the calendar crew?" she jested.

I grabbed her hand and squeezed it. "You don't have to fake it."

Only then did she finally allow the tears to run, and she sobbed. "I'm scared, Omi."

"Me, too," I said, hugging her and patting her back, watching the house burn.

It took an hour of spraying before the firemen contained the fire. And by contain, I mean soaked the area so it wouldn't spread once it ran out of fuel. The house itself was gone. Both Tricia and I flinched when it collapsed in on itself.

When the police chief—a handsome if grizzled fellow wearing glasses and a wedding ring—informed us it would be at least a day or two before the ashes were cool enough to sift, Tricia broke. Given her car had suffered extensive damage, I drove, but rather than take Tricia to her house, I took her to mine. I didn't want her to be alone. She'd need a shoulder to cry on.

She also needed a reality check, because the first thing she said upon seeing Winnie was, "Maddy took Marjorie."

## 24

WHILE I MADE TEA, WINNIE HUGGED A CRYING Trish as the two sat on the couch. I also placed a few fat bombs I'd whipped together using coconut oil, cocoa powder, some stevia, and shredded unsweetened coconut on a plate. A ball of healthy oils and almost no carbs that helped with hunger pangs. I needed something to snack on as Tricia dealt with the grief of her missing lover.

"I don't think she's dead," Winnie declared.

"Me either. I'd know in here." Trish thumped her chest. "But she's in danger; I can feel it. We have to find her."

I wanted to be supportive, but there was reality to consider. "I don't know where you expect us to look." I didn't point out the obvious that her house burned down along with any clues. "Could be she's not missing at all."

"She wouldn't have left without a word," Trish insisted.

"Maybe a visit or appointment ran longer than expected."

"She would have called me."

"Assuming her phone is working."

"Even if it wasn't, she wouldn't have left without saying a word." Tricia got up and paced. "She's been taken by that damned monster."

"You mean Maddy?" I repeated, even as I repressed the urge to roll my eyes.

Even Winnie had a hard time with Tricia's theory. "Aunt Trish, maybe Mom is right. Maybe—"

But Tricia would have none of it. She cracked her fist into her palm "I don't want to hear it. Maddy is real. We have to find her lair."

"No, she's not," was my firm reply.

"Yes, she is. Ask Jace."

"I'm not asking him anything." As if I'd dare. I'd be the one to sound crazy.

"Argh!" Tricia thrust her hand in the air. "Why must you both be so stubborn?"

I looked helplessly at Winnie. I didn't know what to do for my delusional friend. "Let's say you're right and the lake monster took her. What do you suggest we do? How are we supposed to find her lair? Especially if it's underwater?" I didn't point out the fact that Marjorie would have drowned if it were.

"We'll cast a spell of finding." Tricia's face lit. Even worse, Winnie brightened, too.

"A spell? Oh, I did a semester on Wiccan rituals at college. I can help," my daughter offered.

I wanted to bang my head on something. "Magic isn't real."

"Tell that to the closet you claim used to be in your room," my smartass daughter retorted.

I flattened my lips. "I'm not too caught up in my fantasies to realize I must have imagined it." Never mind I had distinct memories of that closet. If no one else saw it, then I must be the delusional one.

"Or you could accept the real truth, which is magic was hiding it," Trish snapped.

Winnie clapped her hands. "A spell left over by Great-Grandma."

"She wasn't a witch." Said without real heat.

No one was listening. Winnie and Tricia were already discussing which ingredients were on hand, pushing the living room table aside, and uncovering another circle etched into the floor.

They were completely serious about this. Whereas I, tired and still smelling the damned smoke, needed to clear my lungs. The fire had brought back too many memories of my own close call with death.

"I'm going for a walk."

"It's dark," Tricia pointed out.

"Yup."

"You have to stay inside. It's not safe out there anymore."

"Now you sound like Jace," I grumbled.

"You should listen to him."

"I need to get some air. I promise to stay away from the lake." I wasn't in the mood to go far, but I had to get outside.

"Marjorie's place wasn't on the lake, and she still went missing." Worry infused her claim.

Rather than argue about the monster, I was crude. "I'm going for a walk. Send for help if I'm not back in an hour." I grabbed a flashlight hanging off a peg by the door. When had it appeared? Maybe Winnie had put it there. Kind of laughable given her messy habits.

I did my best to not recall what Tricia had said about my house being alive and giving me what I needed. I'd needed clothes, and the closet had remained empty. Food, and yet I had to grocery shop.

As for the things that kept popping up? I obviously had some short-term memory problems. Might be time to see a doctor, get some supplements.

The moment I stepped onto the porch I took a deep breath. Fresh air to counter the foulness of the smoke still clogging my nose. I closed the door against the voices inside yet couldn't stem the nightmarish reminder of the roar and crackle of flames.

I moved to the rail and clutched it. Leaning over it, I heaved in deep lungfuls of air.

The fire at Marjorie's house hadn't touched me. I remained unharmed if a bit smoky. There was no proof Marjorie had been at home when it started. But that was twice now I'd seen a house burn down. Two times too many.

I tried to focus on something other than the hungry flames, like Marjorie. If she wasn't home, then where had she gone? Tricia was so certain that she wouldn't have left without saying anything, but she'd also admitted that her lover wasn't comfortable making their relationship public. I sure hoped Marjorie hadn't ghosted her. Once by her best friend should be enough for any lifetime.

The growl of an engine drew my attention as a single headlight appeared. A motorcycle pulled into the driveway, the wide beam of its headlamp cutting the darkness and illuminating me. I put up an arm to cover my eyes from the glare and blinked when it extinguished.

"Hey, Naomi." I knew that soft drawl.

Darryl.

My hand went to my hair, and I wondered how badly I smelled of French fries, coffee, and smoke.

He pulled off his helmet before he swung his leg

free. Say what you will about guys and their toys, there was something sexy about it.

"Hey, Darryl." I acted as cool as I could while wondering why he'd shown up. He'd not yet seen my makeover. Would he like the new hair? I at least wore a new pair of jeans that gave me a bit of a nicer shape. My long sweater hid the bulges at my middle.

I hoped.

"Nice night." He grinned at me after he placed the helmet on his seat.

There was that giddy feeling again. I smiled back. "It is." I wanted to slap myself for sounding like a one-syllable idiot. And then I felt guilty as I realized my reply was less than honest. "Actually, it's a terrible night. Marjorie's place burned down."

"What?" His mouth rounded. "What happened? Is she okay?"

I shrugged. "We don't know. The fire chief said it would take a few days to figure out the cause, and no one knows where Marjorie is."

He frowned. "Well shit. That's not good. I'm sure she's fine, though. She filled up her tank before heading out of town last night."

"Wait a second, you saw her?"

"Yeah, I had to replace Byron last night. She came in just before I closed."

"Did she say anything?"

"Just the normal stuff, like hey, how's it going."

"But she definitely went somewhere," I stated. Late at night and without telling anyone. It was looking more and more like Marjorie had skipped town. Maybe she'd even set the fire as part of some insurance scam. I didn't want to think her capable of it, but being broke made you think of crazy things.

"Guess her leaving is why you had a busy day at the diner."

"You heard?"

His lips quirked. "Small town. I thought about coming by for dinner, but the place was closed."

"The diner ran out of fries and burgers. Apparently, I'm fascinating to the townies. They kept coming in to gawk at me." But I wouldn't complain too much. Perhaps if they realized I was just as normal as them, they'd stop acting weird around me.

"Good to know. Does this mean I should order more stuff for the store? That is, assuming you're still coming to work for me."

"Yes, please." Spoken a tad more exuberant than warranted.

Again, he slayed me with that smile. His teeth flashed, slightly crooked, but I liked the imperfection. How had I ever thought him plain?

"When can you start?" he asked.

"I work for Orville tomorrow, but he said if you give me a schedule, we'll figure something out."

"Guess maybe we should head to the gas station then and get that set up."

"Now?"

He arched a brow at me. "You waiting for a better time?"

I eyed the house. By the sounds of it, Marjorie had left town on her own. Trish had Winnie and their spell casting, whereas I needed this job.

And to be honest, I kind of wanted to talk a bit more with Darryl. The sanest person I knew at this point.

"Give me a second to grab my purse and car keys."

"Or you could just hop on the back." He angled his head to the bike.

My first inclination? No to the hell no. Motorcycles were deadly machines. At my age, I shouldn't even contemplate getting on the back. I was too old. Too—

Chicken.

My do-over was about shedding my cowardly nature and anxieties to try new things. People rode motorcycles every darned day. I could do it, too.

"Give me a second to grab a sweater and tell Trish and my daughter where we're going."

"Your daughter is here?" He knew of Wendy's existence since she'd come up on game night.

"Yeah. She'll be staying for a while." Then

because he appeared stunned, I added, "Is that a problem?"

He shook his head. "No problem at all. That's awesome."

"I hope so." I truly did.

Popping into the cottage, I saw Trish and Winnie in the kitchen, poring over the recipe book they must have fetched from my room, which irritated me for a brief second. I considered the space mine, the books, too. But really, it didn't matter. If they wanted to waste time playing with fake spells, then go ahead. I would be the responsible one.

"Hey, Darryl's here."

"I know. I heard his bike. What's he want?" Trish asked, looking up from the recipe book.

"He says Marjorie gassed her car last night."

Tricia's jaw dropped, so it was Winnie who said, "Did she say where she was going?"

I shook my head. "I thought you should know."

"Who is this Darryl?" Wendy asked. "How do we know he's telling the truth? What if he took her and told you that to muddy the trail?"

"Darryl's not a psycho." Or so I hoped.

"How can you be sure? I thought Erik was a nice guy, too. And look at Dad."

"In this case, your mom is right. Darryl's one of the good guys. I'm wondering what Marjorie was doing going out at night," Trish mused aloud. "She knows better. I'll bet she poked her nose somewhere she shouldn't and that's why she got taken."

I held my tongue rather than announce it seemed more likely she'd ghosted. "Listen, Darryl's going to run me over to the gas station and figure out a work schedule for me. I'll be back in a bit."

"Don't forget to use condoms," stated Tricia.

"Wait, is he expecting you to be a prostitute?" Winnie yelled.

"No!" I hotly exclaimed.

"As if." Trish snickered. "Your mom is way too uptight to make any money at it."

"I am not."

"You are too. I bet you can't even get undressed unless the lights are off."

How did she know? The only time I ever saw my body was before or after a shower, and even then I usually avoid staring.

"This entire topic is gross. I don't care who this Darryl is. Mom isn't having sex. I forbid it!" exclaimed Winnie.

A part of me wanted to tell her I'd do whatever I liked. The part that strove to be the perfect mother lifted her chin and instead managed a very flat, "There won't be any sex happening since he's my boss."

"Please. Forbidden love is the best," Tricia insisted.

"Don't encourage her, Aunt Trish. Moms don't

have sex. Nor do they talk about it. It's wrong."
Winnie had the red cheeks of embarrassment.

I wanted to reassure her that I never planned to
be with anyone in that way again. I didn't need intimacy or some sweaty grunting body atop me.
Instead I said, "My sex life is nobody's business."

That should have been the end of it, but Trish
just had to add something to stir the pot. "Winnie,
don't be a prude. You do realize your mom is a
young and sexy woman who will probably have a
string of lovers now that she's free."

"Okay, I am done here." I waved my hands.
"I'm going with Darryl to get registered as an
employee. Try to not blow up the kitchen or
summon any demons while I'm gone."

"No guarantees," was Trish's reply.

"Depends if the demon is cute," was Winnie's.

Smartasses.

As I stepped outside, Darryl turned toward me
and smiled. He had a habit of doing that every time
I looked in his direction. I didn't know what it
meant or even if it meant anything at all. Perhaps I
read too much into the situation. Could be he really
only wanted another employee. He probably smiled
for everyone.

"Ready?" Already wearing his helmet, he strad-
dled the bike, and his eyes held invitation. The
butterflies went nuts in my belly.

He was my boss. I couldn't think of him any

other way, I reminded myself as I sat behind him on the humming machine.

It was close. Intimate. Scary, too.

"One more thing before we go." He pulled out a spare beanie helmet from a side bag.

Good thing I couldn't see myself in a mirror because I could just imagine how ridiculous I looked. I perched it on my head but struggled to clip the buckles.

"I can't fasten it," I grumbled.

"Lean sideways." He half turned as I tilted and placed his hands over mine on the straps. "Let me."

It took him a nanosecond to clip it into place, but his fingers lingered, trailing over my jaw. I shivered as he turned to face forward again.

"Hold on tight," he advised.

I put my arms around his solid torso and, as the bike began to move, closed my eyes. I didn't scream despite the rapid pounding of my heart. I was very proud of myself. Eventually as our ride smoothed, the dirt drive giving way to asphalt, I even opened my eyes. Not that I saw much in the dark. If I tried leaning out to see what little the headlight picked up, the wind hit me in the face. Much better to keep my head tucked behind Darryl's back.

We didn't talk. It would have required shouting over the rumble of the engine. It was intimate and solitary at the same time.

Different. But not necessarily bad. When I

stopped imagining the ways I would die—falling over being in the lead—I began to enjoy my first ever motorcycle ride. We arrived too soon at the gas station.

"That wasn't so bad," as said as I climbed off the bike.

He grinned. "Just wait until we actually do the speed limit next time."

I wrinkled my nose. "Who says there's going to be a next time?"

"Were you planning on walking home?"

Given it was miles of dark road and forest? "Or you could just drive the same speed again?" I said hopefully.

"We can go as slow as you like."

Was it only me who heard the double meaning? Was it wishful thinking? I didn't have the guts to ask.

After he parked the bike, I handed him my helmet, which he perched on the seat. It looked kind of cute sitting beside his. It made think of maybe saving up for one that was more girly. And pink. Look at me, pretending this might happen on a regular basis.

Darryl raked a hand through his hair. I wanted to smooth it. Instead, I asked questions. "So about the job, does it include gassing cars?"

"Nope. The tanks are self-serve. You just make

sure they pay and, if not, call their plates in to the cops."

"Does that happen often?"

"Not usually. You'll be working mostly inside behind the counter." He extended his arm in the direction of the building. "Let's get you kitted out with some hours."

The gas station was open despite it being after nine.

"What time do you close?"

"Whatever time someone is willing to work to." At my startled glance, he shrugged. "Sometimes people have to leave early. I don't make a stink about it."

"That's really nice of you."

He grimaced at the compliment. "Don't let anyone hear you say that. I have a reputation to uphold."

Obviously, he was trying to overcome his past, too. Like me, he'd also had to restart his life. There was a lot to admire.

The counter was manned by a guy I'd never seen before. Barely more than a teen, his hair was greasy and dyed a vivid orange, his nose pierced. His neck tattoo peeked above the collar of a T-shirt that depicted something so vulgar I had to look away. It bore a pentagram dripping in blood and the words, *See you in hell, asshole.*

Darryl caught my shock and chuckled. "That's Byron."

Eyeing Byron's ensemble, I couldn't stop myself from being judgy. "Should he be wearing a shirt like that?"

"Damned right he's allowed. People think twice about robbing me since he started working nights."

I glanced back at Byron, who twirled a switch-blade. "Do you get robbed often?"

"Not anymore." I'm sure the wink was meant to be reassuring. It failed. He found the right words instead. "You won't be working nights. Days mostly, with me around."

That startled me. "If you're around, why do you need me?"

"Because I can't get shit done. There're things that need fixing, but I'm always being interrupted. And while I do some of it at night when Byron's manning the shop, a man needs some time off, or what's the point of all the work?" He rolled his shoulders.

"Fair enough. Just making sure this isn't a pity hire."

He stared at me, blinked, then laughed. "This is the opposite of pity. When people find out, they'll be saying the same thing about me that they said about Orville when he hired you today."

"What are they saying?" I had a morbid need to know.

"That he's doomed himself. A Rousseaux isn't supposed to pay for anything."

"He didn't pay me, though," I said with a smile. "He let me keep the tips."

"Which might be enough for the curse they all believe in."

"I thought you believed in it, too.

Darryl laughed, but it held a bitter note. "Hard not to have the superstitious herd mentality. I grew up hearing the stories. Heck, I remember the boys talking about you in school. There was a dare over who would ask you out and bets on if that guy would disappear or die."

"Wait, we went to school together?"

"Yup, but we never met. You were several grades ahead of me."

Which made me older than him. Not a big gap and it wouldn't have bothered me if the ages were reversed, but knowing he was younger made me look at him differently. It put our flirting at a more taboo level. A hotter level.

"You obviously changed your mind about the curse, or you wouldn't have offered me a job."

Again, his lips quirked. "Or is it because I interpreted the curse differently? That by denying you something you require, like a job that I can provide, I am in fact activating the very doom I sought to avoid."

Surprisingly enough, I followed his logic. And

my reply? "Curses aren't real." Just runs of really bad luck.

But my luck was turning.

"How many days a week do you need me to work?"

"As many as you like?" he offered. "Pick them, morning or afternoon or both."

"What if I demand twenty hours a week with fifty cents more than minimum wage?" That and the diner shifts would be more than enough to cover me since the cottage was rent free.

"And pay you less than Byron when I hired him and get accused of sexism? I offer a dollar more than minimum wage starting out. Is that acceptable?" He held out his hand.

"Deal." I let him clasp my fingers, wondering if I was the only one who had a jolt of awareness at the brief touch.

He dropped my hand quickly and headed for the counter.

"Any problems?" he asked his night clerk.

"Nah."

"I'll be in my office with our new employee if you need me."

"'Kay." Byron barely paid me any mind as I followed Darryl to a door at the back.

It led into a cramped office with a tiny window. It was tidier than I would have expected and modern with the thin computer screen and a slim keyboard sitting on an Ikea desk.

He sank into the chair. It didn't take him long to log in, a good thing because it took less than thirty seconds to peruse the space. A few posters for various candy treats with interesting designs, like the ones for *Star Wars* and a famous chocolate bar.

There was no bed, not even a couch. There was barely room enough for the desk and single chair because of some boxes stacked against a wall.

"Fill this in, would you, while I pop out front for a minute." He vacated his seat, which brought him close to me for a moment, the scent of soap lingering on his skin. He'd showered before coming to see me. While he passed close enough he could have copped a subtle feel or brush of skin, he was polite instead, skirting me and leaving so I could sit down.

I eyed the screen. The questions started out very basic. Name. Age. Address. Previous work experience. I chewed my lip. I didn't have much, but I had more than I used to when I applied for my first job as a cashier.

It was on the third page the tone of the questions changed.

*Do you have an allergy to iron?*

*Do you say a prayer before killing animals or cutting down trees?*

*Have you ever danced naked in the moonlight?*

The list of oddities went on, and the office grew colder. I glanced around, wondering if the heating system had kicked off, or maybe the cooling system had come on?

I glanced back at the screen.

*Have you ever kissed the devil?*

What the heck?

I rose from the seat and frowned. Was this some kind of joke?

It wasn't funny.

Darryl had left the door ajar when he exited. I sidled to it, the air getting crisper. My breath emerged in light puffs.

Why did this keep happening to me? Was this a sign of perimenopause? My insides heating up to the point everything else felt chilly?

A peek through the door showed the store empty. No tattooed guy behind the desk. No Darryl. Not a single sound either.

Spooky.

I stepped into the store between a rack of diapers with smiling babies across from another with condoms. Even in the boonies, it was all about product placement.

"Darryl?" I couldn't help but say it softly.

A light overhead flickered.

I wouldn't scream. This surely was a prank. First the questions, and now they would try and scare me. Then, when I was crying in terror, they'd take my picture. I'd seen it in a movie. I wouldn't fall for the same trick.

My logic failed to slow my racing heart.

I took a few more steps and made it to the aisle with canned pasta in red sauce and crackers, salted of course because anything else was wrong unless you had Cheez Whiz to spread on it. A glance outside the plate glass window with its dusty, faded posters showed the gas pumps empty. Where had they gone? Would they pop up suddenly and yell, "boo," causing me to pee myself?

Don't judge. Geoff had a large head, and all the exercises in the world never helped given the damage from the spot they had to stich me.

Nothing broke the silence but me. My steps were a slow shuffle. The air that panted from my partially panicking lungs practically hung in icicles. Why was it so cold?

The light overhead flickered again. I glanced upward at the long fluorescent bulbs, buzzing and twitching ominously.

No music played. This was not a horror movie.

I wasn't about to die.

Lights burned out all the time. It just happened to be the wrong time for my nerves.

"Darryl?" I called his name more loudly. "If this is a joke, it's not funny."

A door behind me slammed shut, and I whirled. There were only a few doors. The bathroom, which was sealed. One that read "Employees Only," also closed. And the office door, which I could have sworn I'd left open but was now shut.

The room got dark, which should have been impossible with the light overhead. I glanced upward, but despite the light shining steadily, the room lost its brilliance. Shadows cloaked me. The chill became intense enough my body couldn't stop shivering.

And when a voice said, "Did you know you snore?" I almost peed my pants.

Okay. Not almost. I dribbled a little and wanted to die.

---

## 25

Darryl stared at me, and all I could think was I needed clean underwear.

The weird dream evaporated, and in the blink of an eye, everything was normal. I still sat in the office, staring at a very normal resume. The lights were on.

Darryl appeared amused as he said, "Is this a good time to mention you drool?"

"I do not!" I exclaimed as I wiped my arm over my mouth. "And I wasn't sleeping." At his arched brow, I amended, "I must have just dozed off. I'm sorry. I don't know how it happened."

"Obviously an indication I need to fine-tune my question-asking skills. Looks like you got it all completed."

"I'm really sorry," I felt a need to repeat. "I swear I won't sleep on the job." I still didn't understand how it had happened in the first place. One did not simply start to snooze in the middle of filling out forms. Yet the proof was against me. The air was warm, and my ass was quite definitely planted in the chair, not wandering the store.

"You're tired. Working the food industry is tough."

Why was he so understanding? At times he seemed too nice; however, I couldn't say I preferred Jace's sarcasm. Or even Orville's gruff manner. And why did I only doubt motives when men were involved? Had Martin skewed me so badly?

Yes, he had. I no longer trusted my instincts.

"Orville asked me to work tomorrow, but maybe I could do a few hours in the morning here before heading over to the dinner to handle lunch."

"That would work out great since the refueling truck is coming around ten and I'm the only one that can deal with them." He held out his hand.

I stared at it before slipping my hand into it. It was calloused, the grip firm. He shook my hand. "Welcome to the company."

"About time," was Byron's reply when he heard I'd been hired.

After a quick bathroom break, where I wrapped my wet undies in tissue and shoved them at the bottom of the garbage can, I got a thirty-minute crash course on running the till.

"It's easy stuff," Darryl said when the training

was done, and we headed back outside. "And I won't expect you to remember it all at once."

"I'll figure it out. Thank you."

The night was calm, the moon a crescent in the sky. He stood in front of me, not close, but enough I was aware of him.

Should I move closer? Would he? Why was my mind constantly thinking about it?

My mind alone apparently, because he glanced at his watch. "It's late. I should get you home."

He drove at a sedate speed where nothing happened. Darryl saw me to the door, smiled and said he'd see me tomorrow, then got back on his bike and left.

So much for turning down a kiss.

Upon entering, two pairs of eyes swung my way.

"Well, young lady…what do you have to say for yourself?" Tricia tried to say most seriously, only to crack into giggles. Winnie howled beside her.

"I don't know why you're so amused." I hung up my sweater.

"How did the job interview go?" Trish added air quotes to it.

"If you're implying I had to put out to get hired, then you're wrong."

"Mom, no one says 'put out' anymore. They say 'hooking up.'"

"Or snoggin'," Trish added.

"No one says snoggin'. And when I say nothing happened, it's the truth." I didn't admit the fact I never got to even turn Darryl down. "I filled out an application, and he brought me home." I didn't mention falling asleep. I still couldn't believe that happened.

"That's it?" Trish sounded surprised.

"I'm not some desperate divorcee making out with any guy who looks at me." Even if I eyeballed them all like I did the steak in the supermarket, gauging their fat content and satisfaction factor.

"I don't think I'd call Darryl desperate. For a guy, he is cute," Tricia said.

"How cute?" asked Wendy. "And how come I haven't met him?"

I didn't know whether to be amused or annoyed at the third degree from my daughter. "You want to meet my boss, go to the gas station." I flopped into the armchair. I'd gone from no job to two and was already exhausted.

"Secret workplace sex is the best," Trish advised. "Just remember never to do it against a bulletin board. Those pushpins leave marks."

"And lock the door. Nothing worse than someone walking in and having to murder them and hide the body," Winnie said.

I blinked at Winnie, who grinned. Who was this playful girl?

I smiled back. Then got serious as I noticed the

map spread open on the living room table. "What are you plotting?"

"Nothing yet. Just getting ready for the spell." Tricia appeared serious about the process.

The recipe book was sitting open beside the map. I had to lean closer than I liked to read the flowery script. "Locus Exponentia." The description underneath spoke of using the spell to find things.

I glanced at Trish. "You do know that mixing a recipe of…" I paused to recite from the book, "Hair of the caster, blood of one who has touched what was lost, and—does that say the urine of a faithful companion?"

"Which, I'll admit, I don't have, but I'm pretty sure your cat's pee will count," Trish said.

"And you think mixing those things together will, what? Cause a pin to suddenly appear on the map with Marjorie's location?"

"Of course not," Trish scoffed. "We need to chant, too, and then, if we do it right, we'll get a sign."

"What kind of sign?"

Tricia shrugged. "Depends. We'll know it when we see it or hear it."

"And you're going along with this?" I asked Wendy.

"Give it a chance, Mom. What if it really works?"

"What if it doesn't?"

"Would it kill you to give it a try?" Tricia taunted. "What are you afraid of?"

"She's afraid we're right and she's wrong," Winnie declared.

I was getting tired of them acting like I was the unreasonable one. "Tell you what, we'll cast this spell, and when it fails—which it will because magic isn't real—you'll both stop this nonsense."

"And what if we prove magic exists?" Tricia asked.

Before I could reply, Winnie did. "She has to stop being judgy with us."

My mouth snapped shut.

Tricia winced. "She didn't mean it harshly."

"Don't you dare mope, Mom. I love you, but sometimes you can be a little uptight."

"Because I had no choice." Martin expected me to act a certain way.

"You have a choice now," Trish pointed out.

A not-so-subtle reminder that Martin wasn't here. I could do whatever I liked. Even pretend to cast a silly spell.

I pointed to the book. "Fine, you want us to play witches? Let's do this. How do we start?"

Apparently, there was a cupboard I must have missed, tucked between the stove and fridge with everything I needed. Cauldron—because every good witch had one—a polished wooden mixing spoon, a mortar and pestle for grinding. Even a cat who sat on the kitchen island, tail swishing. I was just missing a pointed hat.

There was a bit of argument over whose hair we should use and who should chant. Tricia wanted to do it, but as Wendy pointed out, "It's our family recipe book. It should be me or Mom donating the hair and chanting."

Trish tapped her lower lip. "You might have a point, especially since Grisou is her familiar."

My what? I glanced at my cat, who chose that moment to lick a paw and slick it over his head. Maybe I should get a dog and see if I could crack his calm demeanor.

Anyhow, that conversation led to me being the one in front of the pot stirring and mumbling some weird words that meant nothing at first. By the time I was on my fourth repetition, I began to understand.

*Find. Find. The missing one.*
*By the blood.*
*Show me.*
*By the spirit.*
*Show me.*
*By my command.*
*Show me.*

It sounded more eloquent in whatever language I was mumbling.

Nothing happened. I stopped stirring and eyed my partners in spell casting.

"Satisfied?"

"No. Let me add a few more strands of Jojo's hair." Trish had a brush in her car that Marjorie had used. She pulled strands from it, the blonde distinctive. They fluttered into the bubbling pot, as did the drops of blood she pricked from her finger as someone who knew her well.

We didn't get any kind of sign. Winnie, watching the map intently, shook her head.

Tricia held up the cleaned brush. "I don't have anything else."

When she would have pricked herself again, I snagged the needle. "My turn to try. I know Marjorie, too, after all." My first poke didn't break skin, and I bit my lower lip. I'd have to jab a lot harder.

I cried out when my next attempt went through skin a little too deep. Blood welled. I dripped it into the boiling pot and began murmuring again,

*Find. Find. The missing one.*

*By the blood.*

*Show me.*

*By the spirit.*

*Show me.*

*By my command.*

*Show me.*

Without intending it, as the last line slipped past

my lips, it emerged low and rumbly. I would have sworn the house trembled. A cold breeze definitely kissed my lips and momentarily frosted my lashes. Looking down into my brew, I noticed it had stopped bubbling.

Odd because the stove was still on. I went to dip my spoon, and the moment it touched the surface, the contents of the cauldron exploded.

I cried out and threw my arm over my eyes, expecting it to scald. Instead, hard cold pellets hit me, and I opened my eyes to see hail inside my house, lumps of the potion already melting where they landed.

"Oh gross. I need a towel." Maybe a few because it had splattered everywhere.

"Um, Mom."

Winnie's words drew me from the mess in my kitchen. As I turned, I gaped at my poor living room.

Water poured from the ceiling, hit the map on the table, and proceeded to flood the floor.

"Oh no!" I yelled. I'd need more than a towel to mop it up. I needed to stem the deluge.

I dashed for the stairs while Trish shrieked, "It worked!"

The plumbing issue had nothing to do with magic and everything to do with the overflowing toilet. Never mind the fact I'd not used it all day. It chose to start running as we played with the recipe, and once it started, the model was too old to know it should stop.

The shut-off valve stopped the flooding, but the watery mess would take longer to fix. As I dumped towels on it, Tricia paced.

"It worked. I knew it would."

"I don't know what you think was proved." I pointed to the soggy map. "The whole thing got wet."

"Which is the clue. She's near water. Only proving what I said. Maddy must have her."

"This proves nothing." I provided the voice of reason. "Only that the toilet is old and should be replaced."

"It's a sign," Trish insisted.

"Of what?" I pointed to the soggy mess. "It was supposed to show her location."

"It was supposed to give us a clue, and it did. It must mean she's by the lake."

What I didn't say, because even I wasn't that cruel, was if that were the case, then Marjorie would be drowned. Aka dead. Instead, the more sensitive me said, "We should go to bed. We both have to work in the morning."

Except I was too restless to sleep.

Had I done magic?

Despite my skepticism, it seemed rather coincidental that the toilet stopped working at that exact moment. Coincidence did not equal magic, and despite what Trish believed, Marjorie wasn't inside the lake.

Rising from my bed, I put on some slippers and a robe and headed downstairs. Maybe some warm milk to help me sleep? Gross as that sounded. But then again, it worked with babies. Perhaps it was a Pavlovian effect for adults.

I tiptoed quietly past the couch where Trish was sleeping and headed for the kitchen. As the cup of milk heated on the stove, I stepped outside onto the front porch.

The air was chilly, but it didn't have that biting cold I'd gotten used to. I wrapped my arms around myself and shuffled to the railing. The trees hid my view of the lake, and yet I knew it was there. Could swear I heard the lapping of water on the shore. The faint rumble of an engine.

At this time of night?

I grabbed a flashlight before heading toward the lake, the thin beam of light worse at times, given how it bounced. I turned it off as I spilled onto the empty beach.

By the edge of the lake, lit only by a crescent sliver, I listened. I heard nothing at first. Water rolled upon the shore. A tiny breeze ruffled some leaves and branches.

Whatever I thought I'd heard was either gone or had never been there to start with. As if someone would go boating this time of night. I probably mistook the rumble of a car for an outboard engine. There was nothing out here but nature and darkness.

Then someone lit a lantern on their prow a few hundred feet from shore. I heard voices, barking, then the hum of engines and more lights as the first boat was joined by others.

Something was happening on the lake, but before I could truly grasp what I was seeing and hearing, a harsh voice barked, "Get back inside the house."

## 26

WHAT A SURPRISE. JACE, AS PLEASANT AS EVER, HAD come to ruin my evening. At least he looked good doing it. Tight jeans, an untucked button-up shirt with a few buttons undone, revealing his firm chest. I preferred to look at that rather than the scowl on his face.

"Good evening to you, too," was my reply to his rudeness.

"You can't be out here."

"I can and will. This is my property, and if I want to look at the lake, I will look at the damned lake." I stamped my foot as if a tantrum would prove my right.

"It's not safe out here at night." He shifted so that he blocked my view of the lake, and I couldn't help but think it was intentional.

He knew something.

"People keep saying to not go out at night, it's dangerous, and yet, if that were really true, why is no one paying attention?" It had occurred to me as I pondered the many oddities, that if there was so much evidence and so many people missing, then surely some higher government entity would be involved. The local police at the very least, and possibly even the RCMP—the guys in red more formally known as the Royal Canadian Mounted Police.

"There are people watching, and believe me when I saw they know how to ensure their secrets are kept."

"Way to sound ominous. Pity you don't have a mustache to twirl."

"I'm serious, Naomi."

"Oh, I believe you are, just like I'm pretty sure you know what's going on and it has to do with those boats out on the water. What are they doing?" I jabbed my finger at him, and even though I didn't touch him, he recoiled.

He also didn't reply.

"Well?"

"They're fishing."

"Liar." My next words emerged in a puff of frost. "There is something happening in Cambden, something people wouldn't approve of, and you know what it is." If this were the ocean, I'd assume black market lobster or crab fishing. But our lake had nothing so exotic, and the fishing was considered subpar.

"There are some secrets in this world that aren't meant for mortals."

"Way to elevate yourself over us mere mortals." I snorted. "Let me guess, next you're going to claim you're some kind of god." Maybe in body, but in character he was severely lacking.

"Not a god, but not human either."

I outright laughed at his claim. "What are you then?"

"A guardian."

I'd read enough books to know what that meant. "Guardian is a polite word for enforcer." Once more I shook my finger. "There's something illegal going on, and you're part of it, helping to cover it up."

Rather than deny the accusation, he changed direction. "What makes you believe anyone is breaking any laws?"

"Why keep warning me away?" I retorted instead of laying out my flimsy reasons.

"Not very successfully," he grumbled.

"What are you involved in, Jace?"

Before he could reply, I heard music. A faint melody playing so softly that I almost wondered if I imagined it. It came from the water. Stepping around Jace, I noticed the boats were no longer the brightest things on the water.

I blinked to make sure I actually saw the water glowing green. It shimmered like an emerald gem lit from within, and it undulated, the waves of the illuminated lake restless. They churned in a way that mesmerized me. I stared, losing myself in the beauty of it. It took getting wet feet to realize I'd begun wading into the water.

It startled me enough that I sprang back onto the shore. I turned to see Jace with his arms crossed over his chest, glowering.

"Were you going to let me wade in and drown?" I asked as I realized he'd done nothing to stop me.

"I knew you'd snap out of it. But now do you believe me when I say there's danger?"

I turned back and noticed the glow appeared fainter, the music almost impossible to hear. "Is this what happened to those missing people? They got lulled into drowning."

"Go home," was his reply.

"I can't because if something on the lake is hurting people, then we need to stop it." And by we, I meant contacting the right kind of folk who knew what to do. Since the locals hadn't done anything thus far, it was time to go higher up than them. Who should I call?

For some reason, I had a hysterical urge to shout, "Ghostbusters!"

"You can't stop what is happening."

"Says you. If there really is some kind of criminal ring using our lake as a nexus point, I want to know because I will stop it. Especially if it's taking people."

"It's not taking people."

"How do you know for sure?" I pounced.

"Because I do. And that's all I can say. You don't know what you're dealing with here. Who you're dealing with," he added in a low, ominous tone. "They've hesitated to act thus far only because of your name, but once they realize you don't have the power your grandmother did…" He looked away. "I won't be able to protect you."

He sounded ridiculous. Melodramatic. Nobody was afraid or coming after me. Except maybe Martin. It would be mighty convenient to his plan if I disappeared before the divorce was final and he inherited everything.

"Is it drugs?" I asked, although why anyone would be doing a deal in the middle of a lake, I had no idea. There were better places to conduct nefarious affairs.

"Forget what you saw."

Kind of impossible, even more so with his warning. I turned back to the lake and noticed the glow was gone. The music, too. The lake appeared calm and normal once more without any shining lights.

But things began to make sense. "Whoever that was on the lake is trying to make people afraid.

They want people to believe in Maddy rather than look deeper into what's actually happening."

"You seem to be sure of many things with mere speculation."

"It wouldn't be speculation if you'd cough up what you know."

"How can I resist when you ask so eloquently?" Sarcastically delivered.

"You're impossible," I spat.

"And you aren't?" he riposted. "You don't listen."

"Why should I listen to you?" I cocked my head. "Hmm. You've been nothing but rude, not to mention bossy."

"I'm trying to protect you out of respect for your family."

"You never knew my family."

"Says who? You?" His turn to make a disparaging noise. "I actually knew your grand-mother. A woman of incredible power and then there's you." He didn't finish the thought. He didn't have to.

How dare he imply I was inadequate?

And why did it sting?

I stalked past him, not saying a word, too mad and too hurt to manage anything.

"About time you listened," was his mumble as I went past.

I whirled and slapped him. At least I meant to,

but he moved too fast for me to see. He held my wrist in a tight grip, and now it was his eyes that glowed. The same color as the lake.

He growled. "I wouldn't."

"Let go of me. I won't be insulted on my own property."

"Are your feelings hurt?" was his rejoinder. He didn't let go but rather reeled me closer. "I don't care. I want you to hate me. I want you to hate this place. Leave."

I didn't feel a need to give him any reason as to why I wanted to stay. All I said was, "No."

"I could make you." He dragged me even closer, the grip of his hand tight, but he wasn't hurting me.

My breath shortened, and I got that quivering feeling again. "Hurt me or my daughter, and I'll have you arrested."

"It wouldn't hurt. The things I can do to persuade… You wouldn't feel a thing but pleasure." He drew closer, and his mouth almost touched mine. I could sense it hovering there, and I shivered.

"Doubtful, given I hate you." I didn't like him. What my body felt wasn't like either.

"Are you going to lie to me, Naomi?" He purred my name, the words soft on my lips. Warm.

And yet I shivered. There was a chill in the air. A frost that limned my lashes. I blinked at him through ice crystals. "Lust isn't like."

"You want me," he stated but didn't seem happy about it.

"I do." I wanted to kiss those teasing lips. Run my hands over those thick arms and down the muscles of his back. Instead, I stepped away and wrenched free. "But I know how to say no to the things that are bad for me." At least now I did. "Good night, Jace."

"Good night?" There was surprise in the words.

Rather than reply, I flipped my flashlight on and headed for the cottage, which I could see clearly, the lights in the windows a beacon unlike the other night when it was so dark.

Lights?

When I'd left, only the small kitchen one over the stove remained.

Oh shoot, the stove. I'd left the pot of milk on it. My pace quickened. As I reached the porch, I noticed a car in the driveway, one that I recognized, which probably explained why Trish was pacing when I walked inside—to a stove that didn't have smoke billowing.

"Where have you been?" Trish snapped as I walked in.

"Out for a walk." I shut the door behind me. "Is that Marjorie's car out front?"

My friend scowled. "Yes. She walked in a few minutes ago. But you didn't answer. Where did you go?"

"Just down by the lake."

"After I told you not to go there?" Tricia exclaimed. "Do you have any idea how much I panicked when I woke up to find milk burning on the stove?"

"Sorry."

"You should be. That shit smells nasty! And you'll need a new pot. I kind of tossed it outside so it would stop making a stink."

"I wasn't thinking."

"Obviously," she said with a roll of her eyes. "And how dare you make me worry. I thought the lake took you."

"No need to be melodramatic. I was just outside."

"Oh, really? Because I tried calling. You didn't answer. Which means I then panicked and had to wake up Winnie. We were just about to go searching for you."

"And I was having the best sleep," my daughter grumbled as she exited her bedroom fully dressed. She flopped onto the couch.

"I'm sorry I didn't hear you. As you can see, I'm fine. And given Marjorie's car is here, I assume she's okay, too?" *I told you so.* I'd been the one to say she was probably fine.

"She's not hurt, but she's not exactly okay."

The non-answer wasn't going to fly. "Where did she go? Does she know about the house?"

Tricia nodded then bit her lip before saying, "She's the one who set it on fire. Not on purpose," she hastened to add. "She figures it was a candle she left burning."

"Where did she go?" I asked.

"Into the city, where she fell off the wagon and got royally wasted."

My mouth rounded. "Oh no! Why? What happened?"

"When she left me the other night, apparently she came home to a letter claiming she needed move out before the end of the next day. That the house didn't belong to her."

"Oh no!" I could see why Marjorie would be upset. In this, at least, I had experience. "Has she called a lawyer? Does she want the name of mine? Martin tried to kick me out, and Mrs. Salvatore got the judge to rule in my favor."

"If only it were that simple." Trish paced. "Turns out the letter was from the new owners of the property. Milo sold it without telling her then skipped off with all the dough. Dough which rightfully also belongs to her."

"She went after him." I could see what happened next. Things didn't go as planned, and she fell off the wagon into a bottle of booze. Understandable.

"I didn't just go after him. I beat the hell out of him." A wan Marjorie emerged from the bathroom. "Rotten jerk. How dare he sell our house. When I met him, he was living with his brother and we used my savings to buy the place. It was more mine than his. And you can bet I told him that."

"You found him?"

Marjorie smirked. "Him and that whore of his. Living in some dump with the nicest car parked out front."

"What did you do?" Because I knew what I'd fantasized about doing to Martin and his girlfriend.

"Keyed the hell out of his new ride and slashed the tires. Insurance will give him a check to fix it, which he's going to use to repay me part of what he owes."

"He agreed to that?" I said somewhat skeptically.

"We had a discussion, and he saw my point."

Tricia cleared her throat. "She's skipping the part where she had a tire iron and threatened to beat his face in and had his girlfriend cowering in a corner."

"Details." Marjorie waved a hand. "The point is, he agreed, and on my way back to my house, I stopped into a bar. Which was a bad idea. I know. I got stressed and ended up getting royally drunk."

"Oh, Marjorie." I sighed her name.

"Don't say it. I'm disappointed in me, too. But I was at least smart enough to not drive, which counts for something, I hope. I spent the night and most of the day sleeping it off in a sleazy motel."

"Wait," I said, trying to make sense of what Tricia had said. "If you were in a motel, then how did the fire start?"

Marjorie's nose wrinkled. "I'm assuming it's the candle I lit in the bathroom the night before to get rid of the smell of puke. When I read the letter, I didn't react very well."

"I know the feeling." The kinship proved instantaneous.

It was Winnie who pointed out the obvious. "It can't have been the candle. It wouldn't take eighteen hours for the fire to start, not to mention the flame would have snuffed out once it ran out of string and hit the wax."

Marjorie shrugged. "It's what I would have thought, too. Plus, it was inside a glass jar. Whatever the case, the place seemed fine when I left. When I heard on the radio on my way back from the city that my house burned down, I panicked. I've been driving around for hours worried I was going to get arrested for arson."

"You won't be arrested," Trish assured. "You have an alibi."

"Who?" I asked because Trish and I were so obviously at the scene of the crime.

"Me," Winnie volunteered.

My eyes widened. My daughter intended to lie!

Marjorie read my expression. "I swear this wasn't my idea, Naomi. I don't want to get your kid involved."

Trust my stubborn daughter to tilt her chin and declare, "Mom can't tell me what to do. And you'll only need an alibi if they try to claim it's arson."

"Which they won't," Trish declared. "I'll make sure of it."

I didn't ask her how she planned to ensure that happened. Instead, I hugged Marjorie. "I'm glad you're okay." The right thing to say. I wasn't about to judge. I was still a steady visitor when it came to dark mental places.

"I'm fine. Better than fine, actually. I hated that house, and now this gives me a reason to do what Tricia's been asking me for the last month. Move in with her." She smiled at Tricia. "That is if she'll still have me."

"Of course, I will, you idiot." She held open her arms, and Marjorie went into them, but I still had some questions.

"Why didn't you let Tricia know where you were, or answer your phone?"

"I forgot it at the house when I went to confront Milo. And then after, I didn't want to disappoint her." Marjorie hung her head.

"Shit happens," was Tricia's reply. "Always know you can call me. No matter what." She grabbed Marjorie's hands, and Marjorie's lips trembled. It was beautiful and sad at the same time.

Would I ever find that kind of acceptance and love?

"It's late," I said as I glanced away from them. "What's the plan?"

"We go home, and you go back to bed."

I liked that idea, but being a smartass, I had to point something out. "I guess the spell didn't work after all because Marjorie's not in the lake."

"Isn't she though? I'd say the cottage is pretty close. Or maybe we did something to change the spell and it brought her to us instead?"

I snorted. "Now you're pushing it."

"Is it that hard for you to believe in magic?"

As I looked around at my friends and daughter, all I could say was, "Magic isn't real."

But dementia was high on the list of possibilities.

## 27

---

Tricia and Marjorie headed to their new home together, and I went back to bed, calmed by the glowing lines I'd painted. No nightmares plagued me and yet I woke later than I wanted to bright sunshine and the birds singing.

What a gorgeous day. However, I didn't have time to lie in bed enjoying it. If I didn't get moving, I'd be late for my first day of work.

A quick shower, clothes, my hair tied back in a clip atop my head. I bit my lower lip before applying a bit of mascara. I eyed myself in the mirror and wondered if it was too much. It did make my eyes appear to have more depth. More definition.

I didn't apply any lip-gloss. Baby steps. I'd not worn makeup much in the last twenty years.

Given I didn't have much time, I had a cup of

coffee for breakfast, grabbed some precooked bacon from the fridge, and packed a salad for later.

The air held a hint of warmth and freshness that filled my lungs and spirit. With Marjorie back, me employed, and Winnie hugging me this morning and saying, "Good luck on the new jobs," I could finally say it was good to be alive.

Damn you, Murphy, evil god best known for kicking people in the face. I should have known my sunny morning wouldn't last.

Arriving at the gas station, I noticed Darryl sweeping up glass. The front window had been smashed, the inside ransacked.

Oh no.

I hopped out of my car. "What happened?" Maybe wind tossed a branch or a vandal smashed it.

"Nothing." The word emerged flat and angry. He also never even raised his head to glance in my direction.

"Darryl?" I said his name with hesitation, my slow steps across the asphalt crunching.

A glance down showed even more debris, snacks that had been ripped open and tossed around and more glass. Even the smell of gas filled the air. I noticed one of the tanks leaning slightly, the puddle under it alarming, but not as frightening as the way Darryl ignored me.

"Why are you ignoring me?"

At last he reacted. His shoulders stiffened, and while he didn't rise, he finally replied, "Why do you think, Naomi? Because helping you screwed me. I gave you everything you asked for, and this is how I am repaid." He swept a hand at the destruction.

My mouth rounded at the attack. "What are you talking about? How is this my fault?" Then I knew. "There is no curse," I said, and I believed it, and yet, I also couldn't deny the destruction.

"No curse, eh?" He dumped a dustbin full of garbage into a bag and began to angrily sweep again, muttering the entire time. "I was told to stay away from you. Told you were nothing but bad luck. But being a stubborn dumbass, I ignored it. I gave you a job like you asked. Even thought..." He trailed off.

I prodded, "Thought what?"

"Nothing." He rose with another bin full of debris. "Go home, Naomi."

"Let me help you clean up."

"Haven't you done enough? What part of go away do you not grasp?" He whirled to face me, and I gasped at the bruising that blackened his eye and mottled his jaw and cheek.

"Who hit you?"

"As if you don't know." His shoulders drooped, a man that I'd seen as confident literally beaten down.

"I don't know anyone who would do such a thing."

At my reply, he snorted. "Sure, you don't."

The sly remark made me flash on Jace. Could he be responsible? He did call himself a guardian, but would he really stoop to wanton destruction and physical attack just because Darryl hired me?

"If you know who did this, tell me. Because I'll tell you right now I think what happened to you is wrong.

"I never saw them. Whoever it was attacked me from behind and then once I was on the ground, I was too busy covering my head while they kicked me." Darryl sighed. "Guess I deserved it. You made me think it was possible."

"What was possible?" I knew what I hoped he'd say.

For a moment, those pale blue eyes regarded me, and my heart fluttered. "Doesn't matter now. In case it wasn't obvious, you're fired."

"Fired? But I haven't done anything wrong."

"Never said you did. But it's been made clear that you can't work here." He swept a hand to encompass the damage. "I can't afford this. If it happens again, I'll lose my business."

I could understand why he did it, but that didn't stop me from exclaiming, "It's not fair."

"Welcome to life. It's been kicking me in the

teeth since I was born," was his last reply before he stepped inside the ruined store.

Rejected. And it hurt.

But unlike with Martin, this time I understood why at least. He'd been vandalized because of me. Attacked and almost ruined because he'd helped me. I could understand why he hated me, and under the hurt was anger and sadness, but most of all frustration.

Why did this keep happening to me? Why was this town determined to make my life miserable?

As I went to my car, crunching puffs of cheesy snacks, my stomach clenched. Was Darryl the only victim?

Despite suspecting what I'd find, I drove into town, straight to the diner with its matching broken window and another job loss before I'd begun.

Orville at least looked sorry about it. "Even if I wanted to ignore the warning, I have no work. It will be a few days before I get this place back in shape." Because the vandals hadn't just destroyed the window but slashed all the seating and then emptied the freezer onto the floor.

Tears brimmed, my stomach roiled, and my steps lagged as I left the diner. My shoulders hunched, and I had to fight the urge to scream as people glanced my way and quickly averted their gazes.

A pariah in my own town. Jace was right. I

should leave. It was obvious no one wanted me here.

If twenty-some years of marriage to Martin had taught me one lesson it was don't allow myself to get beaten down over and over. Why stay and let myself be treated as if there was something wrong with me? If I sold the cottage, I could start over somewhere new, where no one blinked an eye at the name Rousseaux.

It would be easy to give in and slink away; however, since my separation from my husband, I'd discovered a stubborn streak. I was done being bullied. Screw sitting back and letting people, or even history, dictate my future. No more being attacked.

Time to fight back.

In this case, I needed to find the culprits behind the vandalism. Despite the oddity I'd seen on the lake the night before, I remained convinced that there was no monster or ancient witchy spell behind everything. In my mind, this would turn out to be just like a Scooby-Doo mystery, where it seemed supernatural, but in the end, it was just some bad people playing tricks. Find those people, bring them to justice, and the town would realize there was no such thing as a curse.

Where to start looking, though? That question haunted me all the way back to my house. What purpose was served in alienating me? Why make me feel unwelcome and targeted?

*So I'll sell my cottage.*

The answer hit me as I pulled into my driveway. I stared at the hunter green roof and the rooster-shaped wind vane that I somehow had missed seeing before. Odd the little details that kept popping up, things that appealed to my sense of style, like the black shutters framing the window. I'd never noticed those either or the gingerbread lattice between the porch posts and the awning. A Victorian decoration I'd always loved, yet I could have sworn didn't used to exist. My memory must truly be failing for me to forget, because a house didn't just grow accoutrements, no matter what Tricia said.

I stalked inside, ignoring the umbrella stand shaped like a dragon with its mouth open wide. It sat by the shoe mat, which I remembered. I nudged off my runners and padded into the living room. Pacing, I let my brain run.

What if this was about the cottage? The property more specifically. When I refused to sell, someone got peeved and did their best to ensure my existence in this town would be uncomfortable.

I wasn't leaving. This was my home. "I am on to you," I declared out loud, which earned me a fierce "Meow!"

I peeked down at my kitten, who weaved in and

out of my legs. "Poor, baby. I've been so busy stressing lately, I've barely had time for you." I scooped Grisou into my arms. Never mind he'd been sleeping with me and I'd remembered the basics like feeding him and cleaning his box. A cat also needed snuggles and play time. "I'm sorry I've been stressed."

He nudged me with his head.

I sat down on the floor and reached for one of his toys. "Someone is trying to make me leave." I squished his toy, and it crinkled.

A set of ears perked.

I tossed the crinkly ball, and Grisou squirmed from my arms to chase it.

"Question is, who?" The first name that came to mind was Jace. The man with tight lips and a tighter ass. If only I could have gotten him to spill his guts last night. Alas, my feminine wiles were lacking, and I wasn't sure of my ability to put the actual screws to him.

But he definitely knew more than he let on.

I thought of those lights the night before and the agitation of the lake. As if something rose from the deep…

"Me-uu?" Grisou questioned as he dropped the toy in front of me and I took more than a second before I clued in and tossed it.

"Jace will never talk," I muttered aloud. But he didn't work alone. Jace represented a single cog in the machinery of an actual company. If Jace wouldn't spill the beans, then maybe someone else would. Like his brother.

Since our last encounter, I'd had time to convince myself that Kane didn't frighten me. A lie. He terrified me because, despite the fact he might have done something to me, I still remembered the breathless pleasure of his kiss.

Yes, I'd lost control. I still didn't know how, but it would be false of me to pretend I didn't enjoy it.

Would I do it again?

I honestly didn't know. And it might not matter since I didn't have the slightest clue how to find him short of knocking on Jace's door.

I'd gotten brave about many things; however, sauntering over to Jace's house and saying, "Hey, how can I get ahold of your bother?" remained beyond my capabilities.

It was Winnie who had the answer. She walked in with a stack of letters and flyers. "Mom, when was the last time you picked up the mail?"

"Um." I didn't want to admit never. It never even occurred to me I hadn't received any.

Winnie dropped it onto the coffee table and did a rapid sort. "Junk. Junk. Satellite. New windows."

Done playing, Grisou took the crinkle ball he'd conquered to his spot atop the couch. I rose just as Winnie fired a letter at me.

I captured it and almost yelped. The damn

thing managed to give me a paper cut. A line of blood beaded on my finger.

"You got mail," Winnie announced as I sucked the wound.

"I almost got decapitated."

"Don't be a cry baby." For a moment Winnie mimicked her father so well that ice ran through my veins.

Her laughter chased the chill. "You should see your face. He's gone, Mom. You can stop being scared."

"I'm not scared." Not anymore. Martin couldn't touch me now. "It's more that I keep looking back and wondering why I was so blind."

Winnie enveloped me in a hug. "It wasn't always bad."

"It wasn't as good as it should have been either," I said with a sniffle.

"Can't change the past."

"I wish I could, though." Fervently. Not the part where I had Geoff and Winnie. I would never regret them. But I wished I'd left while they were young. Before…everything that happened.

"Our mistakes shape us."

"A nugget of wisdom from college?" I said through a throat choked with tears.

"Fortune cookie, actually. Although, as part of the game, I had to add 'in bed' at the end. So it was actually our mistakes shape us, in bed." She winked.

"Winnie!" I exclaimed.

My daughter grinned at me. "Lighten up. What's done is done. Look at us, two single swinging gals, hanging out, casting spells, me eschewing men and you getting cozy with your boss at work."

I grimaced. "I doubt that will happen. Not only was I fired, Darryl won't have anything to do with me."

"What? Why?" Her inquiry led to me telling her everything as I petted the cat sleeping in my lap.

"I wouldn't usually give in to your anxiety, because you've always been a bit crazy about doing the normal stuff," my daughter said when I was done, "but you might be right about someone intentionally trying to run you out of town."

"What do you mean crazy about normal stuff?"

"Please, as if you don't know." Winnie rolled her eyes. "You always had excuses why you couldn't go out. A headache, stomachache, laundry."

"I always went to the important things."

"And little else. Which is fine. I get it. I learned in college about how some people have a hard time dealing with stuff that stresses them."

I wanted to argue and claim I never did that. It would be a lie. I'd been doing better since my separation, but it was still a struggle to go out and do normal things. "This thing with Darryl isn't about my anxiety, though. It's because of that stupid curse."

She shook her head. "We both know there's no curse."

"I thought you were on Tricia's side about the lake monster and stuff."

"Because it was fun," Winnie said with a roll of her shoulders. "But what happened to Darryl and the diner? That's someone messing with my mom. Not cool."

"Not someone. This company." I waved the letter with yet an even more generous offer. The kind of money that would set me and Wendy up nicely in another city where no one would care my grandma was a witch.

Too much money for a simple cottage sitting on a lake.

I wouldn't accept it. However, I could find out more about the company offering it.

While Wendy went to shower to prepare for training at her new job—she'd been hired by a car dealership in the next town over—I examined the letter and the envelope. The return address was a city two hours away and a postal box to boot. Utterly useless.

The company name, Airgeadsféar, was distinctive enough that an internet search found it, but there was little information. I perused a slick website that stated they were a worldwide company of imports and exports, which to my overactive mind screamed drugs. The legal pharmaceutical kind or the illicit? Or maybe they were gunrunners? Gold smugglers. I even wondered if they could be into the sex slave trade.

I didn't worry for me, not at my age, but Winnie might be in danger.

But at the root of all my fanciful ideas, why Cambden? It seemed farfetched that this sleepy, dead town be the hub of a giant narcotic or flesh trade ring, yet those answers seemed more likely than a lake monster.

More searching only led to dead ends. I couldn't find anything that linked Airgeadsféar to Cambden. So I started looking for information on my neighbor, Jace.

Nothing. The man didn't have an online footprint, but to my surprise, his brother Kane did.

I blinked as he appeared immediately in a search with a Wikipedia page of all things. Renowned American architect born in South Dakota. There was a full page of info on his numerous accomplishments. He'd excelled at school. Been the recipient of awards.

I scrolled hundreds of images showcasing the buildings he'd had a hand in designing, gorgeous works of art created by the extremely talented Kane D'Argent. A man who didn't shy from the camera.

Turned out he had quite the social media presence, Instagram being his favorite, where he posted pictures of projects in progress, along with selfies with model-type women hanging off him. Beautiful women.

It made our interlude in the parking lot more surreal than ever, and Tricia's claim he'd drugged me even more ridiculous. Why would he waste time with me when he could date supermodels?

Never mind he looked bored in those images and, at times, amused. He wasn't a man who had to resort to subterfuge to get into someone's pants. And he'd kissed me.

I wasn't naïve enough to think for one instant he desired me. Not anymore.

*He used me.* The realization hit. He probably knew who I was and thought he could seduce me to get me to sell the cottage. Son of a bitch.

For some reason, I kept scrolling through his social media, moving from Instagram to Facebook, perusing image after image of a glamorous, rich world I couldn't even imagine. It was on his personal Facebook profile page that I hit the jackpot. The caption on the image read, *Check out my newest restoration project.* To my surprise, I recognized that forlorn bookshelf with the scrolled wood. I'd seen it peeking through a bookstore window. A bookstore currently being renovated in downtown Cambden.

Given I wasn't working today, and Wendy had

gone to work, I decided to go take a look. I parked close to the bookstore and sat in my car watching for a minute. Not being stalkerish at all. There was a white, partially rusted van parked out front. The side of it was emblazoned with the company name Mr. Do It and a man with a big mustache holding a hammer.

What I didn't spot was a fancy car. Would Kane still be kicking around? Even if he wasn't, the renovation fellow might know where I could find him. Before I could change my mind, I'd gotten out of the car and crossed the road.

Entering the store, I heard a drill going, and my nose twitched as small motes of sawdust tickled it. The shelves remained in their straight rows, the antique wood partially sanded, and the cracks and divots patched. The bookcases were prepped and ready to be stained.

The lonely books of before, splayed like papery corpses, were gone and, with them, the sense of abandonment. In its place, the calm before the birth.

This bookstore would be fantastic when finished. Full of new purpose but also history. I loved it and wondered if they'd hired anyone yet. Working here would be so satisfying.

The moment I thought it, the crushing realization hit. I would never be hired. The superstitious townsfolk wouldn't allow it. Unless I could prove the curse that kept following me around was fake.

The drill paused. I saw my chance. "Excuse me?" I called out.

A woman stepped into the shop from a door in the back, wearing a plaid shirt hanging open over a plain cotton gray T-shirt and worn jeans.

I blinked in surprise. And was immediately ashamed. I'd made some assumptions in seeing the truck.

"Can I help you?" she asked. She was younger than me but older than Winnie, looking to be in her thirties with her dark hair pulled back and tucked under a ball cap.

"Sorry to bother you. I'm looking for the architect on this project. Kane D'Argent."

"No idea who you mean."

Could it be she'd never met him? That seemed unlikely. "I know he's the one in charge of this renovation."

"So what if he is," she stated, crossing her arms.

I couldn't help but notice the muscular strength of them. "Do you know where I can find him?"

"No." The word was flat.

"He'd want to talk to me," I lied.

"What makes you think that? Because, in my world, people who want to talk to me leave me a method of contacting them."

The letter probably had contact info. If only I'd

not rid myself of them. "We have history." Let her think what she would of that claim.

"Don't we all. Now, if you're done wasting my time, I have things to do." She dismissed me, and I had to think fast.

"You know what. I am done trying. Next letter I get offering to buy my place, I might just reply and explain who's to blame for me not selling my property," I huffed.

"You got an offer?" I finally had her interest.

"Several, as a matter of fact. My name is Naomi Rousseaux." For once I wanted my name to evoke a reaction.

She continued to give me a blank stare.

"You might have heard of my grandma."

"I'm not from around here."

"She was a witch."

"And you're not." Her lip curled, and she eyed me with disdain. "Nor are you very impressive considering."

Why did people feel a need to remind me?

"You might not have heard of me, but trust me when I say my family put a curse on this town, meaning you have to give me what I want or face the consequences," I boldly stated.

She smirked. "Don't care."

"You don't understand," I said a tad desperately. "People get hurt if they don't comply."

"Don't care."

She didn't, but given the offer I'd received that morning, I'd wager Kane's company did. "You might not care, but are you sure your boss doesn't?" I pulled the letter from my pocket. "A million-dollar offer says he really wants my place. And now…" I tore the letter to shreds. "You can explain why I am not ever going to sell." I then prepared to flounce out the door, despite having never flounced in my life.

"Wait."

I froze practically mid step.

"I have no idea who you are but let me give him a shout and see what he says." The woman turned and stepped into the back room. To follow would have been too obvious. I had to content myself with trying to make out soft murmurs then pretending disinterest when she emerged, her face a knot of annoyance, and said, "He'll see you at his office."

"You don't say." I acted cool, even if inside I was almost fainting because it had worked. I was going to get another chance to crack the mystery of this town—and see Kane. "What's the address?"

"He said to tell you he's at the old mill."

Of course, he was, I thought as I headed down the unkempt road to the closed-down factory. He couldn't be in a more public, less spooky place.

I'd been to see it twenty-some-odd years ago, not long after it shut down. It had been eerie to walk through that cavernous space and see the monoliths of the machines left behind. Too big and too old to be of any use. I could only imagine what time had done to it.

The parking lot outside the factory had been mowed back. The asphalt still showed signs of cracks and pits; however, the weeds that I suspected once thrust through the gaps were shorn short, the foliage of the encroaching forest trimmed back.

The number of cars parked along with the fancy sedan surprised. I noticed five, plus more specialty vehicles like an electrician and plumber. Big metal shipping containers sat nearby, and I could hear the squealing of power tools coming from inside. How had I not heard the news of the mill being renovated? Did people even know yet?

As I walked toward the building, I noticed even more signs of renewal. The exterior had been patched and painted, windows replaced. Inside the smell of sawdust and oil filled the air, along with something more pungent. My nose wrinkled. Ugh.

It was cold inside. Colder than expected.

I entered the building and no one tried to stop me. No one appeared either to question my presence so I went from the reception area, with a desk lacking anybody to question me, to the factory proper, where I gaped.

It wouldn't be long, apparently, before this place hummed with life again. I noticed a man working on a conveyer belt, starting and stopping it, watching as it moved a box along to a palette. It fell off the end, which caused the fellow playing with it to wave his arms and yell in a foreign language. The woman who'd not caught the box replied with a rude gesture.

On the far side of the factory floor were open bay doors and a front loader moving shrink-wrapped palettes around. A full glance around showed a giant vat, pressurized and plastered with gauges, emitting several pipes, which ran across to a giant metal machine that fed the conveyer belt. I wondered what they planned to package here.

Walking farther into the factory brought me even with an open box, and looking inside, I noticed empty bottles, but my skin didn't start to itch until I saw the company's sigil on the label. What were they planning to produce? And how was it I hadn't heard anyone talking about it? I went to reach for a bottle so I could read the label when a voice startled me.

"If it isn't Cinderella."

Snatching back my hand, I whirled, and I stared stupidly at Kane, taking in the niceness of his suit, the way his silky gray hair waved back from his face, the wickedness of his smile. "Hi." Every single speech I'd practiced flew out of my brain.

Did he know? Was that why he grinned even wider? "I hear you've been looking for me."

Hard to deny I'd been looking, given that

woman in the bookstore had called him. "I was. I wanted to talk to you." A plan that seemed foolish now with me partially tongue-tied. Did I really expect this man to divulge his secrets? To me?

"Katia said you wanted to sell your land finally?"

"Well…"

He chuckled, the sound deep and rich. "I had a feeling that might not be true."

Rather than confirm or deny, I blurted out, "Did you know who I was that evening at the bar?"

"Yes." He didn't even attempt to lie.

He'd tried to seduce me to soften me to his offer. In other words, he was fake attracted. It deflated me even as it finally made sense.

"Why are you buying up all the property in Cambden?"

"Not me, per se. But the company."

"To do what?" I asked.

"Does it matter if it brings vitality back to the village?" he asked with an arched brow.

"As a matter of fact, it does because I get the impression your business is shady."

"Oh really? Shady how?" he asked, still appearing amused.

"Rumor has it people are dying if they reject your offer." I threw that at him.

He laughed. "That is an absolutely astounding

conclusion. And what proof do you have people are dead?"

Not much when I thought of it. I struggled to repeat what I'd heard. "There was that family who perished in the fire."

He arched a brow. "You mean the McGraws? They aren't dead, but they did relocate. A good thing, too, given what happened."

"And I'm supposed to just take your word they're alive?"

"Would you like to call them?" He held out his phone.

"Why would they move and not tell anyone?"

"Tell who, exactly? My understanding was they were a very private family."

While he was able to offer sensible replies, my accusations got even broader.

"Those guys that drowned fishing?"

He arched a brow. "How is that anybody's fault?"

"Oh yeah, well, right after I decided I wasn't taking your first offer, my old house burned down."

"I have to say, sounds like we've been busy." Kane laughed again, showing white teeth with a hint of canine, his laugh a deep alto that was too sexy for my annoyed state of mind. Why was I attracted to jerks?

It made no sense. Even as they annoyed me, I

felt quivers. Maybe Tricia's magic existed and they were hexing me.

Into their sex toy? Yeah. Okay. It wasn't magic but a mid-life crisis making me horny. I might have to take the plunge and get my first encounter over with. Outside of town so I didn't have to see him again if it failed in spectacular fashion.

What if I was one of those women who cried after sex the first time after divorce?

What if I turned out to be horrible at it?

And then there was the whole taking-off-my-clothes part. I hugged myself. Never.

"Was there anything else you wanted to accuse me of?" he asked.

As a matter of fact, I did have one more thing. "You sent thugs to beat up Darryl and ruin his gas station so he'd fire me." A wild guess and I watched his expression carefully.

"Why would I want you fired from a minimum-wage job?" The curl of his lip held disdain.

"To force me to sell!"

"I don't have to force you to do anything. I don't actually need your property."

"Then why offer me so much money for it?"

"Because it was the only one missing to complete our ring around the lake."

"You own everything else?" I gaped. He had to be lying.

"Is that a problem?"

"It is if you're buying those properties to conduct criminal acts."

His mirth boomed. "So now I'm a criminal."

His mockery of my practiced list of accusations had me blurting out, "I know you're somehow involved with those lights on the lake at night."

Finally, I'd gotten his attention.

"When did you see lights?"

"Last night." I didn't mention the music or the fact the glowing lake held an unearthly sheen. Probably a distortion of the water.

"In that case you must have also seen a giant, three-headed serpent undulating."

My embarrassment grew as he mocked me. "I most certainly did not."

"You should have."

I blinked at his reply. "Excuse me?"

"I'm guessing you didn't watch the lake the entire time we ran the test."

"What test?"

His canines appeared almost wolfish in his next grin. "The test we ran last night with Mechanical Maddy."

## 2 8

I MUST HAVE MISUNDERSTOOD. "DID YOU SAY Mechanical Maddy?"

"I did." Kane held an amused expression.

"Wait, you mean Maddy really exists?" I blinked at the unexpected news.

"Yes and no. She's not the Maddy of legend, obviously." He spread his hands. "This one is made of metal parts and gears. A machine for mining, patent pending. We've been doing some test runs with her at night so as to keep her secret."

"Let me get this straight. You've got a machine that looks like a lake monster?"

"I do. Would you like to see her?"

"Yes?" Hesitant sounding because this conversation hadn't gone at all where I expected.

Despite his teasing and the rumors I'd heard, I had trouble imagining the mechanical monster.

Would it be big or small? Was it truly three headed? Why a serpent shape?

I'd soon find out as Kane led me through the factory, bigger than it seemed from the outside. The more I saw, the more questions I had.

"You're getting this place ready for production."

"I am. Or I should say, the company is."

"Producing what?"

"Mud."

I stumbled. "Why are you bottling mud?"

"Because it's got interesting properties."

"Like?"

"I'd have to get you to sign an NDA before I tell you." He sounded utterly serious.

"I'm going to assume this special mud comes from the lake."

"I'd say that was rather obvious."

I scrambled quickly to make sense of the news and forged ahead. "Isn't it against environmental laws to take the mud?" Given the subterfuge, I didn't get the impression he had permission.

"Why, Naomi, are you accusing me of environmental poaching?" He clasped his chest in mock shock. "Actually, we are a government-sanctioned operation, working in secrecy for the moment and preparing for a controlled revelation to the outside world."

"You have permission from the government?" I might have squeaked that query.

"I do. Why even the mayor has signed off on our business. Very soon, Cambden is going to enjoy a revitalization greater than the mill days. Given that will involve an increase in personnel, we've been rebuilding the town to offer amenities."

I might have asked him more questions but a barked, "What are you doing?" had me turning to see Jace striding across the mill floor, the worn denim of his jeans molding his thick thighs, his expression thunderous.

"Would you look at that. Jace is in another fury. Over you." Kane eyed me and smiled. "One would almost think he's jealous."

I was getting tired of hearing it because I didn't see it. Jace was an angry man. He didn't appear enamored of me, and I highly doubted he was pining with desire either.

"Is that why you kissed me? To one-up your brother?"

That brought a teasing smile to Kane's lips. "I kissed you because you taste like candy."

Well, that was unexpected.

Jace joined us, glowering and growling, "What the fuck are you doing here, Naomi?"

"It's none of your business," I hotly exclaimed.

Whereas Kane purred, "Brother, how unexpected."

"You were supposed to stay away from her," he snapped.

"I didn't go near Ms. Rousseaux. She came to me," was his triumphant claim.

"You just couldn't leave well enough alone, could you?" Jace snapped in my direction.

"Such a temper," Kane tsked. "Why so angry?"

"What is she doing inside? How come the guards didn't stop her?" Jace planted his hands on his hips, and I might have been more intimidated if he'd held his axe, but his glower didn't scare me.

Martin was much better at it.

Kane shrugged. "I guess the guards were all on break. What odd timing." Kane didn't appear perturbed at all that Jace was peeved. And Jace didn't sense my simmering anger.

Especially as he berated Kane for giving me answers.

"This tour is over," Jace growled.

"Already? But I've yet to show her the monster." Kane waved a hand at the stairs leading down to a dock bordering a canal of water that flowed inside the warehouse.

"Are you crazy? You can't show her," Jace hissed, casting me a glance.

I wanted to waggle my fingers. Like, *hello, idiot, I can hear every word*. But I didn't dare say anything because it might interrupt this fascinating discussion.

"On the contrary, brother. I think it's time we showed the world what we're doing. We've been keeping secrets long enough. Do you have a camera?" Kane asked me.

Startled, it took me a second before I reached into my purse and pulled out my cellphone. "I have this."

"Prepare to post to social media the wonder I'm about to reveal."

"I, uh, don't actually have Facebook or anything." Martin said it was dumb. In retrospect, it was just another way to cut me off from the world.

"I do." He whipped out his phone and winked. "Prepare yourself to be amazed."

As we stood on the edge of a concrete dock, I expected many things to emerge from that water. An actual lake monster making the list or some kind of submersible with a periscope maybe.

Instead it was a giant sea serpent made of metal. Overlapping plates with fins that projected from the side and three working heads. One sported a shovel, another a giant claw, and the third a bucket.

It was obviously a machine, but at the same time, put it out on water at night, or far enough from shore that people only got a glimpse, and it would seem like something more. Something of legend.

"Why did you build a metal monster?" I asked.

"Despite its fanciful shape, Maddy was made to mine underwater," Kane said. "And doesn't require a human operator, making her rather unique."

"Drones already exist."

"She is more than a drone. She can actually think," Kane insisted. "Meaning when she gets under water where we lose signal and visibility, she can still work."

"But why our lake?" I insisted. "What's so special about its mud?" The only thing I remembered was how it squished between my toes and Grandma always yelled at me to check for leeches.

He shook a finger at me. "Nice try. I thought we talked about non-disclosure."

At his statement, Jace snorted. "You showed her the monster, why bother hiding the rest? Has he told you yet the mud has interesting properties?"

Kane waggled his fingers as he joked, "Some might say it's full of magic."

"Don't listen to him," Jace growled. "You saw what you came for. Now you need to leave."

"In just a moment, brother. We can't let her leave without a picture. Smile," Kane said, holding up his cellphone. He snapped a pic, and I was convinced I'd blinked.

Then I had to wonder if the image would even do me much good against the curse. Showing Cambden that Maddy actually existed didn't prove I wasn't a witch.

Kane held up his phone. "Posted and hashtagged."

"Are you stupid?" Jace barked. "You can't tell people what we're doing yet."

"Why not?" Kane argued.

"Because you know there are those who will argue our right to dredge, even though we own over ninety-eighty percent of the property around the lake."

"The lake doesn't belong to anyone," was my reply. Not to mention they would never own it one hundred percent because I wasn't selling.

I was sitting on a potential goldmine if that mud was important enough that they'd gotten permission from the government to mine it. Would I need permission, too? Or would the mud on shore be just as good and discreet enough to remove without causing problems?

"Now that I've satisfied your curiosity, I don't suppose you'll help me with something." Kane extended an arm that I might go first on the stairs to the main floor.

"What kind of help?"

"I am famished and hate eating alone. Care to join me?" Kane's smile held the devil in it, all temptation and sin.

Jace's lips were twisted with annoyance as he yanked me toward the exit. "No, she is not having dinner with you."

"Excuse me," I said, trying to pull free of his grip. "That's not your decision."

"Actually, it is. You got the answers you wanted. Now go home."

He was right, I had. Maddy was real and fake at the same time. People weren't getting eaten by a monster; some deaths were just tragedies. Blame small-town inertia for a decline in population.

Now if only I could solve my curse as easily.

Arriving home, I noticed a motorcycle leaning on its stand and Darryl sitting on my porch. Exiting my car, I didn't immediately join him but leaned over my door, recalling the hurtful way he'd treated me that morning.

"What are you doing here?"

He stood and ducked his head sheepishly. "Here to say I'm sorry."

"You said it, now you can go." Did he think the word sorry could fix everything? He'd been mean to me.

"Ah, Naomi, don't be mad. I really am sorry I was such an asshole." He sighed and raked a hand through his hair. "All I could think when I saw you this morning was how much it was gonna cost to fix and how it was my own fault for hiring you."

"Because I'm a cursed witch. Blah-da-blah-blah," I exclaimed, flinging my hands before slamming the car door shut. I stalked toward him, simmering with anger. "I am getting mighty tired of having that thrown at me. I didn't ask to be born into a family of supposed witches, but I will say I'm not one of them. I just want to find myself a little job and live quietly at my cottage. Maybe take up a craft or something." Like pottery. Could the mud in the lake be baked into an ashtray or a vase? I should look into using a kiln.

"Would you let me finish talking?" he snapped. "I'm trying to apologize here."

"Didn't sound like one," I muttered.

"Because I wasn't done. Anyhow, after you left, I started realizing I was being unfair to you. And I started to wonder about the curse. It was obviously a person that smacked me from behind and trashed my place, so I watched the pump cam."

I blinked. "Hold on, you had camera footage?"

"Yeah, only recently installed because I had some issues with overnight theft."

"If you have a video, then that means you saw who did it. Who? Tell me." So I could confront them and ask them why they wanted to ruin my attempt at a new life.

"I didn't recognize the guy, so I thought I'd see if you did."

Darryl held out his phone, meaning I had to approach to reach for it.

As I did, his free hand caught mine. "I really am sorry, Naomi. I hope you'll let me make it up to you."

I could have held on to my hurt. Could have chosen to remain annoyed. It would be easy, but it took a real man, and courage, to admit he was wrong.

"It's going to cost you dinner."

At my words, he grinned. "You're on."

"Let's see this vandal." All I had to do was hit the triangle for the video to play.

I replayed it three times before I called my lawyer, and when she heard what Martin had done…she sent a ridiculous list of demands to Martin's lawyers, and in exchange, we wouldn't sue his ass to hell and back.

He accepted.

Within days, I went from separated and confused to divorced.

I celebrated with a no-sugar, no-crust cheesecake.

# EPILOGUE

Despite Martin giving me my divorce, he ended up in jail. It seemed Darryl and Orville weren't as forgiving. They were kind enough to wait until the divorce papers were signed before they had his picture plastered in the papers as a wanted man.

Within hours, Martin was arrested, and his jowly mugshot made the front page of our local paper, which consisted of eight folded sheets and mostly ads. But there, in black and white, was a list of his crimes, which all revolved around harassing me.

From stalking me at our old house and trying to burn it down with me in it to following me to the new town, stalking me here, and admitting to officers that I was only still alive because of Jace and his nosy habits.

He'd destroyed the gas station and the diner to be vindictive. His true plan was to burn down the cottage with me in it and then, with me out of the way, take Kane's offer to buy the property.

Never mind the fact it would have gone to the kids. Greedy Martin wanted it all.

In an ironic twist, it turned out he'd lied about how much money we actually had socked away. He'd hidden so much from me, but my lawyer ferreted it out. When the divorce cleared, I came into a tidy sum of money. Enough that I didn't need to worry about a job, could buy that kiln and learn to make mud cups, and buy the derelict downtown shop from Mrs. Basinette, who said I reminded her of dear Clementine. Given she meant a goat, I wasn't entirely flattered.

Kane laughed when he found out I'd snared a property out from under him. Then invited me to dinner. I said no. I always said no, even as I secretly enjoyed the attention. Every Friday, Kane sent me a single white bloom with a sharp thorn that almost pricked me the first time. The note made me shake my head and smile. *I'm not afraid to be scratched. Dinner?* One of these days, I might just accept.

While Kane enjoyed running into me, Jace glowered whenever we crossed paths, which thankfully didn't happen often. He kept to his property. I kept to mine. Despite going down to the lake often, even at night, I didn't run into him. Probably for the best.

Orville took a shine to me. He began concocting low-carb creations just for me and bringing them to my pottery shop for tasting. I won't deny I enjoyed every yummy bite.

And finally, the last of what Winnie called my harem, Darryl, who became a steady visitor despite my refusal of a job. He was determined to be my friend and, by his own admission, something more. Saying no to him wasn't all that easy given he'd been working out. The paunch was gone, the jaw still scruffy, but the eyes clear. His grin mischievous.

Maybe I'd say yes to him one day. But not yet. I'd just gotten divorced. I had no idea what I wanted in a man, or a relationship. Did I even want to be with someone? I had so much to figure out. Starting with who I was and what I wanted for myself. A hard question to answer, but I was getting there with the help of my daughter and new friends.

On the good news front, I'd not had any chilly incidents since Martin got locked behind bars. Was the cold my instincts trying to warn me? Or pre-menopause? If the latter, it better stay away. I was still too young for that kind of crap. When it came to life, I preferred to believe I wasn't even halfway there.

And I planned to make every moment I had left

count. Starting with an actual career as a business-woman. If this town was about to fill up with people when the mill came fully back to life, then I wanted to be part of it and not just as a mooching recipient. I was going to work for it by opening my own store. It was Winnie who gave me the idea. Turned out, she'd taken pottery in college, along with business admin and a few other courses. Between the pair of us, we'd muddle along and hopefully ride the coming wave of prosperity.

With the monster debunked and Martin arrested, people started treating me normally. Meaning, I got charged for gas, and gladly. But I still got free pie at the diner. Margorie insisted.

Life was good. Amazing, actually.

Now if only those dreams would stop. Weird dreams where I once more went to that mill and Kane invited me to see his invention at work. Except instead of a machine undulating on the lake, I saw Maddy the lake monster, harnessed in chains, her skin marked by abuse and her eyes begging me for help.

*Not real.* The words on my lips each time I woke, sitting bolt upright in my bed, covered in sweat and shivering.

"Mee-uu?" Grisou queried as I stared at the glowing lines of my ceiling.

"It's nothing," I said, petting his head. Just a nightmare.

Or more proof I was on my way to going crazy.

---

*"I THINK SHE'S STILL BUYING IT," MY LIEUTENANT commented as we met at the mill to go over a few items of interest.*

*I snorted. "Of course, she bought it." The charade had been impeccably wrought. My finest work to date. But then again, I'd not expected anything less than perfection. This entire operation was my doing. My gaze swept over the factory, which I'd been careful to keep as mundane as possible.*

*"What if she comes snooping again?" asked the lieutenant, who'd panicked when it seemed the witch would figure out our secrets. He wouldn't go far up the ranks if he didn't learn to think on his feet.*

*"If she does come around, we'll handle it, but I doubt we need to worry because Ms. Rousseaux is about to become very busy."*

*Because she didn't know yet, but her husband had escaped prison. That should be of great concern to Cambden's witch, given what was written on the wall of Martin Dunrobin's cell in blood.* **Gonna kill that bitch.**

## The End

Yeah, not quite. While Naomi got to enjoy a midlife mulligan—and solved a not-so-paranormal mystery—she's not done with her journey yet. Are you ready to find out what happens to her in *On My Way*?

**For more Eve Langlais books please visit EveLanglais.com**

LOOKING FOR MORE #PWF BOOKS FROM THE FAB13? THEN VISIT OUR WEBSITE AT PARANORMALWOMENSFICTION.NET